Hurled fifty-eight years into the future.
Lives are shattered.
Choices must be made.

In the spring of 1965, a violent storm snatches 20-year-old Laura Malone away from her friend, Paul, and casts her fifty-eight years into the future. Now in 2023, Laura is horrified to learn that due to her unexplained disappearance all those years ago, Paul endured each of those agonizing years ostracized from society with allegations of her murder. She is determined to prevent Paul's deterioration into a frail and sickly recluse, but how can she possibly accomplish it? With the help of a kindhearted stranger, Kevin Donahue, Laura must somehow return to 1965, but her altruism backfires. Not only does Laura come to realize she has fallen in love with Kevin, her decision to leave him behind sets her own timeline on a calamitous course. Laura's fate now rests in Kevin's hands as he sets out on his own life-altering journey in an attempt to save the woman he loves from a bleak and joyless future.

Editorial Reviews of *One Time or Anoth*

D1291038

"...an exciting time travel adventure with romance at its core. Characters jumping through time together offers a new and innovative twist to a familiar genre which fans of time travel will enjoy. The author includes enough science to be believable, but not too much to distract from the storyline. The characters are well drawn and you can't help but root for them! ...a fun, easy read with enough romance, sci-fi, and adventure to appeal to a wide range of readers. And the ending is totally unexpected!"—*Christy Cooper-Burnett, Award-winning author of The Christine Stewart Time Travel Series*

"Ellen Ricciutti's writing is enchanting and engrossing, transporting readers through time with elegance and enthusiasm. And the ending is totally unexpected!"—*Todd McLeish, author of Return of the Sea Otter*

"Ellen Ricciutti's writing style and storyline captivated me right from the start! Her clever intertwining of time periods will have you reminiscing some of the favorite years of your life, while at the same time, cheering the characters on as they must navigate time and space! It is a book for almost all ages. My young teenage granddaughter could not stop reading! This is an incredible book for book clubs across America. Get it soon while you have time!"—*Roberta Walker, author of A Chance of Rainbows*

"If you're a fan of time travel novels, then you're in for a treat with Ellen Ricciutti's delightful novel, *One Time or Another*. The book is filled with memorable characters, surprises, romance, and adventure, and the story will keep you hooked until the very end."—*Elyse Douglas, author of Time Zone and Time Past*

"No matter if your favorite genre is mystery, romance, historical, or science fiction, you'll find it all in Ellen Ricciutti's remarkable debut Time-Travel novel…You'll easily slide back and forth from 1965 to 2023 and get caught up in the lives of well-developed characters who you meet in both decades… Start reading this book early in the day. If you don't, you'll find yourself reading late into the night."—*Agnes Alexander- multi-published author of Rena's Cowboy and Stella's Time*

ONE TIME OR ANOTHER

Ellen Ricciutti

Moonshine Cove Publishing, LLC
Abbeville, South Carolina U.S.A.

Moonshine Cove Edition July 2023

Anne,
Best Wishes Always !

Ellen Ricciutti ♡

ISBN: 9781952439629

Library of Congress LCCN: 2023912286

© Copyright 2023 by Ellen Ricciutti

Cover illustrations copyright 2023 by Leigh-Ann Dauble, wiseartdesigns.com; interior attempt to rescue a girl design by Moonshine Cove staff.

For Jim, Cristina, & Julie
Always

Acknowledgments

To my husband, Jim, whose unwavering love, humor, & incredible patience I could never live without.

To my incredible daughters, Cristina & Julie, who appreciate escaping into the pages of a wonderful story. Keep dreaming those dreams because they really can come true. Love you.

A huge thank you to my parents and two brothers who recognized and encouraged my love of writing all the way back in elementary school.

To my extended family, for offering to read my manuscript only to be told, "It's not ready yet," well, it's ready.

With special thanks to T.W., D.M., R.M. & her husband T.M., who believed in me even when I doubted myself.

I cannot thank Gene D. Robinson of Moonshine Cove Publishing enough for recognizing the potential of *One Time or Another*. Thank you for bringing my story to the light of day.

About the Author

Ellen Ricciutti, a New Jersey native, is a proud graduate of Ithaca College (B.A. in Sociology) and Montclair State University (M.A. in Communication Sciences and Disorders). Currently, she works as a speech-language pathologist in a suburb of New York

City, and in her spare time, she enjoys reading, hiking, and watching every Marvel movie released. Ellen has dabbled in writing over the years, but has not pursued publication until *One Time or Another*, her debut novel. It is the product of many years of intrigue for time travel, initially sparked by the 1974 episode "Elsewhen" of the campy *Land of the Lost* television program. Her Facebook page is onetimeoranothernovel; and her own website is shown below:

ellenricci.com

The important thing is not to stop questioning. Curiosity has its own reason for existing. One cannot help but be in awe when he contemplates the mysteries of eternity, of life, of the marvelous structure of reality

–Albert Einstein

Prologue
1965

Hello listeners—it's your Cousin Brucie back at you on your A.M. dial. We made it through the week, folks—it's finally Friday! You ready for tonight's main event? We've been waiting for this spectacular cosmic light show all week. Here's what our stargazer friends at Lincoln Observatory said, and I quote, 'With the fiery colors of dusk combined with the gravitational forces of the planets' alignment, we're in for a sensational cosmic light display never before witnessed in recent history.' Holy smokes, a historic event! Soooo, at sundown, pull up a lawn chair and check it out. And for you party poopers out there, don't sweat it—you'll get another chance to see it in about fifty years or so. Ho ho!

Reaching across the steering wheel, Paul Calloway turned off the radio with such force the plastic knob pulled clear from the spindle. Goddamn piece of crap. He grunted and wedged the piece back to its proper place, downshifted into park, and turned toward Laura.

"Enough of this alien space shit already. What, did every DJ in existence forget how to play the vinyls? This is bogus."

"Oh, lighten up, Paul. We're about to see something nobody on earth has ever seen before." She squeezed his hand. "C'mon, you know this is cool, admit it."

"Admit what? We're wasting time here in no man's land when we could be hanging with the guys tossing down a few. Let's blow this place and head to Diesel's. He set up some lawn chairs and an ice chest on the driveway, and even rolled out his old man's hi-fi for some Stones. If we split now, you'll see your eclipse thing at Diesel's. What d'ya say?"

"No, there are too many trees there, we'd never see anything. Not like here." She waved an open palm across the scenery. Not a single tree, except at the far edge of the meadow. She glanced at him and sighed. "Hey, I know this isn't your bag, Paul. We'll go to Diesel's as soon as the show's over, okay? Just sit tight for a while, you'll survive a few hours without your boys." She grabbed a rolled-up blanket and a wicker picnic basket from the backseat. "Come on, help me set this up." Pulling the handle, she shoved the door open and stepped onto the grass.

Scowling, Paul peered through the satisfyingly pristine windshield at the long reeds of rich, jade-colored grass and the completely unobstructed expanse of the heavens. Okay, so maybe she had a point hauling them all the way out here. If they were going to see anything at all in the sky, this probably was the best place to see it. The secluded meadow was situated atop a hill on the outskirts of Sullivan's Township, and the only trees were in the woods a good 50 yards from here. Not a soul was around. A perfect make-out point. Maybe this wouldn't be a wasted trip after all.

He eyed Laura as she trudged through the grass with her bundled quilt. As far as he was concerned, the girl was the epitome of perfection—those pouty, sweet lips, the flawless complexion, and that hair ... oh god, that gorgeous mane of auburn hair, begging for him to plunge his hands into the thick of it. But he knew it was her eyes—emerald green with shades of golden amber—that captivated him.

"You coming or what?" she called.

"Fine." He gave the steering wheel an affectionate pat and pushed open his door.

She had already billowed the blanket onto the grass and carefully positioned the basket in the center. The contents, he imagined, were most likely homemade cookies and lemonade. Gorgeous and a good cook.

Laura lowered herself onto the blanket and rolled to her back, her watchful eyes surveying the expansive sky. The sun dipped closer to the horizon and the moon edged toward its place in the alignment.

"See what I mean, Paul? We'll see everything from here." Her sundress shimmied up a bit and she smoothed the flared skirt over her thighs. Oh, those legs. Those long, perfect legs. He imagined running his hand up her smooth silky skin, up and up...

He swallowed.

"Um. Right. Great view. Great." He cleared his throat and hooked his thumbs in the pockets of his Levi's. He couldn't figure her out. He was cool enough, right? His dark brown hair, a shade lighter than black, was combed back on the sides, and a disarray of curls hung over his forehead. Girls usually dug him, but Laura? Yesterday, he asked her to go steady but instead of smothering him with kisses, she said she needed to think about it. Think about it. What's there to think about? It's 1965, they're both 20 years old—it's time to get with the times, baby. And then with her big, green eyes looking all hopeful-like, she had the gall to ask him to come here, to this God-forsaken meadow, to watch the planet hoopla. Like an ass, he agreed, but who knows, maybe this romantic setting would be the ticket he needs. A secluded meadow, maybe alien fireworks...

Paul eased his long frame down on the grass and sat beside her. He kept his eyes fixed on her lips. He was done waiting, of sitting around until she gave the green light. Well, things were about to change, right then and there. He regarded the sky and noted the sun was making its final descent now, casting pastel streaks across the low-lying clouds. Long, eerie shadows, born from the final throes of sunlight, stretched across the fields. Evening was announcing its imminent arrival.

Yes, the time was now. Besides, if he waited too long, the moment would be over.

He rubbed the back of his neck, then swooped in and planted a hard kiss on her mouth. Okay, so it wasn't the most romantic thing he'd ever done, but hey, he was a guy with needs.

"What the hell?" Laura snapped her head away, her eyes wide in disbelief.

"Enough of this, Laura. You know we're good together, right? Just go with it. C'mon, baby."

"Back off!" She gave him a hard shove. "The light show is starting any second now so keep your friggin' pants on. God, you're such a Neanderthal."

Wait, did she actually put her hands on his chest and push him? Who did she think she was?

His fingers tightened into fists. "This is some kinda game for you, isn't it. Christ, you're a piece of work, you know that? You think you're—"

The ground beneath them rumbled, a subtle vibration that he disregarded at first. But gradually, the tremors traveled up through his legs, into his belly and chest, until his heartbeat matched the pulse of the vibrations. His eyes darted around the meadow, searching for something, anything, to keep them safe. He found nothing but goddamn reeds of grass vibrating in a frenzied dance, as if they were guitar strings plucked by the devil.

"Wh-what the hell?" He stumbled to his feet. The earth shifted and groaned, quivering like Jell-O. "We gotta book. Now!"

Wide-eyed and trembling, Laura managed to stand, her face ghastly white.

They amassed a single step.

The mound of grass beneath them convulsed, launching stones and twigs to join an arrhythmic dance. Deep within the earth, the quake lurched spasmodically, launching the two from their feet to collapse on the surface.

Outraged by the disturbance, the delicate breeze transformed into an angry, howling wind, swirling and whipping. Grass and twigs joined the frenzy, striking the couple with stinging bites. The blustering cacophony roared like a freight train careening through a tunnel.

Adrenaline coursed through Paul's body as he fought against the paralyzing fear. He couldn't move, he could barely breathe. All he could manage was a small movement of his head. The gale-force wind was a worthy opponent and had him pinned him to the ground. He bellowed with fury, but his voice was soundless.

He stole a glimpse at Laura. Her eyes were squeezed shut, but her mouth hung open in horror. Her shrieks were nothing more than a whisper carried off into the maelstrom.

Huddled on all fours, he tightened himself into a ball, and buried his head under his arms. His heart pounded furiously in his temples. *No, no, no. I don't wanna die. Please.*

The ground continued its vicious assault and the wind blustered with fury.

Inhalation was a Herculean effort. Every gasp felt like a thousand knives ripping his lungs apart. Amid the turmoil, harsh claps of thunder and the acrid odor of electricity penetrated his consciousness.

He ... couldn't ... breathe ...

Paul strained to inhale his final breath when the tumult abruptly ceased. The captive debris held hostage by the wind plummeted to the ragged landscape.

The sudden silence was deafening.

Fearfully, he raised his head a few inches and peered over his trembling arms. The delicate reeds of grass that once carpeted the meadow were flat or uprooted, leaving the pungent, yet sweet, scent of torn grass. Twigs and shredded leaves were scattered haphazardly all over the meadow. Paul looked over at Laura. He could only see thick, gray dust suspended in the blinding sun, so he forced his body to sit up.

"Laura." His voice sounded strained, harsh. He cleared his throat, tried again. "Laura?" He managed a decibel or two louder.

Silence.

Painfully, he heaved himself to his feet and staggered over to Laura. He peered down at her.

With disbelief, then terror, Paul saw no one.

Instead, he stared at a mound of earth shrouded by a perfect circle of charred, dead grass.

Chapter 1
2023

Fifty-eight Years Later

Rubbing his forehead between his thumb and index finger, Kevin Donahue sighed with heightening exacerbation. He leaned back in the standard, and very uncomfortable, wooden chair known to every college library and his sigh morphed into a loud, and quite long, moan.

"Oh my God! What's wrong with you? Shut up already," a college student said from a nearby cubicle.

Rubbing the back of his neck, Kevin uttered an apology and clamped his lips together. It was an unexpected blow, he thought, that after devoting four solid years to his studies, being honored with a handful of academic awards, and receiving accolades from several seasoned professors, he was going to fail out of college. Okay, maybe he was exaggerating, but he certainly felt like a failure. The research for this final project, the very last of his college career, the culmination of one-thousand-four-hundred-sixty days of study (but who's counting), was getting him nowhere. He had writer's block of the brain, complete shut-down. In a few weeks, he should be graduating summa cum laude, but without the completion of this research paper, he was certain his diploma would be withheld. For all he knew, he wouldn't even be permitted to attend the graduation ceremony. Well, that would be a kick in the teeth. And what would life be like without passing that proverbial finish line? It would be the ultimate defeat. Melodramatic? Could be. But more than anything, he desperately wanted that coveted sheet of paper affirming his dedication to his studies. The first stepping stone to a successful career, a successful life.

How depressing the only thing standing in his way was a brain fart.

He cleared his throat. It was time to buckle down, so he advanced his computer screen to another website. He managed to read five single words, *Theories Related to Celestial Bodies* when a pair of silky arms slipped around his neck and a breathy voice whispered, "Hey, you."

The stress he felt a moment ago was nothing compared to the tension he now experienced. That sexy voice was 100% cortisol injected directly into his veins, skyrocketing his blood pressure into the stratosphere. A pair of lips brush the top of his ear and a waft of Victoria Secret's Scandalous tickled his nose. In small doses, the perfume smelled just like cotton candy, but right now the fragrance was clogging up his nasal passages.

"Hiding out in the library again?" The young woman straightened herself and turned to perch on the table in front of him, blocking his laptop. "You know, Kevin, if I didn't know any better, I'd think you were avoiding me. You haven't answered any of my texts."

"You haven't sent me any texts, Brittany." He pulled his phone from his back pocket and glanced at the screen. Eleven in the past two hours, all from his girlfriend. Eleven. "Oh. Didn't see those." He tossed the phone on the table. "Listen, Britt. I have to concentrate on this paper, okay? I'll call you later. Go meet up with your friends or something."

"Hmm? What, baby?" She slid a pile of worn books stacked on the table and wiggled her butt further onto the table.

"I said, I'm still working here, but—"

"Oh, gross," she said, jumping to her feet. She swiped at her clothing and tiny black flakes adhered to her hand. "This is disgusting."

"Take it easy. They're pieces of leather from the book covers."

"Do I care? Just get them off of me."

He noticed several students turn their heads, and one girl jammed her laptop in her backpack and stormed out.

He reached over and swatted some of the flakes off Brittany's forearm. "It's no big deal, the covers are peeling. They're old."

Wrinkling her nose, she flicked one last speck off her skin and it bounced off his laptop. He barely glanced at the leather flake and knocked it off the table.

"Yeah? Well, they're repulsive and reek like rotten eggs. You do realize every book in a library is a germ-fest." She lowered her voice. "I found a tooth wedged in the pages of a book. For real, an actual tooth. Talk about repulsive. That was the last time I touched a book." She ran her fingers through her hair. "C'mon, Kev, let's just get out of here."

And that's my girlfriend, ladies and gentlemen. Scholar extraordinaire.

"Nah, go on without me. I have to figure something out for this research paper."

"Oh, I know, let's go to Starbucks. I could use a Mocha Frappuccino right about now, how 'bout you?"

Apparently, he was invisible.

"No, Brittany. Read my lips, I have work to do."

Her slender fingers fluffed the pin-straight bangs on her forehead. "Puh-lease. Hit up the internet and copy something off Wikipedia and you'll be done in ten minutes flat." She leaned over and slammed shut a heavy volume entitled *Astronomical Phenomena,* then wiped her hands on her Lycra leggings. "So, let's go."

"Hey. You lost my page. Can't you just—"

"You know what your problem is Kevin?"

Oh, here we go.

"You spend too much time worrying. You worry about getting to class on time, writing your papers, getting anything lower than an A. You're the only person I know who actually does the assigned readings. Nobody does the readings, Kev. Nobody. Learn to live a little and have some fun. Have a Frappuccino and stop reading through ancient history—you'll never find anything worthwhile in the past, and I bet those books are boring as hell."

He could feel his blood pulse in his temples but kept his tone soft and even. "They may be old publications, but you never know what you might learn from years ago. Besides, they're a real kick to read."

She raised an eyebrow.

"Like this one guy," he gestured at one of the smaller books at the top of the pile. "I think it was in the 1960s, he invented self-propelled roller skates to eliminate, as he called it, 'the exhaustion of walking.' He planned to have housewives jet themselves to the market, the beauty parlor, or wherever, without perspiring." He sniffed with amusement. "The thing was, he couldn't get the tiny engines to stop blowing off the wheels. Hit himself in the eye a few times." Chuckling, he pushed his chair back and hoisted the well-used volume. "Wait 'til you see this picture—"

"For crying out loud, Kevin, put it down. You're getting that black crap all over my new top. It's hand embroidered lace."

Rolling his eyes, he tossed the book onto the pile, a billow of air scattering the dark confetti. Kevin slumped back in his seat, feeling the red creep across his face. He couldn't deal with her right now, and he definitely couldn't deal with any research.

"The hell with this," he said, and powered down his laptop.

His girlfriend grinned, seized his wrists and dragged him out of his chair. She then retrieved a small bottle from her Louis Vuitton handbag and squirted a glob into their palms.

"Sanitizer. Believe me, you need it." She dropped the bottle back in her bag, pulled out a tube of marshmallow-flavored lip gloss and pointed it at him, as if reprimanding a small child. "Listen to me. There's nothing in the past that will have any effect on your future." She slathered her pouty lips in iridescent pink and plopped the gloss back into her bag with a flourish. "Copying Wikipedia is the way to go."

He clenched his teeth as he regarded her, mindful of her mile-long legs and pin-straight, obsidian hair cascading down her back to her butt. Sighing heavily, Kevin stacked four large tomes on top of his computer and cradled the pile in one arm. "Fine, you win. We're going. But I'm taking the books with me."

Yep, I'm a wuss.

Brittany smiled triumphantly, clutched his arm, and they exited the library. As they descended the steps, she nudged him toward the on-campus apartments that also housed one of the three university Starbucks.

"After we grab those Frapps, Leo," she crooned, "I'm gonna find all sorts of ways to loosen you up."

Leo. The tiny hairs on his neck stood at attention. For months she obsessed over his resemblance to the actor Leonardo DiCaprio, back when he played Jack Dawson in that old shipwreck movie. It was a comparison that initially flattered him but eventually disquieted him. Seriously? Leo DiCaprio? For one thing, the actor's eyes were blue, and Kevin's were a deep chocolate brown. For another, he heard this DiCaprio dude could dance, whereas Kevin was blessed with two, completely dysfunctional, left feet. He was certain Brittany relished tormenting him, for she started calling him Leo the moment he told her he hated the comparison. To make matters worse, the more he told her to cut it out, the more she used the infuriating nickname. Let's face it, everything about her had been rubbing him the wrong way.

He took a good look at his girlfriend. She was a stunning girl, there was no doubt about it, but he knew her entire self-worth was tied to an overwhelming need to be the center of everybody's attention. She delighted in turning men's heads to gawk when she sauntered past, and she basked in the glory of sowing seeds of envy in resentful women. It baffled him that the attention of strangers was so essential to her well-being. He told her countless times to tone it down, but she'd laughed him off, saying, "When you have it, flaunt it, baby." He was shamefully aware that he, himself, had fallen under her spell when they first met in Tennis 101.

He had signed up for the elective gym class this semester thinking it would be a great way to blow off some steam. Besides, it was only a four-week class, and if he didn't like it, he'd be no worse for wear. On the first day, he stood with a handful students on the court as the teacher rattled off names for attendance when he glanced up... and caught sight of her. Holy shit. The girl was a knockout in her barely-there tennis skirt and spandex tank, and he soon discovered her overhead serve was impressively deadly. Not to mention her coy and relentless flirting. In a matter of days, she had often found an excuse to touch him, whether to give him a victory hug or a squeeze to his arm after a match. "Whoa, nice tricep, Kevin Donahue."

It was tough to admit now, but he had accepted the unsolicited attention wholeheartedly. No stranger to the interest of attractive women, he recalled enjoying a few flings in college, but none of them could have competed with Brittany's jaw-dropping looks. Her sass and self-assuredness were irresistible, and he spent many restless evenings in disbelief over her avid attention in tennis class. What could a woman like her, one as close to perfection as they can come, want with a regular guy like him? Her body had exuded sexuality without effort, and her glossy, midnight black hair had practically demanded to be touched. Even the air around her had seemed electrified. Of course, he was captivated. A few weeks into tennis class and risking humiliation, Kevin mustered his courage and asked Brittany to see *The Guardians of the Galaxy.* He practically dissolved into ecstasy when the human goddess accepted.

Their relationship blossomed at warp speed. He called to mind how he reveled in the intimacy of watching Brittany get herself ready in the mornings. But now? It was like being an animal behaviorist studying the preening rituals of wildlife. For God's sake, she required well over an hour to apply her luxury cosmetics. She disguised her natural beauty beneath layers of spackle— primer, foundation, concealer, bronzer— and had a designated sewing needle with the sole purpose of separating each individual eyelash to avoid gooey mascara clumps she liked to call "goobles." How many times had he begged her to limit the quantity of makeup? She scoffed at his ridiculous idea, claimed he was a stereotypical clueless male, and like an idiot, he took her word for it. Kevin shook his head. Laying bare, those mannerisms he once deemed sexy were veritably pretentious and shallow.

Perhaps it was him all along who was shallow.

They made their way through the library exit, and he regarded her stride which was more like a bounce. She tossed him a megawatt smile, and for the first time, his heart didn't leap in response.

"You think there'll be a line at Starbucks? We better hurry."

"You know what, Britt? He slackened his pace then stopped. He couldn't do this anymore. She exhausted him. He yanked his arm from her grasp and started, "I don't think we should— I think it's time we—"

And then Kevin looked into her bewitching baby blues. Damn.

"I'm really beat," he said. "I'll ... text you later."

I'm a complete and utter wuss.

"Wait, what? Aren't we gonna hang?"

Kevin vehemently shook his head.

"Ugh. You're so annoying. Fine. Whatever." She leaned toward him on her tiptoes and planted a light kiss on his cheek. "Later, Leo."

Brittany turned away with a fragrant spin, and after spotting two of her bombshell friends, jogged to the student union building. "Hey, wait up, girls. Who feels like a Frapp?" she called out, arms waving, and the three hugged before disappearing inside.

Kevin swiped his sandy hair from his eyes, blew out a long, aggravated breath, then bee-lined in the opposite direction toward Ronnie's Pizza and Italian Eatery. No longer the lunchtime rush, only a handful of customers were there, most of whom were finishing up their last few morsels of Ronnie's famous calzones. Kevin easily located an empty stool at the counter. He nodded at an elderly patron seated at the end then dropped his heavy load of books onto a vacant chair behind him.

The establishment was old, having been in business for decades, but well maintained and clean. Kevin eyed the three enormous, iron ovens that lined a wall and emanated enough heat to warrant the air conditioner running all year. A long, wooden countertop typically found in a pub stretched opposite the ovens, giving patrons a place to eat while watching the harried chefs prepare the orders. To the left of the ovens, the restaurant expanded into a larger dining area, with tables in the center and several cozy booths nestled against the windows overlooking the street. Each tabletop sported paper placemats printed with advertisements from local businesses. Halfway decent amateur paintings of Italy's scenery were hung on the paneled walls. And, to the delight of newcomers, hundreds of empty vintage wine bottles that were decorated with coiled fisherman's rope dangled from the ceiling.

Kevin called to a weary cook working near the ovens. "Hey, Ronnie." The heavyset man turned around with a scowl until he saw Kevin, and broke into a charismatic grin.

"Well, if it isn't Kevin Donahue. Good to see you, man," he said. Kevin often wondered if Ronnie was a smoker in a former life, given his trademark gravelly voice.

"You too. Hey, pop in a couple of slices for me, would ya?"

"Sure thing."

Ronnie wiped his hands on the front of his stained apron, snatched two cheese pizza slices from under the counter and tossed them into one of the iron ovens. Despite being in his mid-sixties, Ronnie Giordano exuded the energy of a man thirty years younger. He carried his 6-foot frame in a relaxed, easy-going manner, tempering his imposing form. A 40" waistline was a clear indication that he frequently indulged in his caloric fare, and he often boasted that his authentic Italian gravy was so deliciously thick and hearty that "it'll put hair on your chest." As if to prove his claim, Giordano proudly sported an abundance of curly chest hair that peaked out the top of his crew neck t-shirt. He was also blessed with a full head of hair that was predominantly dark but recently graying above his ears. He kept it short and nonsense-free, and the moment he perceived any tuffs growing longer than an inch, he would arrive at the restaurant the following day with his coiffure severely cropped. Quite a few women had enjoyed running their fingers through that hair, but Ronnie never did find "the one".

Considering the over forty-year age difference, Kevin was well aware theirs was an unlikely friendship. The two had developed a strong bond originating from their mutual passion of baseball. During his freshman year, he was enjoying a slice of Sicilian and a heated conversation with Ronnie about the Mets' mediocre performance that season. Kevin happened to possess an extra ticket for the following week's ballgame, and it only seemed logical to invite the guy. Although the Mets lost, the two men became thick as thieves.

"So, listen Kev." The burly cook leaned across the counter. "I got good news — I scored us a couple of tickets for tonight's game against San Francisco."

"You serious? Thought they were sold out."

"Yeah, well... I know a guy. So, you gonna go or what? I got a few bucks ridin' on this one."

"Oh man, I can't believe I'm sayin' this but I gotta bail on you. No, hold up, before you start griping on me, I've got too much going on. School's been a nightmare lately, and now this thing with Brittany..." Kevin's voice trailed off into a defeated groan. It occurred to him he had been grumbling a lot lately.

"Uh oh. Trouble in paradise?"

"You can say that. Brittany's definitely easy to look at, but lately? She's irritating as hell. I don't think I can take too much more of her, Ron. I'm through."

"Hallelujah. My boy's finally seeing the light. She's mighty fine, I give you that, but damn. The girl thinks Babe Ruth's a candy bar."

Kevin laughed. "Yeah, well, you know Brittany, it's football or bust. I think she gets off from the sound of crushing helmets."

Brittany's father was a co-owner of a professional football team, and it aggravated her when Kevin couldn't bother to remember which team. The Jets? The Giants? Whatever. Football never held any great appeal to him.

Ronnie continued, "I may be a hundred years older than you, but even I know when it's time to cut someone loose."

Kevin shrugged.

"I mean it, man. She's got a hole in the toe."

"She...what?"

"She's got a hole in the toe. The way I see it, girls are like socks. You wear them and you're like, crap, they're too tight. But wear 'em awhile and the elastic will ease up. Or if they're too itchy, you wash them with fabric softener, break 'em in, and life's good again.

But then there's Brittany. She's got a gaping hole, man, and there's no fixin' that, no matter how hard you try to sew that damn thing up. Your big toe's wiggling through, trying to escape."

Kevin stared at his friend.

"Hey, your perfect sock is out there somewhere. Give it time."

"Your analogies are, if nothing else, imaginative. But listen, she's the least of my problems. You know I'm taking an astronomy class, right? The preliminary research is due on Monday. Monday. And I don't even have a proposal."

"So what? You've got all week. Why you stressin' it, man?"

Kevin shrugged. "Damn if I know. Something's holding me back, like they'll withhold my diploma or something."

"Withhold your diploma? Can they really do that?"

"I dunno, I guess. I heard the professor made arrangements with the registrar—they're to hang on to our diplomas for six months if we don't fulfill the requirements for this paper. I swear, this professor has problems."

"Whoa, that sucks."

"You have no idea. It's as if my entire future is hanging on the line over an irrelevant astronomy report."

"Okay, let me think. An astronomy topic, hmmm."

Grabbing a thick oven mitt from a hook, Ronnie heaved the heavy oven door open and tossed the two slices of pizza on paper plates, dropping them on the wooden counter without ceremony. Kevin folded a hot, deliciously aromatic pizza slice into a delightful mess, and bit off a huge stringy chunk. As he chewed, Ronnie poured him a Coke from the soda machine, yanked a rag tucked under his apron strings and began wiping down the countertop.

Kevin gulped down half of the Coke. "And not any old astronomy topic. We're supposed to research an interplanetary or celestial phenomenon and its impact on the earth."

Ronnie nodded. Leaning with his forearms on the counter, he casually crossed his ankles and looked at Kevin thoughtfully. "A celestial phenomenon? How about how the moon messes with the ocean tides?"

Kevin shook his head emphatically. "Nah, I thought about that but my professor wants us to think 'outside the box.' What the hell does that even mean? The only thing I can think of is researching the sun's impact on the earth's seasons."

"Not a bad idea. Why don't ya do it?"

"Oh, c'mon, Ron, this isn't a fourth-grade science fair." He dropped his head on the counter with a thud. "I...give...up."

"An interplanetary or celestial event. What about black holes? There's stuff drifting in space that gets swallowed up by those suckers all the time. Trapped forever, all their energy sapped right out of 'em."

Kevin leaned forward, his voice low. "You just described Brittany."

Ronnie grinned and slapped the countertop with a beefy hand. "Ha. You said it, not me."

"You know, a term paper about black holes isn't a bad idea. I'll check the library later to see if a satellite or something ever disappeared."

"It's worth a try."

"But now that I think about it, black holes don't really have an impact on our planet. Not directly, anyway. My professor would never go for it. Keep thinking, buddy, keep thinking. You're onto something."

Ronnie excused himself to take a patron's food order, then returned with a thought. "Your old man was into astronomy, wasn't he?"

"Mm-hmm. That's why I signed up for the course. I figured since my dad loved studying the stars so much, the class would be pretty cool."

"You still have his notes? Maybe he kept track of, you know, any interesting—what did you call it? Phenomena."

"Doubt it. It was only a fun hobby for him."

"No offense, kid, but, staring at the sky sounds like a pretty lame hobby."

Kevin shrugged. "I guess. But he was really into it. I remember him dragging me outside to point out constellations. I'd be standing there, shivering in my *Wolverine* pajamas and he'd say something like, 'You can't get a better night than this, Kev. Not much light pollution.' or 'There's the Big Dipper, see the North Star on the handle?' The week before his accident he bought a new telescope... you know, the kind with all the bells and whistles 'designed for the home astronomer.' He was so psyched about it. Said we'd be able to gaze into the past and see stars that burned out and died eons ago. Come to think of it, it does sound pretty awesome, doesn't it? To see the past?" Kevin took a long draw of Coke from the straw. "Fate's a funny thing. He never even had a chance to take the damn thing out of the box before he died. Mom left it sitting by the front door for months until she suddenly got rid of it."

A couple of college students entered the restaurant and claimed a booth in the back. As Ronnie grabbed a few menus for their table, he offered a sympathetic smile. "Well, I have an idea. Write about how the full moon causes women to say, 'Not tonight, honey, I've got a headache.' I'm sure you'd find a lot of guys willing to attest to that."

Kevin's worried frown cracked into a grin. "Now that's a topic."

"I do what I can."

As his buddy shuffled over to his customers, Kevin took another large bite from his pizza. He was thinking about googling 'strange interstellar events' when the elderly gentlemen at the end of the counter approached him. Kevin regarded the man's snowy hair and deep brown eyes. His tanned face was weathered with a lifetime of experience, and his pleasant smile alluded to a life fulfilled. Kevin cleared his throat, "Sir? Can I help you with something?"

"I beg your pardon," the gentleman began. "I apologize for overhearing, and I know this is none of my business, but I'd like to offer you a suggestion if I may."

Kevin grabbed a napkin and wiped his mouth while vigorously nodding. He pointed to the empty stool next to him with an open palm, inviting the older man to sit. "Yes. Please have a seat. Anything you can suggest would be fantastic."

The man ignored the invitation. "Years ago, I used to dabble in astronomy." He hesitated, as if trying to decide whether or not to share his idea. He stared at Kevin. "Have you considered researching the planetary alignment?"

Kevin furrowed his brow in disappointment. "You mean the order of the planets' distance from the sun? That's irrelevant, sir."

"No, no, no," said the gentleman. "The impact of Venus, Mars, and our moon in perfect alignment. This happened fifty-eight years ago, almost to the day. Look it up on your fancy computer, for chrissakes."

"I apologize, sir, I meant no disrespect."

"Apology accepted."

The man reached for a sweater on his stool, slowly walked to the door, pulled it open, and departed without another word.

Chapter 2

Kevin gaped at the door. What an odd encounter.

He shrugged, finished his lunch in two enormous swallows, drained his Coke, and scattered a few bills on the counter.

"See ya, pal" Kevin called out.

Ronnie was engrossed in conversation with his customers, but managed a quick wave as Kevin exited the restaurant, lugging his pile of burden back toward the library. Risking a glance at the student union building, Kevin quickened his pace and prayed he wouldn't run into Brittany. Please, not now. He was practically jogging by the time he arrived to the library's remote parking lot. A shiny, black Kawasaki Ninja 300 SE was waiting for him, and he grinned.

"Hello, Lucille. I missed you, sweetheart," he murmured to his bike.

He yanked a bright orange helmet from the rear leather pouch and shoved his belongings in its stead. The helmet was a gift from his widowed mother. "In case the police need to find you in a ditch on the side of a road someplace." His cheeks flushed as he pulled the ABS bubble onto his head, aware that he resembled the obnoxious aerial marker balls on power lines to alert low-flying planes. But now that she was redefining herself in Europe with her new husband, the helmet offered a trace of maternal solace in his lonely, frenzied existence.

Yes, it was easy to admit he was lonely. Even though he had his best friend, Ronnie, it wasn't easy navigating life without the unconditional love of family to support him. Never in a million years would he ever give his mother a hint of his despondency. He would shield her from that burden well after he graduated and settled down. His mom had taken the death of Kevin's dad extraordinarily hard, and had spent years quietly burying her tears while creating a loving, but fatherless childhood for Kevin. It wasn't until Kevin turned fifteen that his mother reclaimed her dynamic personality and pulled a complete 180. She grabbed life by the horns and returned to school, earned a degree in finance, and married a CEO of a Fortune 500 company. If she found a way to enjoy her life again, then he could, too.

He rolled on the throttle, hammered down, and sped for home.

Kevin inhaled the clean, fresh scent of ozone and felt the taut knots of stress softening. Lining both sides of the road, thick foliage gave the illusion of driving through a leaf-covered tunnel, but every now and then he caught the majestic view of the river in the distance. The lull of Lucille's motor was soothing, almost hypnotic, and helped him untangle the disarray in his mind.

First, he had to break up with Brittany, that was a given. Her presence in his life was suffocating, no longer worth the fifteen minutes of intense satisfaction on Saturday nights. Secondly, his indecision about this final paper was ridiculous, and at this point he'd go ahead and select any damn celestial occurrence. He wanted to kick himself for even enrolling in an astronomy class. As a geophysics major, he gravitated toward earth science classes—at least there you're provided solid answers about the earth. Astronomy, on the other hand, was riddled with unanswered questions about the universe as a whole, and he abhorred uncertainty. Life was much easier to navigate when you can see where you're going, with a few surprises along the way to keep you on your toes. But no matter, it wasn't worth dwelling over. After writing this paper, he'd never have to think about celestial bodies ever again.

Kevin veered Lucille into an apartment complex and followed the winding driveway to a two-story brick building at the top of the hillside. He eased the motorcycle into his designated parking spot and kicked out the side-stand. Retrieving his articles from the sack, he stuffed them in his helmet and loped to an entrance labeled 42B. He worked his key in the lock and shoved open the door to his meager one-bedroom apartment. It wasn't much, but it was home.

The walls of his living room were adorned with science related posters, including the infamous photograph of Albert Einstein sticking out his tongue, and a rendering of a man with a pickaxe entitled, "Geophysicists Rock." A worn upholstered couch draped with a NY Giants fleece throw blanket, courtesy of Brittany, was positioned against the wall under the posters. Practically daily, Kevin sprawled on that couch and marveled the unobstructed view of the river through the balcony glass doors. Positioned in front of the couch sat a chunky oak coffee table, ladened with homework assignments and notes strewn haphazardly across its surface. A stained coffee mug imprinted with *Beam me up, Scotty* rested in the corner, threatening to tumble to the rug.

Kevin flung his belongings on the couch and grabbed a chilled can of Bud from the fridge, cracking it open. He chugged a few refreshing mouthfuls and strode to the sliding glass doors to his balcony. Without opening the door, he admired the view of the distant river for a moment, aching to unwind outside and bask in the peace. The undercurrent of anxiety started rearing its ugly head, forcing him to deal with his astronomy dilemma.

That elderly customer at Ronnie's was interesting. Eccentric, but interesting. Kevin never heard of any planetary alignment before, and he had nothing to lose checking out the guy's recommendation, but still—if the alignment had actually had a huge impact on the Earth, wouldn't he have heard about it prior to today? He turned away from the door.

Time to get back to work.

Hastily shoving the paperwork from the coffee table into the semblance of a pile, Kevin pried open the top of his computer and connected to the internet, the word *Google* taunting him. He poised his fingers on the keyboard. "Okay, Google. Let's see what you come up with."

He typed in Planetary Alignment. Wow, 430,000 results popped up. His eyes scanned through the selections, momentarily regarding and dismissing the science fiction sites. Hold on, what was this? His eyes widened to a PDF file from 1965 labeled, *"Planetary Alignment in Northern USA to Wreak Havoc."* He guided the computer mouse to the link and opened it.

April 23, 1965

The Tenakill Tribune - Beware of unexplainable chaos and outlandish behavior tonight. According to the top astronomers at the Lincoln Observatory, these events may be the result of a rare interstellar occurrence, an alignment of planets. As the sun sets at 7:44 p.m., Mars, Venus, and our moon will align to form an entrancing light show over the next few days. However, legends originating from ancient mythology claim the alignment will have dire consequences on our planet. Fanatics believe the earth will enter the final throes of its demise. Zealots predict catastrophic tornadoes, thunderstorms, and earthquakes. Present-day astronomers claim the planetary alignment will merely be a captivating light show. Only time will tell.

Kevin stretched back in his chair with his hands behind his head and heaved a heavy sigh. *Thank you, strange old pizza guy. You may have just saved me.*

He readjusted himself in his seat to continue researching. Obviously, the Earth didn't blow up, but there better be an effect on the Earth, such as neon lightning bolts or even a brief rainstorm, otherwise he'd be back to the drawing board for a topic.

Would a couple of planets lining up with the moon even have an effect at all?

Time to find out.

His fingers tapped the subsequent day across the keyboard, "*April 24, 1965, The Tenakill Tribune*" and opened another scanned copy of the newspaper. Skimming through the pages, he was momentarily distracted by an advertisement, "*Brought to you in living color, NBC presents Frank Sinatra's Fiftieth Birthday Special*," but soon located an ominous article entitled "*Local Boy Suspected of Murder in Sullivan's Meadow.*" Kevin's finger was poised above the arrow icon to advance to the next page, but his eye spotted "planetary alignment" in the news story. He began reading.

Local Boy Suspected of Murder in Sullivan's Meadow
Last night, a 20-year-old male of Sullivan Township was held as a prime suspect in the disappearance and possible murder of his girlfriend, also 20 years of age. Local authorities informed the *Tribune* that the suspect insists the victim had disappeared while attempting to witness the hyped planetary alignment light show. The suspect also described a short-lived storm preceding his girlfriend's disappearance. Authorities say no such storm occurred. Names are not released as a full investigation is underway.

Well, well, well. A murder. Kevin wondered if the boy was convicted, but refocused his thoughts to gather information about the cosmic occurrence for his project. He didn't have much to go on, other than a small possibility of a storm and the appearance of unusual, astronomical lights. He double-checked the date of the phenomenon, and froze.

April 23, 1965. Tomorrow was April 23rd, fifty-eight years later.

Kevin's heart quickened and his mind raced. Chances were there'd be no replication of a planetary alignment tomorrow, otherwise he'd have heard about it in the news. But what if he wrote how the planetary alignment in 1965 caused a kid to commit murder? Afterall, the previous article warned its readers about outlandish behavior, and committing murder definitely fit that bill. He could head up to Sullivan's meadow, fifty-eight years to the day, and wrap up his paper with first-hand observations of the sky for comparison purposes.

Definitely not a bad idea. Before he could change his mind, Kevin hovered his computer mouse over the Yahoo mail icon and clicked. If Dr. Archer gave the go-ahead, he had until tomorrow evening to get ready. He cracked his knuckles and flexed his fingers, then tapped the keys.

Five minutes later, his email chimed. *Proposed topic approved.*

"Yes." Kevin pumped his fist in the air and whooped.

Chapter 3

Sunday progressed at a snail's pace but Kevin was preoccupied with his projected strategy for this evening. For the bulk of the day, he holed up in the university's library searching for resources and organizing a rough outline for his paper. He managed to locate an abundance of material written in the 1960s by astrophysicists who were renowned for their studies on syzygy, or the occurrence of three or more cosmic bodies aligning in the same gravitational system. Several novice scientists, he learned, were convinced an alignment would trigger a reverse in the Earth's rotation, thereby creating a shift in the planet's polarity. Reading these ludicrous scenarios, he decided to devote an entire section of his report to the superstitious beliefs related to syzygy.

After exhausting his pile of periodicals for any relevant information, Kevin perused current NASA publications for a mention of the alignment's anniversary. He was skimming the third feature in *Spaceport Magazine* when he arrived at the following line: *After fifty-eight years of orbit,* the author stated, *Mars, Venus, and the Earth's moon will once again be aligned at sunset on April 23, 2023.*

He stopped. And blinked.

It was going to happen...again?

Thunderstruck, he read the article in its entirety then let it drop in his lap. He was actually going to see it, first-hand. He eagerly rifled through the remaining sources but there was no other mention of tonight's alignment. Sadly, society had lost its passion for outer space and instead developed a penchant for vulgar Reality TV.

Pursing his lips, Kevin stared at his outline on the computer screen. A section detailing his observations tonight was necessary, especially since he'd bear witness to the event. He allotted time before sunset to canvass the meadow, jot down a few notes and log any abnormalities. He wasn't quite sure what to expect, if anything. Sparkling stars? Or stretches of prismatic light like the Aurora Borealis?

His phone chirped. A text from Brittany. Argh, great timing, Britt. Kevin responded, *Busy now TTYL,* and checked the time. Oh crap, 5:30. He hastily gathered his books and papers together and hustled home.

There wasn't much time before dusk, but an exhilarating rush of adrenaline coursed through his body. He was no longer wallowing in the inky pit of despair, because finally, yes finally, he developed a solid plan for his term paper. With the plan out of the way, he anticipated the celestial event with renewed energy, certain it would be monumental. Not to mention the added mystery and intrigue of a fifty-eight-year-old murder. It was certainly possible that the timing of the murder and the alignment was completely coincidental. But on the other hand, the planetary alignment might have caused an influx of hormones in the perpetrator and awakened latent, deranged tendencies—

The phone chirped. *Leo. U ghosting me?*

Seriously? Kevin fired back, *Busy. Catch you tomorrow.* Okay, he was being a jackass, but he really didn't have time for this.

Scurrying around the apartment like a lab mouse in a maze, he grabbed various supplies for the night's escapade, even remembering to grab a flashlight. He scarfed down his go-to meal on the run, Lucky Charms, and the phone chimed yet again.

No, not 2morrow. 2night. Ur taking me to the new Vietnamese place. Pick me up at 7. No jeans.

Vietnamese food? She knew he hated the stuff. Impatiently, he typed another quick note of dismissal, and as he stuffed the phone into the back pocket of his jeans, it began ringing. No, not a text but an actual phone call. He yanked it out of his pocket and glanced at the screen. Brittany. That was bizarre. She didn't believe in phone conversations.

"Hey, Britt, I'm on my way out—"

"Kevin. Before you say anything, I need to get this off my chest. This thing we have going on? This so-called relationship? It's not working for me. I'm not feeling the same connection with you anymore and I want to move on. No offense. I thought I'd be a decent human being and actually tell you face-to-face on the phone. So, goodbye, Leo baby. Maybe someday we can be, like, friends."

He heard feminine laughter in the background as she abruptly ended the call. He was rooted to the spot.

Wait. Did that just happen? She broke up with him?

He shook his head, stunned. Apparently, Brittany was much more aware of his irritation and impatience than he assumed. She managed to cut things off with him before he had the chance to do it himself—she would never subject herself to the humiliation of being dumped.

His stomach somersaulted with a twinge of guilt. He'd acted like a complete jerk to her today. Sure, their relationship was spiraling to its doom for a few weeks, and he only postponed the inevitable breakup to avoid her tears and histrionics. No, that wasn't true. Let's face it, he had chickened out. Regardless, he needed to shake off the guilts and be thankful the relationship was finally over.

Kevin slid the phone in his back pocket, muttering, "Face-to-face...on a phone call? Really?" He snagged his keys off the coffee table and allowed the door to slam behind him.

Twenty minutes later, Lucille's GPS guided him to a remote section of Sullivan Township that he never knew existed. Fortunately, the motorcycle was capable of handling off-road terrain, as the last half mile twisted through a wooded area laden with ancient trees supporting a thick, leafy canopy. Abruptly, the roadway ended at the threshold of a glorious meadow, seemingly endless acres of luscious, vivid green grass delicately swaying in the breeze. He inhaled deeply, appreciating the fresh aroma of the landscape. After rolling his bike to a stop and positioning it next to an imposing oak tree, he removed his helmet and secured it to the handlebars. Carefully, he pulled his laptop out of the sack while admiring the tranquility and serenity in the isolated pasture before him.

A few paces into the field, Kevin spotted an old, dilapidated cottage about a hundred yards to his left. The building appeared abandoned and uninhabitable, but instead of running the risk of trespassing on private property, he opted to approach the house to find its owner. If someone actually lived in Sullivan's Meadow, he'd better ask permission before he traipsed around the property.

The graying shingles attached to the cabin were in shambles, many of which had fallen to the dirt, rotten. The uneven path to the front door was choked with bushy clumps of dead weeds in the crevices, and he found himself circumnavigating large rocks and branches strewn across the path. The front door appeared to be made of wood, but decades in the sun had bleached the hue into a dull, miserable ash.

He couldn't rationalize his trepidation, so he raised a fist to the door and lightly rapped on the frame. No response. He attempted again, this time knocking sharply. Silence. Kevin turned his head and surveyed the sweeping grasses of the meadow but located no one.

After a brief hesitation, he edged his way along the front of the house and inspected the area to its side. There, a worn, dusty footpath extended into the grass and ended at an ornate wrought iron bench. Seated on the bench was an aged man, completely unaware of Kevin's presence.

Kevin cleared his throat. "Excuse me? Sir?"

The man slowly lifted his head and peered at him with watery eyes. "Hmm? Who the hell are you? This is private property, kid." His voice was thin, weak, as if unaccustomed to speaking.

"Um, I'm sorry to bother you, sir. My name's Kevin Donahue and I'm a senior at Sullivan U. I was wondering if I could walk around your property for a research project."

"Did 'ya say Sullivan University? That shit-for-brains school? Ha. The morons there don't know their asses from their elbows."

Dumb-struck, Kevin stood there.

"What's the matter? You surprised? Your precious institution is run by a bunch of bureaucratic morons whose heads are up their a-holes." The man snorted and rubbed his nose with the back of his hand. "Take my advice and get out now, while you can. Unless hanging out with those idiots is your scene."

Okay, so the guy clearly didn't like Sullivan U.

"Uhh yeah, right, they're a bunch of idiots. But, the meadow? Is it okay if I walk around?"

"My meadow. My glorious meadow. You like it here, huh? Lots of secrets hidden here, I can tell you that. Even the secrets have secrets." The old man set his gaze onto Kevin. "What d'ya want with my meadow, kid?"

"I don't want anything. I'm conducting research for a class, that's all."

"Research, that's a hoot. You're not gonna find anything. Nothin' to see here. Not a damn thing." He turned his head away.

"Oh, I'm not so sure about that." With the intent to intrigue the man, Kevin added, "I'm investigating the planetary alignment. You've heard of it?"

The ailing man's head shot up and he gaped at Kevin. He struggled to raise himself from the bench and balanced his weary body on unsteady legs.

"What the hell you sayin'? You a cop? It's been fifty some-odd years, damn it, and you want to harass me again? Why can't you people leave me alone." His wavering voice gathered strength and volume. "I told you all that I know, damn you."

"No. No, I'm not a cop. I told you, I'm a college student, remember? From Sullivan U?" Stunned by the guy's enraged reaction, Kevin aborted his research and turned to make his escape. "It doesn't matter anyway, I'm leaving. See ya."

Crazy old coot.

"Ahhh, that's right, that's right. You're a college student, a big man on campus." The withered derelict ruminated. "And you want to look into that god-damn planetary alignment. What for, you wanna dance with the devil? Hey, it's your neck, kid." He shuffled toward Kevin. "But be my guest, look around. You're not gonna find anything worth a damn. I've been searching for fifty-eight years and never got a whiff of a clue. Fifty-eight years. You know what fifty-eight years is? More than half a god-damn century, that's what." He raised a trembling finger at Kevin's head. "You listen here, college boy, you do your research and find answers. I wanna know the truth." He was hollering now, with lines of spittle tracing down his chin.

Kevin took a few steps back.

I'm alone with a psycho. Oh, fabulous.

He knew he should get away from this deranged loon, but he told himself to hang in there. He needed this observation. "Hey, I'm here to look around, take a few notes, that's it. I don't have any idea what truths you're talking about, mister, but it has nothing to do with me."

"Uh-uh, you listen to me, bub. You find anything, I wanna hear about it. It's my meadow."

Kevin shivered. The guy's piercing stare unnerved him. "Fine, fine. Whatever you say. I'll be outta your hair after the sunset."

Appeased, the man removed his liquid blue eyes from his uninvited guest and watched the long reeds of grass flutter. "They're all connected, you see, all of it— the alignment, the meadow, the storms. Don't know how, swear I don't." He snatched a walking stick resting on the back of the bench and staggered closer to him. "But by God, they're connected."

Kevin studied the man. His face was aged with deep lines of a wretched existence, his thin lips drawn in a permanent grimace. The man's thinning hair was drab, the identical ashy tint of the shack's shingles, and a gray stubble shrouded his quivering jaw. Kevin could detect the thin, malnourished frame beneath the soiled t-shirt and dungarees and concluded from the anguished, hardened appearance the guy had never experienced the frivolities of youth.

The man summoned him to the bench. "Get your butt over here and sit."

Hesitating for a moment, Kevin stepped over to the seat and eased himself down. A pungent, sour odor penetrated his nostrils and he willed himself not to gag. He swallowed several times, fighting the urge to puke.

"Right. Now, look, kid. What do you see?"

Kevin peered at a vast field of bright green grass waving lazily in the soft blowing wind, then he looked into the sky for anything celestial. Nothing.

"Don't be a dimwit. Look down."

Several feet in front of him, he could just about make out a deviation in the dancing grass. Kevin rose from the bench and inched forward for an unobstructed view. A five-foot circle of singed, yellow grass lay before him, scarring the earth. He squatted closer to the flaw and extended his hand to touch the dead grass. The blades felt waxy and unreal.

His eyes focused on the lifeless grass. "Strange. What is this?"

The elderly man snorted contemptuously. "You said you're studying the planetary alignment."

Kevin straightened himself into a standing position. "Yeah, I did. And you're showing me a patch of dead grass."

With a trembling sigh, the old man lowered himself to the bench and visibly withered. If the seat had cushions, he would've melted into the tufts of foam rubber and fabric, disappearing completely.

"You don't get it. Nobody gets it." He raised his filmy eyes to meet Kevin's. "I already told you, they're all connected. The planetary alignment, this meadow. I came here fifty-eight years ago. She wanted to see the light show. Who the hell cares about a light show? But she wanted to see it. A light show in Sullivan's Meadow, with a clear view of the sky. So why not. Figured she'd find a way to thank me later. Heh, what's the worst that could happen?" He sniffed. "I'll tell you what's the worst that could happen. A storm from hell, that's what."

And he began his tale.

"It was 1965, and this crazy planetary light show was to be all the rage..."

Chapter 4
1965

Paul spun in frantic circles searching for her. "Laura!" he screamed with desperation. At one point the sun had dissolved into the horizon and the sky darkened into navy. Two pinpoints of starlight, one brilliant white and the other a rusty red crowded the crescent moon. He roared at the heavens, wildly and incessantly, "Laura!" and listened periodically for a response. He strained to hear a voice in return. Nothing.

Exhausted, he collapsed next to the scorched grass, panting. His brain attempted to find a logical explanation for her disappearance, but couldn't grasp any tangible threads. He knew she'd been cowering beside him, shrieking in panic. Could she have somehow escaped the storm? Impossible. The winds were too powerful. The charred circle was all that was left of her.

Staggering through the reeds of shredded grass, he was barely aware of the various shades of violet progressing across the night sky. Stars punctuated the darkness, providing hazy illumination across the meadow. Hearing nothing but his own desperate breaths shattering the silence, he stumbled through the fields. She was right next to him, wasn't she? She was right next to him and then she was gone, as if she never existed.

"Laura!" His voice, hoarse with dismay, shouted through the emptiness and returned as echoes, mocking him. Even his legs were betraying him, his thighs and calves were like Jell-O, and he collapsed near the blackened patch of grass. His chest heaved with every breath.

Think, Calloway, think. Stop acting like a dork.

He forced himself to slow his breathing, calm the hell down, and think this through.

Nothing made any sense. A freak storm. What the hell did it do to her? He was certain, absolutely certain, she vanished into oblivion. But maybe she'd come back just as suddenly. Of course. He'd wait right there, in the grass, until she returned. They'd hop into the car and it would be like this harrowing shit never happened.

So, he waited, and he would not leave without her.

The overnight hours passed into morning and afternoon, and Paul remained in the meadow, vigilant and alert. The surge of panic eased over time, giving him a reasonably clear head to analyze every aspect of the evening. Did the chaos of the storm mess with his brain? Turned him into a birdbrained dweeb? Oh, come off it, he was a Calloway. They were the strongest, brightest family in town. Besides, nobody simply goes 'poof' out of existence. He laughed at his own moronic stupidity, until he heard a high-pitched, crazed, shriek, kind of like a hyena's laugh. He recoiled. The hyena's laugh was his.

Pulling his back his shoulders, he lifted his chin. He had to stop acting like a fool and think. More than likely, Laura had crawled out of the tumult and escaped to the woods. The rationale was sound. The poor girl was probably lost somewhere in the acres of trees, terrified and alone. That had to be it. Did he freak her out by kissing her? Nah, deep down she knew they were good together. Playing hard-to-get, that's what she was doing. Women. Now that he had it all figured out, he'd better get his butt up and search for her in the woods. She'd be all over him once he found her. Matter of fact, he'd be a hero. Everyone in Sullivan Township would look up to him. Heck, the entire country would declare him a hero. They'd have a celebratory hero's parade, and President Lyndon B. Johnson himself would clap his shoulder and tell him how lucky our country was to have such a fine fellow. He'd thank

Paul for his courage, his persistence, and for saving a young girl's life against all odds. Then, the president would open one of those fancy velvet boxes with those ornate hinges and award Paul with the Medal of Valor.

With a renewed sense of purpose, Paul spent the next several hours scouring the woods calling Laura's name. He combed through the trees, searched inside hollow logs, and checked behind boulders. Nothing. Not a single trace of her. The forest was expansive. It would take weeks to search it properly. What if he couldn't find her? What then? He couldn't show his face in town without her. He needed to be the hero, for cryin' out loud.

Day turned into night, and as he emerged from the thicket and back into the meadow, Paul looked up at the inky black sky. She was gone. He settled himself against a young sapling, his cheeks wet with salty tears. He failed. He was no hero.

Tenacity spent, Paul dozed.

* * *

The sun rose once again over the meadow, and with one last glance at the waving reeds, Paul wiped his eyes. He climbed into his parked Corvair at the edge of the trees and followed the long, winding trail away from Sullivan's Meadow into town. He needed help.

He burst through the door at the police station, his chest heaving, and stumbled to the dispatcher's desk. The room was eerily quiet, broken by the sound of shuffling papers and an occasional cough. The fluorescent lights hummed overhead, casting an artificial glow across the room. Paul's heart pounded against his ribcage, his face etched with desperation.

"H-help me. My girlfriend. Sh-she's gone."

The officer looked up from his desk, pen still poised. Taking in Paul's disheveled appearance, he scowled and returned to his work.

Paul slammed his hand on the desk, ratting a cup of pencils. "I said, my girlfriend's gone. I need your help."

"What I need is your name, kid," the officer said, impassively.

"You don't understand..."

The officer peered over his reading glasses and leveled his gaze at Paul.

"Your. Name."

"I'm Paul Ca—" He fixed his eyes on a man and woman across the room and cried out, "Mr. and Mrs. Malone!"

Seated in the hard plastic chairs against the cinderblock wall, Laura's parents were cradling Styrofoam cups of lukewarm coffee. Wearily, they raised their eyes in response.

Mr. Malone's eyes widened in surprise. His lips parted as if ready to answer a question as he handed his coffee to his wife as he stood up. He was at Paul's side in three long strides.

"You son of a bitch!" the man yelled, and threw a right cross that connected with Paul's jaw. His wife shrieked and the station erupted in bedlam. Chairs scraped across the linoleum as people rushed from their seats, confused and alarmed. Officers rushed in, shouting commands that couldn't be heard over the pandemonium.

Spewing venom, the livid father unloaded on Paul. "Where is my daughter, you degenerate? Answer me, God damn it!" His face was contorted with loathing.

Three officers grabbed Mr. Malone and hauled him away from Paul, blood running down his chin. Mrs. Malone unleashed a raw, guttural howl.

Blinking rapidly, Paul could barely feel his split lip. "Why'd you—"

"Shut up," hollered a brawny officer. "Not a word outta you, kid."

He seized Paul's forearm and twisted it painfully behind his back, then slammed him over a desk. Papers scattered like confetti all over the floor. "Head down. I said, keep your head down. On the desk." He turned his head toward Mr. Malone. "This the fella you were tellin' me 'bout?"

"Yeah, yeah, that's the kid. He kidnapped my daughter! I'm gonna kill him!"

Mrs. Malone wailed a jarring, high-pitched scream.

"Will someone shut that woman up? God damn it."

The cries and shouts heightened to an ungodly volume, feeding the overall commotion.

"Get 'em both outta here!"

Mr. Malone hollered obscenities as he was escorted through a doorway, and his sobbing wife followed behind.

The auditory assault faded.

"Until we get to the bottom of this, you little shit, you've got the right to remain silent." Paul whimpered as his head was bashed onto the wooden desktop and held there, his cheek pressed painfully on a paperclip. "Anything you say can and will be held against you..."

Five minutes later, beefy hands shoved him into an interrogation room, his shins cracking against an aluminum fold-out chair. Trembling, he peered around the cinderblock room, noting another chair on the other side of a nondescript wooden table. The solid door creaked open and a uniformed policeman entered, tossing him a few ice cubes wrapped in a rag.

"Here. Thought you might need this. Take a seat."

Wincing, Paul pressed the ice to his lip, while the cop sat across from him, examining his driver's license. He was dressed in a standard navy-blue uniform with a wide utility belt fastened around his waist. Paul noticed a pair of handcuffs tucked into the belt and swallowed. After an agonizing minute of silence, the officer placed the license on the table and began speaking.

"I'm Detective Garrison. Any idea why you're being held?"

Paul slowly shook his head and his swollen lip throbbed in protest.

"You were the last person to be seen with Laura Malone. She's been missing for over forty-eight hours. As you can imagine, her parents are panic-stricken. No phone call, not a word from their daughter. So, tell me, Mr. Calloway, where is she? Where is Laura Malone?"

"I swear, mister, I don't know, you gotta believe me—"

"Somethin' wrong with your ears? It's detective. Detective Garrison. And for the record, I don't 'gotta believe' you. So, here's what you're gonna do, see. You're gonna tell me exactly what happened on April 23rd, every detail, from the moment you woke up in the morning, to when you you ate your friggin' Wheaties. The whole day. You got me?"

Blinking back his tears, Paul raked his fingers in his hair and began his account, aware that his words were a jumbled mess. The detective scratched illegible notes on his pad, expressionless.

"Let me get this straight. You say you were working all day at Esso on Sunday, then picked Miss Malone up at the malt shop at 7 that evening. You drove to Sullivan's Meadow and thirty minutes later experienced an earthquake in the fields prior to the victim's disappearance."

"Well, yes, an earthquake and a tornado. It was really windy."

Detective Garrison peered over his notepad. "Which was it, Mr. Calloway, an earthquake or a tornado?"

"Uh, both."

The officer's hardened stare bore into Paul. "Let's try this again. You and Miss Malone were in Sullivan's Meadow shortly after 7 p.m. on the 23rd. Then, out of nowhere, you experienced an earthquake and a tornado, and Miss Malone disappeared. Is this your statement?"

48

Paul dropped his chin to his chest and squeezed his eyes shut. The truth was farfetched, and he recognized his fate was no longer certain.

An hour later, as Paul sat miserably on the edge of a rickety cot with his head in his hands, a booming voice echoed off the cinderblocks of the holding cell.

"Where the hell is he? Where's my son, goddamn it?"

A young, skittish police officer escorted Paul's father to the bars of the jail cell, and said, "Uh, I can only allow you a few minutes with him, sir, while we finalize the paperwork."

Paul saw his father and rushed to his feet. "Dad."

Dressed in an immaculate herringbone-woven suit, Richard Calloway radiated self-importance and conceit. He scowled at the officer then turned his icy glare at Paul.

Aware he was cowering in his father's presence, Paul squared his shoulders and cleared his throat. "I'm glad you're here, Dad. There's been a misunderstanding—"

"Stop. Just, stop. Do not insult my intelligence with another excuse. You've gone too far this time."

"I didn't—"

"Cut the crap. What, you think I was born yesterday? You're a fucking disgrace and have been a colossal embarrassment to me and your mother for years. How many times are you going to fuck up, huh? Let's forget about your shenanigans in high school, shall we, and talk about how you got kicked out of college. How the hell do you get expelled from a school I donate thousands of dollars to every single year? I'll tell you how. You're a good-for-nothing jackass. A lazy, unambitious jackass who thought he could get away with assaulting a scrawny kid for a useless fraternity. You're supposed to be above that."

Paul opened his mouth to respond but thought better of it.

"No. You do not get to speak, you get to listen. We had a deal. You were supposed to straighten yourself out, get your crappy old job back, prove you're a man. Land a girl who isn't a goddamn slut. And what the fuck do you do? You land a decent enough girl but confabulate this preposterous story that she vanished in a puff of smoke. Where is she, Paul, huh? Did it even occur to you if she doesn't come home the blame is all on you? Jesus Christ, what the hell were you thinking?" The elder Calloway raked his hair back with his hands. "This latest stunt of yours is going to cost me a fortune in legal bills."

"Dad—"

"I've had enough of you." He turned his back and began walking away. "You stew on it as the detective processes your paperwork. You better figure out how to explain this to your mother by the time we get home." A few strides later, he added, "And wipe that goddamn blood off your face!"

* * *

Laura never returned, and the next few years were agonizing. Paul suffered through accusations of kidnapping and murder, but law enforcement was unable to obtain sufficient evidence for a formal charge. Respected seismologists and meteorologists refuted Paul's claims. There was no earthquake, and there certainly was no tornado. It was all in his head.

In the evenings, Paul holed up with his parents in their home, attempting to ignore the recurrent vandalism of their property and phone calls of death threats. Skeptical of his science fiction story and a desire to disassociate themselves from a suspected criminal, his friends deserted him, one by one. Girls who had once pined over his rugged good looks, mischievous smile, and wealth, trotted to the other side of the street to avoid him. "Steer clear of that one," a girl whispered to her gaggle of friends. "He killed his girlfriend, can you believe it?"

Eventually, Paul lost his part-time job at the Esso station. "So sorry, kid. I know you didn't do it, but I have a business to run. You know how it is, right?"

He began spending long, wasteful hours at the tavern, searching for comfort in Budweiser. Shortly after his parents died, Sullivan's Meadow was up for sale. His bid was the only offer, as nobody wanted to purchase land where a dead body was likely hidden.

Paul built a small cottage and remained in a self-inflicted exile for decades.

Chapter 5
2023

The old man cast a wary eye onto Kevin. "You don't believe me? What the hell, no one else does either. It happened so long ago I doubt the story myself."

Kevin inhaled deeply while attempting to digest the implausible story. It certainly was a tall tale. Sundown was expected in a few minutes so he tried his best to be interested.

"Sounds like you've had it rough, especially losing your girlfriend like that."

The man scrutinized Kevin, his lips trembling. "And what do you mean, exactly?"

Kevin shrugged. "Well, sorry for stating the obvious, but you lost your girlfriend and that's hard enough. But then for people to put the blame on you? That's rough, man." He glanced at the sky. Any minute now.

Voice cracking, Calloway responded, "It's taken fifty-eight years. Fifty-eight. Not one person before you had ever acknowledged my pain. Not even my father." He raised himself from the bench and hobbled toward the house. "I'm going inside. Do whatever you want out here."

The door closed with barely a whisper. Even though the anecdote was preposterous, he felt sorry for the eccentric old guy and could almost feel his pain. Losing the person you love, whether they disappeared into thin air or not, would leave anyone feeling shattered. Looking up, Kevin saw pink streaks spanning across the atmosphere. Sundown was moments away. He emitted a heavy sigh and got to work.

Opening the laptop and placing it on the bench, Kevin prepared a blank Word document to record his observations then he gazed up at the heavens. The sky was darkening ever so slightly, pastel hues deepening into threads of fiery oranges and reds. A warm gust of spring air tickled the reeds of grass, and as they shimmied to and fro, he marveled at their brilliant green blades. Dusk managed to transform the world before him into a dazzling landscape of brilliancy.

The sun dipped lower and hovered at the horizon, stretching the tethered bands of golden amber and orange across the skyline. Directly above him, the sky was now a rich navy blue speckled with the first hint of distant stars. His breath caught in his throat. Never before had he witnessed a sunset so glorious.

Holy shit. It's really happening. The celestial light show.

Searching his small pack of supplies, Kevin cursed himself for neglecting to pack binoculars and was praying the remaining effects of the phenomenon could be witnessed with the naked eye. It occurred to him Calloway might own a pair of binoculars. He'd run and ask him.

He turned toward the cottage and managed to take a single step when the earth began to rumble.

"Uh oh."

The tremors vibrated the earth beneath him, but soon the pulses magnified exponentially. The powerful rage of the quake tumbled Kevin to the ground. At that instant, fierce winds spiraled and whirled with such force they caused the sturdy wrought iron bench to vibrate, then fall over. The storm roared with a nightmarish fury, screeching as it whipped through the whipping grass. He cowered in the dirt, praying for the torment to end. High-pitched howls screamed at him.

Oh God, he couldn't breathe—

As if somebody flicked a switch, the intensity of the winds subsided and the earth ceased its rolling.

His ears, though, continued ringing from the wind's terrifying shriek, a sound that mimicked a person's terrified cries in the face of catastrophe.

Breathe, Kevin instructed himself. Keep on breathing.

He gasped for air until, finally, he inhaled a sufficient lungful.

He heaved his unsteady body upright and noticed the shrieking noise had diminished into sobs.

Turning toward the whimper, he forced his eyes to look at the scorched circle of grass. In its epicenter, what appeared to be a human figure, was curled in a fetal position.

He furrowed his brow. No, that couldn't be right.

What the hell is that thing?

Kevin squinted at the mound, hoping to bring the shape into focus, when it suddenly became quite evident what he was staring at. He dropped open his mouth.

It was a woman.

Despite the shroud of night, Kevin saw tears trailing from striking green eyes. Convinced he was hallucinating, he squeezed his eyes shut, and as far as hallucinations go, this one was a real doozy. But when the hallucination began to speak, Kevin snapped open his eyes and staggered backwards. A shiver ran down his spine, every nerve in his body on high alert.

The woman, whose arms encircled her knees to her chest, lifted her head slightly.

"Oh my God, is it over?" She turned her head and said, "Paul? You okay?" Her eyes settled on a vacant patch of grass beside her. She looked up. Hastily wiping the tears from her cheeks, the girl scanned the dark meadow only to find Kevin. "Oh," she exclaimed, startled, and scrambled to her feet. "I, uh, didn't know anybody else was here. You got caught in the storm too, huh?"

The moon had taken its rightful position in the night's sky and was glowing behind her, providing enough illumination to accentuate her trembling body. She looked ethereal. "I was with someone. Did you see where he went?"

Rooted to the spot and speechless, Kevin was completely baffled. How in God's name did a woman magically appear out of, well, nothing?

"Hey, did you see him? I'm pretty freaked out and I need to find him."

He cleared his throat. His words were slow, effortful.

"Uh, nobody was here."

She used the back of her hand to wipe her cheeks. "Yeah, he was. He's a tall kid, dark hair, name's Paul. He was with me a minute ago."

Kevin shook his head. He couldn't find the words to reply. What the hell was going on? His mind grappled for a tangible thread of a logical explanation. Had she snuck into the meadow without him knowing? Unlikely. Was she taking a nap in the grass? Yeah, right. He bit his lip.

"He was right next to me. There's no way he walked out of these fields during an earthquake."

"I- I never saw him."

She turned to Kevin, lips pressed tightly together. "Well, he's pretty hard to miss and he's gotta be around here. He could be lying in the grass right now, bleeding to death."

She spun away from Kevin and faced the grand expanse of the meadow, cupping her hands around her mouth. "Paul! Where are you? Let's go home."

A gentle gust of air answered her, and she shivered. There was no sign of the man.

She lifted her chin and strode through the meadow of high grass, calling out to a nonexistent person. Kevin, rooted in place, watched her pause for a moment with her head tilted, listening for a response. She then pushed aside some of the tall reeds, searching for clues or something, maybe the dude's body for all he knew. Finding nothing, she returned to Kevin. "I...I...don't understand. Did he leave without me?"

Kevin massaged his temples while he searched for words. "I don't have the foggiest idea what you're talking about. I was standing here watching the sunset, all quiet and peaceful, when, bam! In comes a storm from left field, bringing you with it." He locked eyes with her. "It's like you materialized out of nowhere."

"What on earth are you talking about? We were right here when the storm started. How come we didn't see you, huh? Were you spying on us?" A few flyaway strands of auburn hair escaped her headband, and the girl smoothed them back.

"Of course not. I'm telling you I was here alone. Alone!" His voice, initially soft with uncertainty, began to quiver with impatience. For the life of him, he couldn't figure it out. His logical mind was throbbing. What was going on?

"Fine, you were alone, I don't care. All I want is to go home and Paul is my ride."

The girl looked toward the edge of the woods and threw her arms in the air, exacerbated. "You've got to be kidding me. The creep took off with our wheels. My parents are going to kill me. Late for curfew, once again."

"And that's another thing. No car was ever there. Only my motorcycle."

"You think we walked here? You crazy? We drove in Paul's Corvair."

Kevin raked his fingers through his sandy hair. "Don't you get it? I keep telling you I was standing here alone and you arrived out of nowhere. Something's not right."

"Uh-huh. So, you're telling me you were sitting here all by yourself, and voila. I appeared."

"That's pretty much it."

She slapped her hand to her forehead. "You're crazy. What, you think we're in the *Twilight Zone?* Why are you doing this to me?"

"Doing what? I'm not doing anything to you."

"Riiight," she said, stretching out the word. "Paul's gone and you just happened to be here. Tell me who you are."

"I go to school at Sullivan U and came to study the planetary alignment. My name's Kevin. Now, how about you?"

"Laura. I came to see the alignment too. With Paul."

"Huh. Same name as the crazy old dude in the shack." He threw his thumb over his shoulder.

She turned, and her jaw dropped. "Th-there's never been a house in this meadow, not ever."

"Sure, there has," he said, shrugging. "Let's go talk to the guy who lives there. Maybe he knows what's going on, and then I'll give you a lift home since your ride ghosted you. Come on."

She walked beside him, her gait stiff and robotic, and the two made their way to the front door of the cottage, fifty yards away. Either the old geezer was a heavy sleeper or profoundly deaf. How did he miss the storm? Kevin pounded on the battered door.

Laura said, "This house looks ancient, like it's been here forever, but it never existed before now." Her voiced cracked. "It's not possible."

The weathered door groaned as it was nudged open, its rusty hinges creaking a mournful cry. The feeble old man peered through the entryway and glared at Kevin.

Then his cloudy blue eyes settled onto the girl beside him and widened in disbelief.

"Laura?" he sputtered.

"P-P-Paul?"

She inhaled sharply, her eyes rolled back, and she crumbled to the ground.

Chapter 6

Leaning stiffly against the armrest of a tattered couch, Kevin watched Paul Calloway place a cool, wet rag on the young woman's forehead with reverence. Her eyes fluttered open to the sight of the old man crouching beside her. Drawing a sharp breath, she scrambled to her feet, nearly knocking the guy to the floor. She hurried over to Kevin, a look of desperation on her face.

"This can't be," she whimpered, "What's going on. Tell me. Please."

Kevin's eyes darted between Laura and Paul. "You're telling me this is the Paul you came with?"

"Well, yeah, he's... no. It' impossible."

"Laura, it's me, Paul," said the elderly man. Despite his efforts to speak loudly, his voice remained weak and unsteady. "My love for you wasn't enough and now you've entered my penance, my purgatory. I'm being punished for crimes I didn't even know I committed, and your presence is an additional castigation." His voice trailed into a raspy wheeze.

Laura locked eyes with Kevin. "Purgatory? Is this guy out of his mind? No, this isn't Paul. I have no idea who he is, but he's not Paul Calloway. He can't be."

The frail man stretched his withered arms toward Laura. "You have to believe me. We came here over fifty years ago to see the alignment. Remember? We were so good together, you and me."

She inhaled sharply. "What did you just say?"

"We were so good together. You didn't believe me, but I knew, I knew."

Her entire body sagged to the faded couch. "Paul. Oh, God, no. What the hell happened to you?" She turned to Kevin. "What happened to him?"

"You came here? With this old guy?"

"No. Well, yes, but he wasn't old. He was my age. It's like he aged sixty years in a matter of minutes."

The elderly man extended a finger toward Laura's face, murmuring unintelligibly. She squirmed away.

Kevin's analytic mind rummaged through the events of this bizarre evening in an attempt to piece together an explanation. Nothing was adding up.

"So, here's what we know. You came to the meadow to see the light show." She nodded while eyeing the old man. "We also know you didn't come today because I was the only person present in the meadow. Well, nobody else was around except for this dude." He flipped his chin toward the skinny old guy, who was sitting perched on the edge of the couch wringing his hands together.

"No, that's where you're wrong. We came today. It's been on the radio all week. They said the light show would happen at sundown on April 23rd, and what a rockin' way to welcome The Four Tops brand-new song, *I Can't Help Myself.*"

Kevin blinked. "That song was released in 1965.

She rolled her eyes. "Obviously."

"You came to Sullivan's Meadow on April 23rd, 1965?"

"Oh my God, yes. A thousand times yes. Why is this so hard for you to believe? I'm more concerned with what happened to Paul. Care to explain that?"

Jesus, the old geezer's story was true. He wasn't a murderer. No, he was something much, much, less probable.

He cleared his throat. "I, uh, think I've got it figured out." *She'd never believe me.* "As you said, today is April 23rd, right?"

She nodded and folded her arms across her chest.

"But it's not, um—1965. It's 2023."

Laura gaped at him.

"Today is April 23rd, 2023. I came to see the alignment too, but fifty-eight years after you did. It looks like the planetary alignment was more than a little light show in the sky."

He emitted a nervous laugh. Go figure. That skinny old man, who was currently rocking back and forth, was the sole observer of a celestial phenomenon of epic proportions—he had actually witnessed time travel.

"No. That's not possible. You're loony. Both of you. You and, and, that man, are both wackos." Laura swung her legs off the side of the couch in an attempt to stand while sucking in rapid breaths of air. "I—I can't breathe—" Her entire body trembled.

Kevin hurried over to Laura and pushed her head between her knees, throwing an arm around her shoulders. He could feel her draw in a few deep breaths until she muttered, "Paul's right. This is purgatory. I'm in purgatory with a crazy old crackpot and some weird science dork."

Paul opened his paper-thin lips to speak but Kevin silenced him with a raised palm.

"No, Laura, don't listen to him. This isn't purgatory. I know it sounds ridiculous, but you were somehow pulled out of 1965 and dropped here, into 2023."

The elderly man leaned toward Kevin. "Send her back, boy. I served my time. Find a way to send her back." He launched himself at Laura, grabbing her by the shoulders. "Send her back, goddamn it."

Eyes wide, she backed herself into Kevin. "Oh, God, get me outta here. Please. I'll believe anything you say, I don't care. But get me out of here." She clutched Kevin's arm and tugged him to the exit, yanking the warped wooden door open.

As the two rushed out of the cabin, they could hear Paul Calloway's raving plea. "Do you hear me, boy? Send her back. Send her back to me!"

They escaped to the edge of the woods, and Kevin thrust his orange helmet into Laura's hands and she tugged it over her head. They both jumped on the motorcycle and raced down the winding path.

"Take me home, Kevin."

* * *

At last, they rolled onto a paved thoroughfare. Kevin could feel Laura clutching his waist in a death grip as they passed vehicles and buildings that were not in existence over fifty years ago. Despite the incongruities, Laura called out directions to her house. He began to realize his imagination had gotten the best of him. This whole ordeal couldn't possibly be related to time-travel. It was most likely a colossal misunderstanding, and the girl's parents would sort it out.

Unfamiliar with this particular section of Sullivan Township, his passenger had to guide him through the various roadways that were lined with large, brick McMansions. Newcomers to the town had preferred to demolish the preexisting homes in favor of constructing new, tasteless monstrosities. She lifted a finger and pointed out an ostentatious house boasting a thick carpet of sod for a front lawn. Ornamental bushes, shaped like malformed lollipops, grew adjacent to the steps leading to the main entry. Looking up at a palatial window above the doorway, he could see an ornate crystal chandelier suspended from the ceiling.

He pulled over to the curb and shut the motor. "You live here? Wow." The engine ticked as it started to cool.

Swinging her leg over the bike, Laura stood in front of the dwelling. "Wha...? Where's my house?" She stepped back, knocking herself against the motorcycle. "This isn't my house. None of these houses are right."

Unabashed, her eyes filled with tears, and her slender arms hung limply at her sides.

Kevin's chest tightened, and as he studied her, the truth crashed down upon him. There was no dismissing this as a mere misunderstanding or an elaborate hallucination. Somehow, the poor girl had traveled nearly sixty years into the future, and there was no foreseeable way she could return home. Her face bore the marks of terror and helplessness while her entire body trembled with fear. He had to help her. He was all she had.

He straightened himself and clasped her hand.

"Come on, Laura. I've got you." He hoisted her onto the back of the motorcycle, slid onto the seat in front of her, and rammed the key into the ignition.

Fortunately, few cars were on the road, and as the early evening transformed into the dark of night, Kevin guided the bike home. The ride was tranquil, the hum of the engine soothing. He settled Lucille into her parking spot and the motor sputtered to a stop. The stillness around them was disconcerting after experiencing the preternatural upheaval an hour earlier. Laura placed the helmet on the bike's metal backrest while she surveyed the landscape beyond the parking lot. She stopped.

"I know where we are." She looked around. "Yeah, I'm sure of it. My dad took me here when I was little. I can't believe this." Her voice faltered. "When I was about seven or eight, we'd come here with sandwiches, a whole picnic really." She raised her arm and pointed to a cluster of oaks. "See that row of trees? I used to pretend I was getting married there. My dad was such a good sport. Every time we came here, he went along with it. I'd stick daisies in my hair and hold a bouquet of wildflowers and weeds. He'd walked me down the aisle to my future husband, which happened to be a big, fat tree." She wrapped her arms tightly around herself, as if preventing her body from breaking apart into a million tiny pieces. "It's wild, really. The view of the tree line across the river is practically the same, except for the buildings, of course. There's not supposed to be any buildings."

Her eyes welled, and one lone tear trailed down her cheek. She swiped it away with the back of her hand and raised a trembling finger at Kevin's apartment the door.

He nodded and inserted the key into his door, but before pushing it ajar, looked at her.

"There's a Holiday Inn or a Ramada nearby. I'll go online and reserve you a room, take you there and help you settle you in. You'll be fine. Hang in there, and we'll meet up tomorrow."

"What? No!" she cried in alarm, "No motel. I-I don't want to be alone. Let me stay here, please. Oh God, I can't be alone."

"You want to stay here, in my apartment? With me?"

Like a bobble-head toy, she nodded.

"Um, okay, sure. We'll, uh, hang here."

She exhaled heavily.

Kevin kicked the stubborn door open saying, "Ladies first," and she stepped into his home.

Laura hovered in the center of the living room, biting her fingernails and quivering. He skirted past her to snatch his favorite, but quite ripe, SU sweatshirt wedged in the cushions of the couch. Yep, laundry was not a priority. He rolled it into a ball and lobbed it into his bedroom. He turned to her and found her staring at the landline phone on the side table. She lunged.

"Laura, wait. That's not a good idea—" He moved for the receiver but she'd already snatched it.

She waved him away. "Get lost. I'm calling my parents. Where's the stupid dial?"

"Uh, no dial. There's a keypad on the handset. Use that. Push the green button first."

She regarded the buttons, punched seven digits, then placed it to her ear. "C'mon, c'mon... pick up..." A moment later she carefully returned the handset to the cradle. "It won't go through. The call won't go through."

Kevin opened his mouth to speak, but what could he say? He snapped it shut.

She started sobbing. "I-I don't know what's going on."

Kevin gently placed his hand on her shoulder and led her to the breakfast counter. "We'll think of something. I have a few connections at the university so they'll give us a hand. But for right now, how about we get something to eat? Not much of a selection. Afraid all I have is Lucky Charms but I can pick up take-out. You like Taco Bell?"

Laura pressed a tissue to her nose and blew hard.

Mumbling, she said, "Lucky Charms. That's the so-called magically delicious cereal, right? The one with the little elf?"

"A leprechaun."

"Right. I could use a little magic right about now."

"Help yourself. Pour a bowl of magic and make a wish." Kevin handed her a clean bowl from the kitchenette and they settled onto stools at the counter. She slid the box over, kissed her finger and placed it on the cereal's mascot, Lucky the Leprechaun. Then she filled her bowl.

Laura nibbled her cereal and her muscles slowly ceased their nervous quiver.

"Mmm, not bad. Except my wish didn't come true since I'm still here in this nightmare." She crunched another morsel of cereal. "I guess I'll wake up when I'm good and ready. I mean, come on. Fifty-eight years in the future? Get serious." She yanked another tissue from the box and wiped her eyes. "Seems pretty real, I'll give you that, except Paul would never grow into a foul hermit like that man—he's too hung up on physical appearance."

Kevin started coughing on a marshmallow. "What? Say that again?"

She emitted a hollow, strained laugh. "It's true. Paul's every girl's dream. He's handsome, not to mention rich, and can charm the socks off of anybody. My parents love him." She popped a marshmallow moon in her mouth. "I'm not sure why he wants to go steady with me. I'm definitely not his type, but the more I put him off the harder he tries to win me over."

She could not possibly have been referring to that repellent fossil. Try as he might, he couldn't envision a young, handsome version of that man. It was simply not feasible.

"Well, he must've loved you an awful lot. I mean, he basically became a hermit after he lost you."

She swallowed. "I guess he did." She sniffed. "You know, I never really believed him when he told me he loved me. I kinda figured he wanted to chalk me up as another conquest. Man, this is crazy."

He picked up the empty bowls and carried them to the kitchenette. "This whole thing is crazy. I went to the meadow tonight to research something sensational, like some unusual multicolored lights in the sky or even comets, but your appearance from 1965? Yeah, sensational is an understatement. Your appearance pretty much blows my mind."

He glanced at Laura and noticed her body had resumed trembling.

"Oh crap, I'm sorry. I wasn't thinking." He dropped the bowls in the sink. "But listen, Laura, I have contacts at the university. I've taken a ton of science classes with decent professors, but there's one who I really think can help us, my astronomy professor, who's incredibly brilliant but a bit intense. I figure we'll go talk to him tomorrow morning before my class. He's into celestial phenomena, so I'd bet good money if anybody could shed light on this, uh, predicament, it's him." As an afterthought, he mumbled, "Only, don't look him straight in the eye."

She barely nodded her response.

"Okay, good. At least we have a plan. Don't know about you, but that makes me feel a bit better." He stood. "Anyway. Give me a sec, I'm gonna throw clean sheets on my bed for you. I'll take the couch."

He trotted to his bedroom, rummaged through his drawers, and handed her a pair of faded sweatpants and a Walking Dead T-shirt.

"For you to sleep in. They're not much, but they're clean."

She stood there, displaced, and Kevin clumsily extended his arms and gave her some awkward pats on her back.

"We'll figure this out, I promise you," he said as she quietly sobbed.

Chapter 7

Monday morning was sunny and unseasonably warm, making their jaunt into the center of town quite pleasant. Kevin could feel Laura swivel her head this way and that, daring to absorb the nearly sixty years of change in her surroundings. Yet, she remained wordless. Fortunately, he located an available parking spot for Lucille, then the two strolled past the shops along Main Street. Kevin had suggested they purchase a modern outfit for her, although he couldn't help but note how captivating she looked in her vintage sundress.

A jingle of bells in the store's doorway welcomed the pair into the Past Meets Present thrift shop. A middle-aged woman approached, bearing the sharp, pungent odor of mothballs that burned his nostrils. He whispered to Laura that he'd wait for her in the front of the store, and plopped himself down in a folding chair. He watched her peruse the racks, intent on her task. She pulled a floral, fringe-lined top from the collection and held it out in front of her, examining it. Shaking her head, she replaced the garment to the rack and shuffled through the others. Kevin settled deeper into his seat and crossed his ankles. This was going to take a while, and it gave him plenty of time to think.

He relished the few minutes of idleness, and, naturally, his thoughts drifted to the turn of events over the past twenty-four hours. Yesterday morning he'd been obsessing over a research topic for astronomy class, yet today the assignment had been relegated to the bottom of his mental list of concerns. Even his anxiety over his girlfriend had been resolved. Scratch that. Ex-girlfriend. Sure, he was a wimp for not initiating the break-up, but grateful the burden had been unloaded.

Kevin yawned and stretched his arms over his head. He watched Laura, her arms laden with clothes, speaking to the saleswoman who pointed to a curtained area in the rear of the establishment. Laura turned and smiled radiantly at him, then disappeared into the dressing room.

 Kevin swallowed hard as his heart skipped a beat.

Even though he knew practically nothing about Laura, he was certain of one thing. In physical appearance and personality, she bore no resemblance to Brittany and that alone was extraordinarily appealing.

A few minutes later, Laura emerged from a changing room, bouncing on her toes and beckoning him over.

"Well? What d'ya think?

He couldn't resist smiling as she turned and posed in front of the three-way mirror, admiring her outfit. He had to admit, she looked rather spectacular. The thing was, she didn't choose the type of clothes he was hoping she'd find.

"Um, I thought the idea was to choose something a bit more contemporary, so you blend in."

Laura had donned a pair of snug denim jeans that sat a tad below her waistline, the pant legs flaring out at the bottom. She had paired it with a cropped pink and white ribbed sweater that hugged her body as if designed solely for her.

"Huh?" she turned and confronted him. "But hip huggers are the coolest." She turned to the mirror and scrutinized her reflection. "I'm digging this poor-boy sweater too, but I kinda look like Gidget." She spun again. "No, not Gidget, I look like the chick from *Bewitched.* What's her name again? Samantha? Yeah, she's cool."

Thrilled with her outfit, Laura returned the other garments to the rack then joined him at the register. He handed the oblivious cashier a wad of bills, accepted the plastic shopping bag containing Laura's yellow sundress, and the two exited the shop.

"Thanks for the clothes, Kevin, I love them. My mother would flip out if she saw me in this. Too mod for her taste."

"I don't have a clue what *too mod* means, but you look great, Laura, you really do."

Their next destination was Sullivan U, hoping to catch Kevin's professor prior to class. Fortunately, Dr. Archer was setting up his "Stars, Galaxies, and the Universe" presentation in the lecture hall. The slight, balding gentleman was squatting next to a podium, plugging in an electrical extension cord.

"Mr. Donahue," he stated after straightening himself. "You're a bit early for class, I see." He squinted at Kevin's companion through a pair of Windsor eyeglasses. "A new student?"

"No, Professor. I'd like to introduce you to my friend, Laura Malone. Laura, this is my Astronomy professor, Dr. Archer." The pair lightly shook hands.

"And to what do I owe this pleasure?" questioned the professor. Behind the thick lenses, his eyes oscillated involuntarily, so Kevin redirected his gaze on a distant point behind Dr. Archer's head.

"Well, sir, I've been researching the required assignment and have come across a rather strange twist." Kevin hesitated. How was he supposed to phrase this? He looked over at Laura, who nodded, encouraging him to continue. "What I mean is, I've stumbled upon something completely unexpected. Well, no, the word unexpected isn't exactly fitting, more like unusual. No, that's not quite it either. Jarring. Let's go with jarring."

Laura blew out a breath. "Kevin, really?" She turned to the professor. "Dr. Archer, all those words are fitting, but what he wants to know is if you believe in time travel, Sorry, Kevin, but we don't have time to beat around the bush. That's still an expression nowadays, isn't it?"

The room was suddenly silent, sans the hum of the Smartboard speakers. Laura bit her lip and looked sideways at Kevin. "Sorry," she said.

Dr. Archer removed his eyeglasses and rubbed the bridge of his nose for a moment. The tremulous movements of his eyes intensified, but then he replaced his glasses and contemplated Kevin.

"To simplify Einstein's theories into one short sentence is a disservice to his work. However, my answer is yes, I do presume time travel, in addition to the natural forward flow of time, is possible."

The two burst into relieved laughter.

"However," the professor continued, raising his voice, "As an educator of a university prone to fraternity hazing rituals, one can never be too cautious. You seem like a decent fellow, Mr. Donahue, but I assure you, any insight to my personal beliefs on time travel will remain my own."

"But sir," said Laura. "The planetary alignment. Surely you can answer a question about that?"

Dr. Archer paused. "Certainly. You submitted the alignment as your topic for the final research paper, isn't that correct, Mr. Donahue?"

"Yes. Yes, it is."

"Then ask your question because class is scheduled to begin in a few minutes."

Sensing Laura's apprehension and in attempt to sound remotely plausible, Kevin articulated his thoughts in a manner worthy of the professor's respect. "Fifty-eight years ago, an astronomical phenomenon involving the alignment of Venus, Mars, and our moon was documented and undisputed. In addition to being a spectacular visual event, a localized storm had occurred at the moment of the alignment. This storm involved high winds and geological disturbances."

"And the question is?"

Kevin continued. "Yesterday marked the fifty-eighth anniversary of the original alignment, and an exact duplication of the disturbances occurred in Sullivan's Meadow. The storm was not only identical in its characteristics, but it occurred at exactly the same instance of time as the original event, at sundown. I'm asking you, professor, can this phenomenon occur in reverse? Is it possible to somehow artificially recreate a similar storm in 2023 that will result in an effect in 1965?"

The professor contemplated the query and responded with a resounding, "No."

Kevin chanced a look at his companion, whose hopeful expression crumbled before him.

"However," the professor added, "if there truly was a seismic tremor in 1965 that resonated into 2023, perhaps a powerful aftershock could also bridge the two points in time. Hypothetically speaking, of course."

Several students entered the lecture hall and settled into their cushioned auditorium seats. Dr. Archer picked up his notes for his presentation and remarked, "You are welcome to stay for the class, Miss Malone. As for you, Mr. Donahue, please take your seat. Your presence is mandatory and class will begin shortly."

Choosing a spot on the aisle, Kevin placed the shopping bag on the collapsible side desk and heaved a long, heavy sigh.

"Staying for this lecture feels like a waste of time. We have to find out if there was an aftershock in 1965."

"Don't sweat it. I'll go to the library and see what I can find."

Kevin debated. "I don't think so, Laura. Libraries have changed a lot since the '60s. Why don't you stay here with me, see if we learn anything useful from this lecture, and go to the library afterwards?"

"No. Time isn't on our side, Kevin. Your library has books, doesn't it? Then it may come as a surprise to you that I know how to read." Laura nudged passed a few students lingering in the narrow aisle and headed for the door.

"Okay, okay," Kevin called after her, "Let me help you get set up. Geesh." *They were headstrong in 1965 too*, he thought, and chased after her.

Together, they bounded up the library steps, pushed through the revolving door, and entered the peaceful sanctuary of the library. He drew in a slow, cleansing breath, and as it released, felt his shoulders relax. It felt like he'd been holding his breath for a week.

He strode up to the front desk to consult with a media specialist, giving Laura a moment to survey her surroundings. He was certain this library would barely resemble those of the 1960s, so as he waited for assistance, he watched Laura with interest.

She had circled around the computer nook where individual PCs were placed in partitioned study corrals, affording the patrons a small degree of privacy. Peering around a divider, she seemed fascinated by a student reading information on a computer screen and using a mouse to scroll through the pages. The student pushed back his chair and headed for the shelves against the far wall, home to hundreds of DVDs. The kid returned to his seat with one in hand, snapped open the plastic case and popped the disk into the drive. The boy twisted around to his backpack, and noticing Laura standing there, gave her a brief nod then yanked a pair of earbuds out of a zippered pocket. He settled into his chair and launched a documentary. But then the hum of a machine caught her attention, and she turned to watch a laser printer spit out multiple, colored pages of a document. Someone walked past and grabbed their printouts from the output tray.

Laura was mesmerized.

Kevin didn't have the heart to tell her DVDs were already outdated, pretty much obsolete. Maybe he'd take her to one of the university's 3D printers and completely blow her away.

Laura backed away from the technology and joined Kevin at the desk.

"Stupid library doesn't even have a card catalog," she whispered. He bit back his smile.

"Need help?" asked a young librarian. She appeared to be a freshman, probably working in the library to earning a few dollars of spending money. The girl finished checking in the last book in her pile, replaced the bar code scanner in its base, and looked up.

He was about to answer her when he noticed Laura gawking at the librarian's upper lip and felt her elbowing him in the ribs.

He fixed Laura with a reproachful glare and said, "Uh, yeah. My friend here has to research a paper, but here's the thing. She was brought up in an old-fashioned town— no computers, no tablets, no cellphones. Pretty much no kind of technology. Is there any way you can help her with research?"

The girl smiled and, barely taking breaths between sentences, replied, "Of course I can help. A town with no tech? That's totally awesome. I didn't know there were any places left on this planet that weren't connected. Well, I guess in a country far away, like in a jungle in Africa, but not here in the good old U.S. of A. My grandmother's constantly complaining people don't know how to talk to each other anymore because technology is taking over the world, life isn't the way it used to be, and yadda-yadda. But we're certainly proving her wrong now, aren't we? I mean, we're having a bonafide conversation, right? Anyway, are you familiar with microfilm and microfiche?" she asked Laura.

Laura merely nodded her reply. She was struggling to avoid staring at a tiny gold hoop pierced through the librarian's upper lip. So that's why she was bug-eyed.

"Come with me. My name is Ashley, and I'll get you whatever you need. So, no tech at all, huh? Lovin' it."

As she was whisked away by the loquacious librarian, Laura turned around at Kevin and he said, "I'll be back in two hours. Try not to stare."

Laura nodded and disappeared around a bookshelf.

Chapter 8

By the time he emerged from the longest, most mundane lecture he had ever experienced, Kevin had a well-developed plan for the afternoon. Mostly, the plan involved lunch. He jogged to the library, clumsily toting the shopping bag that continually twisted around itself and smacking him in the leg. He found Laura sitting on the stone steps, watching groups of students walk by. Instantly recognizing him, she stood from her perch.

"Any luck?" he asked.

Laura shook her head. "Not a thing about aftershocks."

"Damn it. Nothing?"

"Most of the articles crucified Paul, the poor guy. When he insisted there was an earthquake and a tornado in the meadow, the chief of police called him a raving lunatic."

"Harsh," he said. "Well, it does sound odd, don't you think? An intense earthquake and a tornado felt by only one person in a meadow?"

"Two people, Kevin. Two people."

"Sorry. I know, two people. How about we grab lunch, then pay a visit to our friendly, neighborhood recluse and see what he knows about any aftershock."

"I thought you had another class," she said.

Kevin shook his head. "As you free spirits would say in the '60s, I'm ditching."

Her lips tugged into a short-lived, quivering smile, reminding him that this world, this time, was still foreign to her. He didn't know why he was so invested in helping her, and didn't care to know why. He was in, all in.

The pair headed for sustenance and Ronnie greeted them as they entered the restaurant.

"Hey, Kevin. How ya doin', man?" Ronnie approached Kevin and gave his shoulder a friendly squeeze. "And who's this beautiful young lady?" he asked, extending his hand to Laura. Kevin introduced them, as Ronnie lifted her hand and planted a sloppy kiss on its dorsal.

"Back off dude, you're not her type." Kevin proffered his stocky friend a good-natured shove and the guy didn't even stumble. Solid muscle underneath all the pudge.

"Every woman's my type, pal." He laughed, and motioned for them to take any open table.

They chose a booth by the window and settled themselves on the red vinyl padding. Ronnie squeezed in next to Laura, the vinyl crackling under his weight.

"All right if I hang with you for a few?" he asked, winking at her.

"Doesn't look like we have a choice," Kevin said, but she laughed and gave Ronnie more room.

"Well, thank you, darlin'. My man Kevin here should really learn his manners. Hey Kev, how about I tell you where you should go."

"Watch it, Ronnie—not in front of the lady."

The heavy-set man chuffed. "Nah, I'm nothing if not a gentleman. My sweet Italian mother taught me well."

"Oh, brother," Kevin said, rolling his eyes. "So, what's been happening with you, Ron?"

"Ah, nothing much. You missed a great game, though. We were making a comeback until San Francisco scored another run near the end and took the win. It was heartbreaking."

"Ouch, another loss for the Mets. Bummer that I couldn't go yesterday, though. Too much going on."

"Mm-hmm. Oh, I can see what's been going on. Glad that research project isn't stressing you out anymore, 'cause it appears this gorgeous girl's got you a little distracted." He jabbed his thumb playfully at Laura and grinned like a Cheshire cat. "How'd you two meet?"

"Oh, we were, uh, hanging around the same meadow," said Laura.

"No kidding? You in Kevin's astronomy class?"

"Nope," Kevin said. "It's kind of a long story, I'll fill you in later. The short version is she heard about the planetary light show and wanted to check it out."

"Well, well. Lucky for you, right Kev? So, Laura, I know it won't be easy, but try to keep my boy outta trouble." He looked up and noticed a group of customers entering the restaurant.

"I'll do my best," she replied as Ronnie slid out of the booth.

"Time to get back to work. Nice meetin' you, Laura. Hope to see you again, soon. And if you decide Kevin's not the one, I'm available." He flashed her another wink then headed over to the waiting customers.

"Don't mind Ronnie. Underneath his warped sense of humor and that greasy apron is a heart of gold."

Laura opened her menu. "I really like him. He's a gas."

A gas. He loved the '60s slang.

Placing a couple of water glasses on the table, a harried waitress scribbled down their food order, collected their menus, and scrambled over to other customers.

Kevin studied Laura as she gazed out the window, probably eyeing all the changes in town. Was anything familiar to her? He knew the small shops along Main Street have been renovated over the years, and their transformation into modern day structures had to be unnerving. Yet, here she sat, casually sipping her soda.

"Laura, I need to ask you something." She pulled her eyes from the view of storefronts and looked at him with curiosity. "I'm not sure how to put this. Well, let me start off by saying that you're the bravest person I've ever met. I mean it. It was only yesterday by a miracle or whatever, you catapulted nearly sixty years into the future, and yet, somehow, you're not freaking out. I mean, I know you were scared at first, terrified is more accurate, but to look at you now? You're actually dealing with it. So, here's my question. I've been wondering, how are you doing it? How are you able to handle being in the future?"

She collected her thoughts a moment.

"I'm not handling anything, I'm too exhausted. Here's what I think. I must've dropped some acid because I'm in the middle of an elaborate hallucination." She inhaled a quavering breath and slowly phrased her next words. "No. That's not true. In my heart, I'm certain all of this is real." She swept her arms to encompass the world, and sniffed. "Besides, I don't think my subconscious is creative enough to invent anything I'm seeing. The restaurant we're sitting in right now? It's supposed to be a malt shop where I work during the summer." Laura pointed out the window. "See that Apple store that doesn't sell any apples? It's really a far-out record shop called Flip Side. Oh, and that vacant lot around the corner? That's where the Esso station should be, where Paul works."

Tears welled in her eyes, but she continued.

"The people here wear dorky clothes and most of the time I don't know what anybody's talking about." She leaned in and her voice rose. "Oh, oh, and listen to this. When I was hanging out on the library steps, a group of girls walked by, but they weren't messing around like normal kids. They were staring down at cigarette packs and beating their thumbs on them, sorta like this." Laura pounded her thumbs on the table in a chaotic dance.

"On cigarette boxes?"

"Yeah. Then, out of the blue, this one chick holds up her ciggy pack and shouts something like, 'selfie.' and the three of them smush their faces together and acted like goldfish in a fishbowl." In imitation, she sucked in her cheeks and pursed her lips into an exaggerated fish-gape pout. "Weirdos."

Kevin disguised his smile with a cough.

She grabbed a napkin from the dispenser, wiped her eyes, and thrust her chin to the window. "I mean, really. Look at those cars. They belong on the Jetsons." She turned to him, and a tear rolled from her eye and trailed down her cheek. "So no, I don't think I'm handling this all too well. I'm trying to convince myself I'll return home soon enough and that this whole thing is— "

"Well, well, well. How quickly you move on, Kevin Donahue."

A cold shiver rippled down his spine.

"And who might you be, girly?" asked a churlish voice. Kevin opened his mouth to speak, but Brittany flipped him her 'talk to the hand' gesture. "Oh no, don't tell me. Did you find him on match-dot-com? Or Speed date? Oh, I know, you googled Loser Beyond Repair and Kevin's name popped up." Brittany's eyes bore into Laura. "One word of advice, girlfriend, don't expect Boy Scout here to ever text you back. LBR doesn't believe in texting. Or, for that matter, sexting. Tootles." Brittany abruptly flipped her pitch-black tresses and bounced her way over to her throng of friends in the corner.

Kevin found his voice. He dropped his eyes to the table and ran his fingers through his hair. "Listen, Laura, I—"

Laura cut him off with a raised palm of her own.

"See what I mean? I have absolutely no idea what that chick said."

He couldn't help but laugh. Her torment earned his sympathy, but her naiveté was undoubtedly refreshing.

After enjoying a mouthwatering pepperoni pizza with extra cheese, the two meandered through the crowded restaurant toward the front door. Ronnie was behind the counter, sprinkling mozzarella cheese on a pie as they approached him. "Thanks for the grub, Ron. Catch ya later."

"You better," he replied. "Hey, take care of that pretty lady, Kevin, or I'm making a move." Laura blew Ronnie a kiss and his face beamed in delight.

Outside, she donned the bright orange helmet and straddled the bike as Kevin placed the leftover pizza for Paul in the leather saddlebag. The old-timer could use to put on a few pounds. It was a good thing he was in the shack during the storm, or he would've been blown into the next county.

Before Kevin had an opportunity to turn the ignition key, a voice called out to him from down the block. Dr. Archer was hurrying toward them, out of breath and quite disheveled. Puzzled, Kevin watched him approach.

"Glad ... I caught ... you ... Hold on. Let me catch my breath. Phew. Jogging is not my forte."

Laura fumbled with the clasp to release the helmet's safety strap, so Kevin squeezed the plastic side releases to free her and they both dismounted the bike.

"Thank you, both of you, for waiting. Let's sit over there. We need to talk."

They darted across the street, and the professor dropped himself on a vacant park bench. Yanking a crisp, white handkerchief from his blazer's pocket, the professor dabbed drops of perspiration from his forehead.

"I'm glad I, quite literally, ran into you both. First, I'd like to apologize for my abruptness earlier, Mr. Donahue, Miss Malone, but when our discussion tapped into my affinity for Einstein's work, I was caught completely off guard. I'll admit I've been giving our conversation a fair amount of thought, and now that we're no longer on university campus, I need to ask you this. What could possibly be the impetus of your questions?" He studied Kevin from behind his glasses, his eyes quivering like a candle flame caught in a draft.

Kevin drew in a deep breath and slowly released it. "We need your help, Professor, but I'm worried you're not going to believe what we have to say."

"Try me. My curiosity is piqued and that works in your favor."

Kevin cleared his throat, stalling. "All right. Laura and I have this situation, and..."

His words hung. Archer was going to think they were certifiably bonkers.

"Let me make this easier for you, Kevin. You entered my lecture hall, initially asking me if I believe time travel is possible. I answered in the affirmative, and the two of you unabashedly rejoiced. I'm intrigued. Care to fill in the blanks?"

"Okay, here goes nothing. We have reason to believe that the planetary alignment yesterday somehow transported Laura through time." As an afterthought, he added quickly, "And this is no fraternity prank."

The professor didn't respond. Then, slowly, he said, "You're telling me your question this morning was not academic?"

"No, sir, it wasn't. In fact, I saw Laura appear directly in front of me from sheer... nothingness."

In the brief silence, Kevin could hear the steady tick-tick-tick of Aster's wind-up wristwatch, a relic from another age.

Go on, tell me I'm nuts. Haul out the straightjacket and let's be done with this.

Dr. Archer chewed on his bottom lip. "I've often speculated time travel as a possibility, but I find it preposterous that you're suggesting it achievable."

"I know, I know. I'm aware this sounds ludicrous. I barely believe it myself, but it's true. Yesterday morning, Laura was home in 1965."

"And now I'm here," she said. "Where every person and every place I know, are gone."

Dr. Archer crossed his arms and studied Laura. "I'm sure you're aware how this all sounds. Your claims are outrageous and bear the bitter scent of a hoax."

"No hoax, I can promise you that," said Kevin.

The professor inhaled deeply. "Then show me proof."

"Proof? We can take you where she appeared ..."

The professor shook his head. "No. Something more immediate. Give me your hand, young lady." Laura frowned, clearly perplexed, but held out her hand to the professor. "Several years ago, an author used this method in a novel to prove a character was a time-traveler. Although rooted in fiction, the idea has merit." He gripped her hand in his, then lifted the short sleeve of her left arm and exposed a circular, nickel-sized scar.

"Well, I'll be damned," muttered the professor.

"Dr. Archer, I've had that scar as long as I remember. It has nothing to do with time travel."

"Oh, my dear, it has everything to do with your claims." He rubbed his finger over the indentation on her skin. "This circle is not a run-of-the-mill scar, it's the result of a smallpox vaccination. Prior to the 1970s, the vaccine caused the formation of a blister at the inoculation site, and ultimately this pockmark. Those born after the early '70s wouldn't have such a scar. But you have it." He lifted his eyes from her arm and looked at her. "For years, I've hoped verifiable proof of time travel would present itself during my lifetime. Maybe it's wishful thinking or maybe I just want to believe my own fantasy, but I'm making the bold and completely out-of-character decision to believe you."

Kevin and Laura looked at each other and whooped. They fell into each other's arms and embraced, laughing and sobbing, while Dr. Archer flushed with apparent discomfort.

"Yes, well. I suppose Diana Gabaldon would be patting me on the back about now."

With a long, drawn-out sniff, Laura asked, "How do I get home, Professor?"

"Ah, that's the million-dollar question, isn't it? How to get you home. You said you traveled from when? 1965? Hmm, fifty-eight years. I, too, traveled fifty-eight years, but I took the long, traditional route. I didn't age quite well, but no matter, you're as pretty as a picture. But enough of that. Kevin, tell me the location and specific details of Laura's miraculous appearance."

Kevin shared his observations of the phenomenon and Laura provided information from her perspective, including the details about Paul Calloway. The professor listened with avid attention, nodding and stroking his chin, uttering an occasional 'remarkable' and 'of course.'

"Well then. Our first order of business is to determine if there was, indeed, an aftershock after the original event, a temporal echo if you will, which may be a viable solution. Isn't this your area of expertise, Kevin?"

"Seismic activity extending through time?" Kevin asked. "Hardly."

Dr. Archer smiled. "No, but as a geophysics major, aren't there methods to determine an upcoming seismic aftershock in the meadow?"

"Well, sure, but the procedures are time consuming. We can ask Old Man Calloway if he remembers an aftershock."

"A discussion with Mr. Calloway's a fine place to start, but don't dismiss scientific methods for detecting seismic activity. After all, there's a good chance the man wasn't present in the meadow at the time of an aftershock or, more likely, has no recollection. In the meantime, I'll head to my office and delve into my material for an explanation. And Laura? I thrive on challenges. We'll get you home. Now, put that orange monstrosity back on your head and drive safely."

A short while later, the twosome wove their way through the woods. Kevin parked Lucille at the edge of the tree line next to a majestic oak, retrieved the take-out container, and reached for Laura's hand. In response, she gave it a squeeze, generating an unexpected but pleasant flutter in the pit of his stomach. Whoa. He glanced at her, but she was already focusing on the battered structure ahead.

The two approached the decrepit shack and located a solitary figure seated on the wrought iron bench. Even as they drew near, Calloway remained oblivious to their presence. His liquid blue eyes fixated on the branded circle of sallow grass while his lips tremored with inaudible words.

"Mr. Calloway?" Kevin called.

Shifting in his seat, Paul turned and cast a distrustful glance toward the uninvited visitors, and then he saw Laura. His furrowed brow suddenly relaxed, allowing the deep crease between his eyes to soften. "You came back," he cried.

"Hi, Paul. It's nice to see you. You hungry? We brought you a doggy bag." She took the paper sack from Kevin and extended it to the old man. He ignored the proffered food and rubbed his grimy hands through dingy, stringy hair. Laura placed the bag on the bench and retreated a few paces, as if confronted by a rabid animal.

"Mr. Calloway, remember me? My name's Kevin and I was here yesterday."

"Of course I know who you are, you punk." A trace of spittle leaked from the corner of Paul's mouth. "You think I'm some kind of moron?" The furrowed brow reappeared.

"We need to ask you a question. It's about the planetary alignment in 1965." He took a few steps closer to the man and encountered a malodorous stench, then deliberately positioned himself upwind.

"Yes, yes, the alignment."

"By any chance, do you remember experiencing an aftershock?"

"Aftershock. Aftershock." Paul squeezed his eyes shut and his body began to shake. Even his thin lips quivered like gelatin.

Laura leaned in and whispered to Kevin, "Look at him, he's terrified. This is cruel."

He whispered back, "I know, but we need to find out. He might be our only chance."

Paul's face drained of color and his forehead broke out with beads of sweat. Haunted by a memory Kevin couldn't imagine, the man uttered words in short gasps, barely audible. "Petrifying. It was petrifying. The storm. The storm shook the earth. The winds. So strong. I couldn't stand. I couldn't breathe."

"But was there an aftershock?"

He opened his eyes. "Damn right, I was in shock. I was screaming for Laura. Where'd she go?" The old man began shrieking at the sky. "Laura!"

"Oh my God, this is getting us nowhere." Frustrated, Kevin grasped the man's arm. "Tell me, Calloway. Was there an aftershock? Another storm or earthquake?"

Paul's wild eyes darted about, viewing images no longer present. "The world's exploding. Where the hell are you?"

Laura intervened. "Paul, honey. Look at me." Paul's eyes shifted to Laura and he smiled at her, perhaps returning to the present. "Was there an aftershock, Paul? Think."

"An aftershock?" Paul's mouth dropped open. "Of course, that's what it was. An aftershock. I came back a couple of days later to search for you, Laura. I had to find you. They were accusing me. Me. Can you believe it? The cops, my buddies, even your parents blamed me. They badgered me with the same irritating, harassing questions, over and over. 'How did you kill her, Calloway?' 'Where'd you hide her body, boy?' 'Don't you even think of leaving town, or you're a dead man.'" He inhaled a deep breath. His limbs trembled erratically.

"Go on, Paul. Tell us about the aftershock," she said.

"The cops had nothin' on me, so after they let me out of jail, I came straight here. I knew I must've missed something in the meadow, some sort of a clue. I didn't know if I'd find anything, I mean, it was already two whole days after you disappeared. Even so, I came back to this God-forsaken place. Sat right over there, next to that blasted circle. And right when the sun was beginning to set, all of a sudden it started happening again. Oh God, the storm was back and this time it was going to take me." On unbalanced legs, Paul stood, howling in agony at the cloudless sky. "But you didn't take me, goddamnit. You left me here to rot. damn you. Damn you to hell!"

Laura recoiled in horror.

"Laura, let's go. He answered our question. We gotta get out of here."

"We can't leave him like this. Look at him."

Paul whirled around and confronted Laura. "Why did you do this to me, huh? This is all your fault. Why did you leave me? Why?" He lunged for her, but considering he lacked agility, the man merely staggered a few paces.

With a pained expression, Laura grabbed Kevin's hand and they ran back to the motorcycle. As they clambered on, Calloway was sobbing at the heavens, "Laura!"

His horrifying anguish was distressing to witness, and as a result, Kevin and Laura drove back to the apartment in a stunned silence. Wordlessly, she entered the bedroom and quietly closed the door and Kevin collapsed on the couch in an exhausted heap. His thoughts were a disorganized jumble, but there was one thought above all others that was unmistakably lucid. Laura might have a ticket home tomorrow at sundown.

Chapter 9

After a restless night, Kevin welcomed the new morning. He had suffered through the predawn hours by replaying their visit to Sullivan's Meadow. Crazed though he was, Calloway's assertions that an aftershock occurred seemed legitimate, but perhaps that was wishful thinking. Anyway, if Kevin was honest with himself, there was a tiny part of him that was hoping there would be no aftershock, and that Laura would remain in 2023. Sure, he recognized these feelings were extremely selfish, but his mind continually returned to the moment Laura's touch had ignited a sensation akin to desire. A mere squeeze to his hand, but its impact was staggering. Had she, too, experienced that momentary spark? The sun nudged Kevin from his reverie and forced him from his bed.

He brewed himself a cup of the strongest coffee he could tolerate, then slid open the glass doors to his balcony, mindful not to wake his houseguest. The river in the distance glistened under the rays of the morning sun, highlighting a handful of sailboats peppering its surface. The boats projected a carefree spirit, liberating their passengers from the harsh realities of worry and responsibility, reminding him of his mother. He could virtually guarantee that at this very moment, Mom was sunning herself on a yacht off the coast of France, nursing a tropical drink adorned with one of those miniature paper umbrellas. Kevin turned from the scene and grabbed his cellphone. He needed to hear her voice, a touchstone to a feeling of family. It was late afternoon in Europe, an opportune time to speak with her. She answered on the third ring.

"Hello?"

"Hey, Ma, it's me."

"Oh, sweetheart. I'm so happy to hear your voice. Are you doing all right? School good?"

Kevin smiled and allowed himself a cleansing breath. "Things are fine, Ma. I figured we haven't chatted in a while. How's France?"

"France? It was spectacular. We left Cannes last week and now we're in the Italian Riviera. Oh, it's breathtaking here, Kevin. *Molto bello.*"

"I'm glad you're enjoying yourself. You deserve it."

"Well, thank you, honey. What's new with you? Things going well with your beautiful girlfriend?"

He laughed. "She's only a friend, but I guess you can say it's going well. She's an old soul, no head games. It's funny, I can actually be myself with her."

"Oh good, son. I'm so relieved you finally found someone. Please give my best to Brittany."

"Brittany? Oh God, definitely not Brittany. That didn't work out. I'm talking about Laura. Hold up, Ma, before you ask me a ton of questions about her, she's a friend. A relationship isn't in the cards."

She softened. "Don't write her off so quickly, Kevin. Any healthy relationship worth having starts off as a friendship."

"I'm hearing you, but it's pointless. I like her. In fact, I like her a lot, but she's not from around here."

"Oh, sweetheart. Distance isn't relevant. For goodness' sake, if not for my choices I would be sitting home wallowing in self-pity. But look where I am instead, sailing the Mediterranean with a man I adore. All I'm trying to say, Kevin, is it's okay to choose with your head but don't disregard your heart. Make bold choices."

If only it was his heart that was the hold up.

They spoke for a few more minutes, talking about Italy's medieval hilltop hamlets and expansive vistas.

"Listen, I gotta go now, son. Will I be seeing you for the holidays? You know the invitations still stands. Come fly out and meet us."

He promised he would give it thought and pressed the off icon. At that moment, Laura, clad in his sweats, slid open the glass doors and joined him on the balcony. Stretching languidly, she asked, "Who you talking to out here?"

"My mom. She says hello."

She gasped. "Your mother is here? Oh God, I have to get dressed." She grabbed the door handle to make a hasty retreat but Kevin took ahold of her hand to stop her. The faintest touch of her skin sparked that rippling feeling deep in his gut, startling him.

"Uh, no, not here, she was on the phone."

"You were talking to your mother on the telephone ... outside?"

Kevin maneuvered his hand into the back pocket of his jeans and withdrew his phone. Laura gaped at it.

"It's my cellphone. I was talking to my mom on the cellphone. No need to worry."

"A cell-o-phone." She tugged the door open. "Far out."

* * *

Kevin decided to go on a supermarket run and allow Laura time to herself. He managed to cram two bags of groceries into Lucille's satchels when his phone began ringing.

"Yeah," he answered.

"Kevin, Thomas Archer here. Are you and Laura available to meet me in my office this morning? I've stumbled upon something that you really ought to see."

Leaning against the bike, Kevin said, "Really? That's great."

"I've been working through the theories most of the night. The majority of my hypotheses are completely farfetched and downright impossible, and hover the line between science and fiction..."

Kevin held his breath. This was a breakthrough?

"...making my conclusions all the more plausible. We are, after all, dealing with time travel. In any case, when can I expect you?"

"I'm on my way home now. We can be there in, let's say, an hour."

"An hour is fine. By the way, did you make any headway with Mr. Calloway? I'm assuming his recollections were cloudy."

"As a matter of fact, Professor, Calloway turned out to be surprisingly precise. He said the aftershock occurred exactly two days after the alignment, at sundown."

"Two days? That brings us to this evening." A pause. "I'll see you in an hour. And Kevin? Tell Laura to wear her 1965 attire."

* * *

Kevin unlocked his apartment door while balancing his parcels in one arm. He called out to his houseguest as he slammed the door with a foot.

"Laura, good news. I spoke to Dr. Archer a few minutes ago."

She emerged from the steamy bathroom towel-drying her hair, wearing one of his tattered flannel robes. She could've been wearing a grimy burlap sack and still look resplendent.

"Yeah? What he say?"

He swallowed, then briefly summarized their conversation and added, "He wants you to wear your dress from 1965."

"The dress I had on? Why?"

"He didn't say. But, by the sound of it, I think you're going home."

She shrieked with joy and flung herself into his arms. "I'm going home!"

Kevin enveloped her in his arms, aware once again of the electrical jolt in his gut. "Hold on, Laura. I'm only guessing. I don't know for sure."

She retreated a step and lifted an eyebrow. "Then why else would he ask me to wear my old dress?"

"Maybe he's into the retro look? Whatever. I'm pretty sure he's onto something, so in case this really is your last day here, let's make it a memorable one." He began emptying the contents of the grocery bags naming each item. "Brie cheese, Ritz crackers, a bunch of grapes, and a bottle of cabernet. But wait, there's more. Fried chicken, biscuits, fruit salad, and last but not least, freshly baked chocolate chip cookies," he announced with a flourish.

"We're having a party with Dr. Archer?"

"Uh, well, no, I was figuring more of a party of two. We'll go hear what he has to say and then go on a picnic. Okay with you?"

She grinned and padded into the bathroom. Meanwhile, Kevin rummaged through his closet for a cooler and by the time he located one, Laura was dressed in her charming yellow sundress.

* * *

"Sit, sit. Make yourself comfortable." Dr. Archer stepped to the side, motioning for the two visitors to enter.

Kevin hesitated in the entranceway of the professor's office and Laura hovered behind him, peering over his shoulder. The room was about the size of a shoebox, barely large enough to hold three adults. A metal desk was wedged in the corner and riddled with opened textbooks and scientific journals. An oversized ceramic mug stained from years of coffee sat atop a tattered notebook near an ancient computer. Three of the four walls were lined with floor-to-ceiling pressboard bookcases crammed with a disarray of publications, knickknacks, and loose papers. The fourth wall was plastered with a multitude of framed diplomas and certificates that surrounded the doorway. Kevin was particularly drawn to an official-looking certificate entitled: *Star Trek Fan Club Acknowledges Their Newest Trekkie, Thomas Archer, November 1967.*

The pair squeezed through the threshold, settled into the two leatherette chairs adjacent to the desk, and waited for the professor to stop shuffling papers.

"My office isn't usually this cluttered, but I've been pulling pieces of material from my personal arsenal to unravel this cosmic mystery. Now then, let's begin with an explanation to the question, 'How did Laura transport from 1965 to the present?'"

His chair squeaked as he swiveled to face a bookcase to retrieve a 3-dimensional model of the solar system.

"Here we have Mars and Venus, and of course our Earth and its moon. As you know, the planetary alignment involves these entities. I pre-adjusted the positions of their rotation to duplicate those at the onset of the storm." The professor then began sorting through the multiple piles on his desk and located a long, thin wire and held it up. "This wire represents a perfect alignment, albeit crude. Watch as I thread it through the center of each sphere. First through Mars ... and now Venus ... and finally our moon. Pay attention as I continue feeding the wire towards Earth. Where on our planet does the wire penetrate?"

"The eastern coast of North America," Kevin said.

"Exactly. So, entering data such as the date, time, and astronomical coordinates, I created a computer simulation of the actual planetary alignment."

Spinning the laptop to face the young couple, the professor tapped the Play key. "As you can see, the cosmic bodies are maintaining their respective orbits. Watch as they begin to align in space ... there." He paused the enactment. "This red line clearly shows they are in perfect alignment. Now let's zoom into planet Earth." They watched, mesmerized, as the size of Earth expanded. The red line zeroed in on the eastern coast of the United States, and as the image continued to magnify, the red line bore straight through the tri-state area, Sullivan Township, and finally, Sullivan's Meadow. "And, as I continue to zoom in, the line pierces the epicenter where Laura materialized."

Silence permeated the room as the three studied the screen. The professor then removed his eyeglasses for a moment, his fluttering eyes visible. "Now bear with me as I explain further. The planetary phenomenon could only occur given an intense concentration of power, and I needed to identify the source. After extrapolating and isolating various energy forces, I have determined that the phenomenon is gravitationally based. With me so far? As the cosmic bodies moved into position, the gravitational energy accumulated and, at the precise moment the alignment was complete, the force of this energy focused into a pinpoint, like a magnifying glass compressing a beam of light. You, young lady, were standing in its central core in 1965."

Laura and Kevin were captivated. "But how did she travel through time?"

"Ah, yes, our original question. This is how I see it. The gravitational energy was so powerful, so focused, that it fractured time and created a pathway between 1965 and 2023. Why fifty-eight years to the day, you may ask? Celestial bodies are in constant motion, rotating and revolving. Fifty-eight earth years amassed before Mars, Venus, and our moon could reconfigure into the original formation, thereby generating a direct line between the two endpoints, 1965 and 2023."

Stopping for a moment, the professor sipped lukewarm coffee from his chipped mug. "Now, to get you home, Laura, I am convinced the aftershock Mr. Calloway experienced will be useful to us. Imagine, if you will, standing atop a mountain with a panoramic view of a canyon. As you holler, 'Hello out there,' the sound waves travel across the canyon, bounce against a solid formation, then boomerang back to the sound source."

"An echo," said Kevin.

"Yes indeed, an echo. For argument's sake, let's imagine a 'time wave' instead of 'sound wave'. With the help of the intense gravitational forces I previously mentioned, a time wave originating in 1965 penetrated 2023. Through the upcoming aftershock, the time wave will rebound to the original event in 1965, like an echo of sound. I am convinced the aftershock is a time echo destined to return to 1965. When it does, the temporal circle will fuse, thereby healing the break in time."

He faced Laura. "You, and you alone, need to be standing in the epicenter at sundown during the aftershock tonight, and if my theory is correct, you will be transported to the exact moment you left in 1965, to the origin of the time wave."

Kevin shifted uneasily in his chair. "Is this dangerous, professor? Can she be hurt?"

The professor cleared his throat. "I don't know. But if she doesn't make the attempt tonight, she'll never have another opportunity to go back. Is this a chance worth taking, Laura?"

Kevin tried to hold her gaze, but she quickly diverted her eyes. "Yeah. It is," she whispered.

Chapter 10

A short while later, the pair trekked up a small slope that overlooked a sweeping expanse of the river. Laura spread the threadbare blanket across a patch of grass while Kevin unpacked the wine. He uncorked the bottle, poured two generous glasses of the aromatic Cabernet, and handed one to Laura.

He raised his glass for a toast. "Here's to the past couple of days, the most frightening but extraordinary days I've ever experienced."

"I'll drink to that." They both drew a long sip of wine.

Unspoken emotion and anxiety hovered in the air between them, but Kevin was well aware she'd be on her way home tonight, so what would be the use of starting something they couldn't possibly finish? In a matter of hours, he would be back living his doldrum life. He'd finish the paper he'd forgotten about, graduate, and then what? Really, what did the future hold for him?

He cast these thoughts aside and focused on the present.

"So, Archer told me he's been working on an alternative plan in case there's no aftershock," he said.

"Oh, there'll be an aftershock. Paul may be a lot of things, but when he's sure of something, he's usually on the mark."

"Even so, we have a lot riding on Calloway's questionable memory."

"I'm counting on this aftershock, Kevin," Laura said. "But I'd be lying if I said I wasn't terrified. The storm I lived through the other night was excruciating."

"What do you mean?"

"Well for one thing, the wind was strong, so unbelievably strong, it tried to lift me off the ground and carry me away. I held onto chunks of grass, which as you can imagine, was useless." She swallowed hard. "And it was loud. Deafeningly loud, like a high-pitched screech inside my brain. And it kept getting louder and louder, until I could feel vibrations course through my entire body. Down my arms and into my fingers, down through my toes, even my teeth. It was the most agonizing experience I've ever lived through, and the thought of doing it again ..." She shuddered and let the thought hang. "You and Dr. Archer will have to hold me down to keep me from running away."

"Of course you're scared," Kevin said. "Who wouldn't be? At least this time you know what's coming and can brace yourself. You're brave, Laura, there's no doubt about it. You survived two full days in this crazy-assed future, and you're holding your own. But now you have a chance, a real solid chance, to go home, and I'll be there every step of the way with you. The professor, well, he won't be coming to the meadow later. He said he'd rather not add an unknown variable to the mix."

"And that means ...?" She swirled the wine in her glass.

"Basically, he's concerned his presence in the meadow could impact the echo and jeopardize your trip to 1965. Something about paradoxes."

"Just what I need, something else to wig out about." She chewed on a thumbnail and looked at Kevin. "Promise you'll be there?"

"Scouts honor. I'll be right there with you, until you ... leave." He didn't tell her that the professor warned him to keep away as well, but he'd be careful and keep his distance from the epicenter, that's all.

"What happens if it doesn't work, huh? Will I be trapped in a future that makes no sense?" Her breath caught. "You're wrong about me. I'm not holding my own. I'm barely hanging on by a single thread. You have no idea what this storm is like, Kevin, it almost killed me! And I have this God-awful feeling that something terrible's going to happen this time, I just know it."

"You're not going to die, Laura. I'll be right there to bail you out if things head south. Besides, if it doesn't work, we'll have Plan B. Archer's working on it as we speak."

"That's another thing. A backup plan? Why does he feel like we need a backup plan? He doesn't think this'll work, does he?" Her chest rose and fell with her rapid breaths.

"It'll work. I promise you, it'll work," he said.

She threw her arms in the air. "Stop it! Stop it! Stop making promises you can't possibly keep."

"Okay, you're right." He caught her eye, and froze. "Laura? Are you okay?"

Her hand clutched her chest while she struggled to inhale. She strained to breathe, only achieving short and insufficient gasps. Tiny droplets of perspiration appeared on her forehead. She looked at Kevin, eyes wide and pleading.

In that moment, he reached for her hands and held them. They felt ice cold and damp to the touch.

"Laura. Focus on my voice. I need you to take slow, deep breaths." He buried his worry and spoke to her in gentle, soothing tones. "Slow and steady." He held her gaze as they breathed together. "It's going to be fine. When I make promises, I intend to keep them. When I say you're going home, you will go home. I will do everything in my power not to let anything bad happen to you." He meant every word.

Her breathing slowed, and at last she drew in a deep, quavering breath and exhaled, her body releasing its tension.

"I'm ... I'm so sorry. I knew I was nervous, but ..." Her voice trailed off and she glanced down at their hands, her fingers intertwined with his. She didn't let go. "I think I'm okay now. I'm going to choose to believe you. You're always making promises I know you can't guarantee, but right now, I have to choose to believe you." She shivered, then lowered her eyes. "You say I'm strong and brave, but look at me. I'm a mess. I never would have survived this future without you, Kevin. I've been on the brink of losing my mind. But being around you, the way you talk to me ..." She paused. "From the moment I met you in the meadow, you're the one keeping me grounded. I feel safe with you."

Her body stopped trembling.

"Well, what kind of knight in shining armor would I be if I left you in the hands of that crazy old hermit?"

She smiled and slipped her hands from his grasp.

"How did he do it?" she asked. "How did Paul live over fifty long years all alone like that? That's no life. When I get back home, I promise you, I'll do whatever it takes to stop this from happening to him. I mean it."

"Now look who's making promises." Kevin chuckled, then gulped a mouthful of wine. How he wished she would stay here, with him, in 2023. He could already feel the heartache of his loss. But he knew she was right. She didn't belong here.

After a satisfying meal, they lounged on the blanket, satiated.

Rubbing her belly, she said, "I had no idea I was that hungry. Three pieces of fried chicken is a new record for me. As my dad says, 'Good food is good for the soul.' Hey, look— I'm not shaking anymore."

"Nice to hear, but I'd lay my money down on the restorative powers of the wine."

He raised the bottle to ask her if she'd like a refill. She shook her head and lifted her gaze to the sky. A slight breeze nudged a pair of puffy, white clouds to meet, and they merged them into one.

"Glad the sky hasn't changed in fifty-eight years." Laura pointed up. "Look at that cloud, right above us. See it? It looks like Magilla Gorilla." She pointed at another puff. "Oh, and look at that one. It's a doughnut, or maybe a really fat hoola hoop."

"Or more like that branded circle of grass in Sullivan's Meadow."

She rolled to her side and regarded Kevin. "No, I don't want to waste our time thinking about that meadow. How about, for now, the place doesn't exist."

"Works for me."

"And we're on a date," she said.

Kevin coughed. "Um, a date?"

"Sure, why not? And since we're on a date, I want to know more about Kevin Donahue, and not just you're a really nice guy who likes Lucky Charms."

"And Taco Bell. You can't forget about Taco Bell."

"Right. And Taco Bell."

"So, there you have it. That about sums me up," he said.

Laura scowled at him. "Let's start with where you grew up. Did you grow up in Sullivan Township?"

"Nope. I grew up in a small town in Vermont called East Middlebury. I only go to school in Sullivan Township."

"Oh right, Sullivan U."

"That's the one. I'm finishing up my senior year with a major in geophysics. Sounds impressive, I know." He hesitated. "Well, I'm supposed to be finishing up my senior year, after I finish a term paper for our good friend, Dr. Archer. You think he'll give me an extension?" He chuckled.

She said, "The professor. He's a good man."

"Yeah, he is. A little misunderstood, but a good man."

"Tell me, what was it like growing up in ... where did you say? East Middlebury? Anything like Sullivan Township?"

Kevin inhaled and described his idyllic childhood in rural Vermont. He told her about the many summers he spent building treehouses with his friends, swimming and fishing in the nearby brook, and playing baseball with his dad. As an only child, Kevin thrived on the loving attention he received from both parents.

"My father was a pharmacist and owned a small drugstore in the center of town. He made a decent living. I mean, we never struggled for money or anything. When I was ten, my dad was crossing the street in front of the pharmacy. He was halfway across when a supply truck came barreling down the road."

"Oh no ..."

"The driver slammed on the brakes, but it was too late. My dad died instantly. You know, I don't think my father even had the time to know he was hit. At least, that's what I keep telling myself."

"I'm so sorry, Kevin." She leaned across the picnic blanket and slid her hand into his. Their fingers automatically laced together, and as Kevin resumed talking, his thumb tenderly stroked her fingers.

"My mom took my father's death pretty hard, but she tried her best not to let her grief affect me. Don't get me wrong, I missed him, still do, but I was a little kid and bounced back relatively easily. My mother, well, she had a much harder time. After she dropped me off at elementary school, she locked herself in the house with only her despair to keep her company."

Kevin recounted how his mother, after six years of mourning, changed her life. She eventually enrolled in a local college, earned a degree in marketing and was hired by a prestigious advertising firm in New York City.

"The fast pace of the corporate world restored her spirit and she soon fell in love with a wealthy businessman. She and Bob have been happily married for two years."

"Wow. I don't know what to say. Such a tragedy."

He waved her off. "Don't worry about it. It's ancient history."

"Your mom's okay now?"

"Mm-hmm. Bob's a good guy, I guess. He makes her happy. She's concerned that I'm falling into her old patterns, living life without really living life ..." He ended abruptly. "Enough of that. Hey, I want to show you something."

Laura straightened herself. "Okay."

He slipped his hand into his back pocket for his wallet. "Hold up a sec, it's in here someplace." He rifled through the small papers and retrieved a card. "Check this out."

Laura examined the card in confusion. "What? I don't understand. How'd you get this?" He had handed her a Selective Service System Classification Certificate, or a draft card dated March 19, 1965 in the name of Kevin Andrew Donahue.

"Looks authentic, doesn't it?" He peered over her shoulder at the card. "I took a computer graphics design class last semester, and assigned to replicate an official document. It had to be one from the distant past, at least fifty years ago, and we were required to use the apps we'd been learning. So, I created this draft card, but look here." He tapped a line of text on the card. "I classified myself as 4F. I gave myself a popped eardrum in my right ear."

"Wait, you're saying this is fake? It looks so real."

"I know, right? I got an A on this project." He stuffed the card back into his wallet.

"Huh. Well, let me see the real one."

"The real what?"

"Your real draft card, goofball."

"Oh, there is no real one. There's technically no more draft."

"What are you talking about? There's no more draft?"

"Well, it's only a formality now. The army enlists volunteers and registration for draft is merely a backup plan."

She paused a couple of beats, shaking her head. "My God. All of those anti-war protests, kids burning their draft cards. This fella I know swears he's going to split to Canada rather than go to war. And now you don't even have a draft? You're blowing my mind," she said.

"Nearly sixty years of change and you've only seen the tip of the iceberg. But, Laura, don't worry about it, you're going home soon. In a few short hours, you'll be sitting with your family drinking orange-flavored Tang and eating a Swanson TV dinner." He gave her hand a squeeze. "Speaking of which, tell me about them. What's your family like?"

Laura inhaled deeply, adjusted her sitting position, and began. "Okay. There's a television program called *Father Knows Best* and my family is sorta like the Andersons. My dad goes to work wearing a suit and tie, my mother stays home to cook and clean, and my little brother, Charlie, is ... a pest."

"Hold on, you have a brother?"

"Uh huh, seven years old. Anyway, my folks expect me to follow in my mother's footsteps. I'm supposed to get married, have children, and then spend the rest of my life taking care of the house. I know they love me but they're such a drag. 'You're 20 years old, Laura, you better start thinking about settling down.'"

"Ah, yes, the old 'a woman's place is in the home' adage," said Kevin.

She pressed on. "Ever since Paul asked to go steady with me, it's a dream come true for my parents because his family is rich. I bet they have a million dollars. I think they own half of Sullivan Township or close to it. So, my mom and dad are constantly on my case, explaining how tough it was for them to live through the Great Depression with barely enough money to make ends meet. If I stay with Paul and end up marrying him, I'll never have to struggle to get by. The thing is, I'm not crazy about him." She paused. "But I certainly don't want him to turn into that greasy old hermit."

She then spoke about her job in the malt shop and her hope to make enough money to go to college, not unheard of in the sixties, but not quite common either.

"I'd really like to be a school teacher, although I doubt my parents would allow me to go to college. They'd be afraid I'd get wrapped up in the anti-war movement on campus." Laura drained her wine and extended the cup for a refill. "They're probably right. I only wish they didn't act like old fogies all of the time."

Kevin laughed.

"Man, they're so strict," she said. "I wonder what they'd do if I was like that dark-haired floozy we saw at Ronnie's. Gads, Kevin, how on earth did you get involved with her?"

He groaned. "Brittany? Oh no, major mistake. Let's not talk about her."

"Hey, I told you about Paul. C'mon, tell me. What's the word with her?"

"I don't want you to get the wrong idea. I met her in a gym class and she, for whatever reason, liked me. Yeah, we dated, but it wasn't going to lead anywhere. She's too plastic."

"Uh huh. You boys can't resist those flirty, curvy girls, can you?"

"What are you talking about?"

"That chick of yours didn't walk, she wiggled. A brunette Marilyn Monroe."

"I guess so. She was definitely hard to resist at first."

"Boys. You're all the same. So ... so .... shallow. It doesn't matter what year you're from, your eyes can't help but pop out of your head whenever a skirt walks by. What is it with you boys? It ticks me off."

"Laura, what are you talking about? Are you ... jealous?"

"No, of course not! I only met you a few days ago. Why would I be jealous? It doesn't matter anyway." She snatched her hand from his and stood up, slightly unsteady on her feet.

He grinned. "Let's pack this stuff up. And, as a special treat, a little music to help with the clean-up." He pulled out his phone and searched his playlist.

Outrage forgotten, she said, "Whoa, that's neat," and plopped down next to Kevin. "Your cell-o-phone is a tiny record player?"

"Sorta —"

"What albums do you have? You got anything by The Orchids?"

"Probably. I'll have to search for it though. Give me a song title."

"Okay, how about 'Gonna Make Him Mine?' I'll teach you how to dance The Hitchhiker."

It was supposed to be an easy lesson, with Laura demonstrating how to shimmy the hips and toss a thumb over each shoulder. Kevin's attempts were hysterically lame, as his hips were unable to rock with the beat and his thumbs jabbed at the air behind him. She howled with snorty laughter, clutching her sides as tears streamed down her cheeks.

"Oh God, so funny, so funny." She wiped her cheeks. "Let's try something slower. A box step."

Kevin searched for "Unchained Melody" and settled his hands on either side of her pelvis. She giggled. "No, your hands go like this." She placed her right hand in his left. The instant their hands touched, his heartbeat quickened, and a hundred butterflies fluttered in his belly. He inhaled deeply and as she described the steps, he did his best to concentrate, but couldn't ignore the effect her close proximity was having on him. He shuffled his clumsy feet, moving completely out of sync with the music.

"Kevin, are you listening? You're moving your feet all wrong."

"You know what, Laura? Let's try doing this dance my way, a la 2023." He pulled her close and heard her gasp. He raised her hands up to his shoulders and wrapped his arms around her waist. Slowly, the couple swayed and danced, their bodies pressed against each other, and the heat between the two enveloped them.

The music bathed them with mournful lyrics of everlasting love, a love so strong it connected two souls separated by time and space.

He embraced her, inhaling the fresh scent of her hair as she nuzzled her head against him. Gently, he pulled slightly away and rested his eyes on her delicate features— her slender nose, the rosy blush of her cheeks, her full lips. She was captivating. He searched her eyes— striking emerald green with flecks of gold— hoping to find an indication that she, too, felt this unspoken connection. Releasing her waist, he raised his hand to her cheek and ever so softly caressed her lips with his thumb. Before he could change his mind, he lowered his face to hers until their lips barely touched. He could feel Laura's body tremble as she pressed her lips against his, kissing him.

* * *

Entering Sullivan's Meadow, Kevin took note of the sun's position in the sky. It hovered close to the horizon and projected a soft, pinkish tint on the clouds. Laura strode beside him through the long grass, her eyes dull and lifeless, her face, ghostly pale. He wished there was a way to ease her mind, to somehow erase her fear, but he couldn't. He could barely keep a lid on his own dread. They both knew the storm would be violent, and there was no guarantee it'll transport her back home. What would he do if the raging storm threatened to kill her? How was he supposed to keep her safe then? Or, what if the storm cast her into some sort of timeless abyss, like the quantum realm in the Ant-man movie? He could feel his heart pounding, so he closed his eyes, took a measured breath, and told himself to cut the crap and man-up.

Laura stepped over to the wrought iron bench and sat, summoning him to join her. Eyeing the battered house, she said, "I'm surprised Paul isn't out here. I hope he's all right."

"Nah, he's fine." Kevin waved his hand dismissively.

Silence. The breeze, barely perceptible, swept the blades of grass into a lazy dance of their own. Streaks of lavender and orange stretched across the sky.

Kevin released a tremulous sigh. "Any chance you'll reconsider? Stay in 2023?"

Laura didn't answer him.

"Of course not. Didn't hurt to ask, though," he said, clearing his throat. "I'll walk you over."

Laura remained mute, tears welling in her eyes. She slowly rose and he guided her to the center of the charred circle.

"Now, remember what Dr. Archer said — you'll most likely return to the moment you left in 1965." He kissed her forehead then distanced himself from the epicenter.

The golden orb sank deeper and grazed the horizon. At that very moment, a deep rumble vibrated beneath their feet.

The two locked eyes.

A violent roar emanated around them, the intensity increasing exponentially. She screamed and started toward him.

"No, Laura. stay there!"

The thunderous noise and percussive forces reverberated the air around them. It was a cacophony of a thousand bass drums beating at such a magnitude, the soundwaves penetrated his body, ready to explode and shatter his existence.

Fighting against the wind, he shouted to Laura. "Keep looking at me!" Could she even hear him?

The intensity and sheer power of the supernatural force continued to amplify. The wind picked up speed, gusts slashed and threatened to wrench Laura from the circle.

"It's okay!" he hollered. "Keep your eyes on me!"

The earth groaned and convulsed, and Kevin crashed to the ground close to Laura, never releasing his eyes from her. He thought he heard a blood-curdling scream, so he extended his arm toward her. The wind whipped into his face causing his vision to blur. He blinked hard—

And she was gone.

The storm ceased as suddenly as it began, tree branches and twigs dropped to the ground. Kevin found himself lying in the grass, shivering. He crawled over to the circle and searched the area, but could detect no evidence of Laura's fate.

He stood, and with a profound emptiness he stumbled past the house toward the woods. The orange-red rays of the setting sun bathed the flowerbeds lining the walkway in a warm glow.

If he didn't know better, Kevin would have said the dilapidated home looked quaint.

Head hanging, he left.

Chapter 11

His alarm buzzed at 8 a.m., waking him from a remarkably deep sleep. Exhaustion permeated his bones, yet Kevin grudgingly moved from the bed to the shower. The hot spray he had directed into his face nudged him awake, and by the time he lathered and rinsed he was rejuvenated. With a cotton bath towel wrapped around his waist, he slid the closet door open to grab a collared shirt.

He stopped.

Where was Laura's Poor Boy sweater and hip huggers? Could she have taken them with her? The clothing was all he had left of her, and his sentimental side had wanted to keep them. He shrugged off his melodrama and pulled a shirt from its hanger. He missed her already, but more importantly, did she arrive in 1965 safely?

It dawned on him to conduct a Google search for her. He yanked the laptop from his sack, connected to the Internet and entered '*Laura Malone April 1965*'. A moment later, in bright blue font, the words 'No results found' appeared on the screen. Kevin tried '*Paul Calloway April 1965*' and the identical message, 'No results found,' flashed on his laptop. Perplexed, he googled '*Planetary Alignment, April 23, 1965*' and the PDF file he had read a few days ago emerged. He clicked on the article and read the familiar words, learning nothing new.

At this point, Kevin was ready to throw his computer across the room. He inhaled deeply, and for his final attempt he typed, '*April 24, 1965, The Tenakill Tribune*' and was rewarded with a copy of the newspaper, the day after the alignment. A quick perusal brought him to a relevant news story.

The Planetary Alignment: A Big Bust

Last night the celestial lightshow that astronomers have been widely publicizing as the 'Interstellar Event of the Century' turned out to be the 'Interstellar Bust of the Century'. Stargazers throughout Sullivan Township, equipped with binoculars and telescopes, were sorely disappointed. "I was expecting starbursts or comets," commented an unidentified source. Another gentleman claimed to have felt an earthquake at the time of the alignment, however geologists have indicated a geological disturbance was impossible and not detected. The astronomers of Lincoln Observatory were unavailable for comment.

His jaw dropped. The paper didn't contain one word about Laura's disappearance or Paul's indictment for murder. Completely unaware his destiny had been balancing on a precipice, the son-of-a-bitch had been exonerated.

But what about Laura? Had she survived the trip back?

He craved information about her, so he slammed his laptop shut and hastily collected his classwork for the day. He had enough time to visit the library's microfilm department prior to his Wednesday Astronomy class. He stuffed his materials in a sack and bolted for the door.

Kevin drove Lucille to the library's parking lot and sprinted up the steps into the building. He scanned the front desk and was relieved to see the student librarian, Ashley, working today.

Breathless, he strode to the desk and called out, "Hey, Ashley."

The young girl looked up and beamed a superwatt smile at Kevin.

"Thanks for helping my friend with her research the other morning. You were a lifesaver," he said.

"You're totally welcome, but I'm pretty sure I never helped you." Ashley expanded her smile to full tilt.

"Oh, not me. My friend, Laura. The red-head who knows nothing about technology?"

"Hmmm, nope, not ringing any bells, but you know what? I bet you're thinking of Melinda, not me."

He eyed Ashley's golden lip ring and shook his head. "Uh, I'm certain it was you."

This kid needs to take some Gingko, he thought.

"Nope, wasn't me."

"Uhh, yes it was. You're kinda hard to forget."

Ashley squealed with delight, her grin now resembled a split watermelon. "Are you trying to pick me up?"

"What?" Kevin's mouth dropped open.

She slid her fingers through her wispy chestnut hair. "Oh my God, you are. You're picking me up. Aren't you a cute one."

"No. No. I'm thanking you for your help on Monday, that's all."

"Oh, don't be embarrassed. It's okay if you hit on me. But, no offense, you need a better pickup line. You see, I never work Mondays, well, except for today. I'm covering for Melinda because she called in sick with the flu. My money's on the 24-hour Singapore Sling flu, if you know what I mean," she said.

"Ashley, today is Wednesday, not Monday. Never mind. I'm heading to the microfilm department."

"No, it's Monday, my silly new friend. You must've had one helluva a bender this weekend. Look here, at my screensaver."

She spun her monitor to face Kevin and large glaring letters scrolled across the monitor, mocking him, 'Welcome to another Manic Monday at Sullivan U'.

"See? Monday."

Kevin stared at the computer. "You guys need to update your computer settings," he said, and started to walk away.

"Hey! Where you going?"

"Like I said, the microfilm department."

"Hold up, give me a sec and I'll take you there."

Kevin lifted his palm to her. "Oh no, I can find it. Thanks anyway. See ya."

He hurried to the back of the library and heard her shout, "Don't forget, I'm usually off on Mondays."

Kevin sighed as he entered a large room filled with giant metal monstrosities, the microfilm machines. He settled into one of the seats. Was today really Monday? Maybe he lost track of time with all the craziness of the past few days. He shrugged, sorted through the microfilm canisters, and located 1965.

Forty-five minutes later, his eyes could no longer focus on the microfilm. He found absolutely nothing.

Laura. Where are you?

He rubbed his face with his hands while he contemplated his next move. If he tried an internet search using a different combination of keywords, he might have better results. He pulled his laptop from the sack and wedged it on the table next to the huge microfilm machine. *Google* popped up on the screen, and Kevin typed in '*Malone and Calloway*'. He did not include a date this time. Kevin tapped the Enter key and was surprised to see a small blurb on his screen.

June 30, 1965
The Tenakill Tribune
Mr. and Mrs. Frank Malone are pleased to announce the marriage of their daughter, Laura Grace, to Mr. Paul Douglas Calloway, son of Mr. and Mrs. Richard Calloway on June 25th. Following an extravagant reception at Sullivan Township Country Club, the happy couple honeymooned in Tahiti.

Kevin tore his eyes from the computer and stared absently at the wall. Well, she made it back safely. But damn it, she married that scumbag, Paul.

He pushed the thought from his mind, collected his things, and ran to the Astronomy lecture hall. He arrived early and sauntered up to the podium. He bet Dr. Archer was ready to bust with anticipation about last night's outcome in the meadow.

"Mr. Donahue," the professor proclaimed. "You're a bit early for class,"

"Hi, Professor. No, I don't attend your class on Wednesdays. I stopped by to give you the good news. It worked! Laura made it back to 1965. The storm was really intense, she almost chickened out. I probably would have ..." Kevin fell silent. "Professor? What's wrong?"

Peering over his glasses, the professor's vibrating eyes bore into Kevin's. "I may be aging more quickly than I would like, but I haven't lost my sense of time. Today is Monday. I am not acquainted with a Laura nor understand the relevance of 1965. Does this have anything to do with your research project?"

"But sir, Laura—" Kevin's words dried up. Something was wrong. First, the librarian insisted today was Monday, and now Archer? Was everybody's memory gone? Deciding to play this by ear, he responded, "Uh, yes, sir, it does have to do with my project. I was hoping to pick your brain about the planetary alignment."

"Go on, please."

Kevin thought fast. "Yeah, so, I've encountered a few unforeseen obstacles." Now, that was the understatement of the year.

"You're describing a situation frequently encountered when researching. Care to elaborate, Mr. Donahue?"

"Could the planetary alignment create a kind of rift?" Kevin asked slowly.

"A rift? A rift of what?"

Careful not to tread on Dr. Archer's suspicion of fraternity hazing rites, Kevin replied, "Um, a temporal rift, perhaps?"

Dr. Archer removed his eyeglasses and placed them on the podium. "Ah, I see you've decided to take the space-time perspective for your term paper. It's risky, I grant you that, and not typically well-received. Indeed, there are schools of thought that entertain temporal anomalies. Often, science fiction authors dabble in space-time conjecture, but there is an element of truth to their fantastical ideas. Maybe it's possible for an interstellar or cosmic phenomenon to conjure enough power to create a pathway between two timeframes. However, this is pure conjecture and would not apply to your research topic."

"Right. The pathway would be like a time-wave," Kevin said.

"Yes, quite good, Mr. Donahue, my thoughts exactly. And, if the power is forceful enough to generate a reverberation, a second wormhole could be formed, and a complete temporal circle would result. Hypothetically speaking, of course."

The temporal circle. But that didn't explain why everyone's memory of the past few days had been erased. Even the professor was affected. Dr. Archer was completely unaware of Laura's visit to the present and all of their efforts to return her to the past. His mind churned. Wait a minute. When he was with Laura last night, was he standing too close to the wormhole and got sucked in? Was he thrown back to an earlier date? It was possible. Hell, at this point anything was possible.

"I can see another question forming in your mind, Mr. Donahue. Please be quick, class is beginning shortly."

"Yes, sir. I was wondering, hypothetically, if an object can travel to another timeframe during a cosmic phenomenon, could a nearby object or person be dragged into the time portal?" Maybe he was dragged back in time a week or so.

Dr. Archer heaved a sigh. "Insightful question, but highly unlikely. I'd venture that nothing could enter the wormhole unless positioned at the exact point of entry."

Kevin's stomach plunged. Then what the hell had happened? As if hearing his unspoken question, the professor pushed on.

"Interestingly, the space-time dimension will not permit a paradox to exist. It finds a way to stabilize itself, and if that means starting over, it will reset the clock to the moment the paradox began. I would imagine no one would be aware of the events that transpired, unless, of course, they were standing near the origin, or mouth, of the wormhole. I'm reminded of the philosophical question, 'If a tree falls in a forest and no one is around to hear it, does it make a sound?' Similarly, if time is rewound and no one is around at the source, would anybody notice?"

"Wait, what? If a person was standing near the wormhole ..."

"He would be the only person on earth cognizant of the paradox's elimination."

Kevin whispered to himself, "I'm the only one who knows."

The professor reclaimed his eyeglasses and placed them on his nose. "As I said, this is pure conjecture on my part. Please take your seat, Mr. Donahue. Chances are my lecture on 'Stars, Galaxies, and the Universe' may interest you. Need I remind you, your presence is mandatory."

Stars, Galaxies, and the Universe? That was two days ago. The paradox adjusted the timeline by two days. Kevin deposited himself in an aisle seat, not sure where else he should go.

He was Bill Murray in "Groundhog Day." Except this time around he must relive the past few days without Laura.

Barely registering Archer's lecture for the second time, he focused his mind on the current dilemma. Apparently, the moment she returned to 1965, her existence in 2023 was conveniently obliterated, paradox resolved. It was as if she never existed here.

At the conclusion of the lecture, Kevin decided to cut classes again. Why not, since he had skipped them on his first Monday go-around. He raced from the lecture hall to the parking area, hopped on Lucille, and declared it lunchtime.

As he peeled out of the lot, another thought puzzled him: Dr. Archer was uncharacteristically verbose with his thoughts pertaining to time travel.

Chapter 12

Kevin arrived at the restaurant as Ronnie finished tossing a pizza into the oven. The friendly cook flashed a smile and called out, "Hey, Kevin. How ya doing, man." He approached Kevin and gave his shoulder a friendly squeeze. Kevin was chilled with a profound sense of déjà vu.

"Doing well, my friend. Would you mind throwing in a few slices for me?"

"Will do. Hey, don't look now, but your little hottie is walking in with her cohorts." Ronnie, playing host, turned to coolly greet Brittany then wiped down the countertop in front of Kevin.

"Well, well, if it isn't my boyfriend. Oh, that's right, ex-boyfriend. I hope you're enjoying your solitude because there's no coming back to this." She palmed the curves of her body with her hands. "Tootles."

Kevin closed his eyes in disgust but could easily recall the image of her dismissive hair flip from the previous time he experienced this Monday.

Floozy.

"Kev, dumping her was the wisest choice you've ever made," said Ronnie.

"Yeah, except she dumped me." They both burst out laughing.

* * *

Shortly after devouring the pizza, Kevin meandered up the winding trail in the woods and parked Lucille. He rested a moment against the old oak and admired the luscious green meadow stretched out before him. Strangely, he felt closer to Laura by being here, despite the heartache it caused him. How had he developed such strong feelings for her after knowing her for only a few days? Maybe it was the result of sharing a harrowing event, but whatever it was, he knew he had never felt this way before, and feared he might never feel it again.

As the tall reeds of grass swayed in the breeze, Kevin stood motionless. He saw not a single shred of evidence that a violent storm had ever occurred here. Even Calloway had remained oblivious to the commotion occurring a few yards from his door. Might as well see how the old geezer's doing.

He strolled up the front walk, but slowed his pace as he trailed his eyes along the pathway. The cracked asphalt held captive by clumps of dead weeds had been replaced by a decorative brick walkway lined with flowerbeds of pansies.

Strange. This wasn't here before.

He lifted his eyes to the cabin and gulped, staggering backwards. The shack was no longer a deteriorating mess, but a cozy cottage with butter-hued shingles and a front door stained a welcoming, cherry red. Decorative wooden shutters framed the windows and handcrafted window planters, home to happily blooming pansies, hung on the sills. Mouth hanging open, Kevin slapped a hand to his forehead.

He stumbled to the entrance, hesitating a moment before rapping on the doorframe. There was no reply, so he strode to the side of the house expecting to find the charred circle of grass. Instead, he saw a person wearing an oversized straw hat squatting in a well-tended garden of multicolored wildflowers and daisies. The individual, unaware of his presence, dug in the soil with a small spade. As he neared, he could detect the soft, sweet sounds of humming. His eyes adjusted to the scene, and he recognized the infamous circle and the irrefutable wrought iron bench. The figure stood and stretched languidly.

An older woman removed her hat and wiped the perspiration from her brow. She had long white hair, braided to the side, and her bright green eyes sparkled in the sunlight. She noticed Kevin and her face lit up with a huge smile. "I was wondering when you'd get here."

He blinked several times but there was no denying it. This woman standing before him was Laura. Somehow, she looked the same. Her face emanated self-assurance only granted with age and experience. Kevin's mind struggled to blend the image of the youthful 20-year-old girl with the silver-haired woman standing before him.

"Well, Kevin, you haven't changed a bit," she said.

"Laura." Her packaging had been altered, but it was still her.

"Now you're catching on. Would it be all right if this old woman tells you that she's missed you?"

Rattled, he stepped closer and offered a stiffened hug. "Um, this is going to take me a few minutes. You've aged close to sixty years overnight."

"I guess that's true, from your point of view anyway. Take your time, adjust." She took a stride or two toward the house. "Come in, let's have a glass of lemonade."

Laura entered the house but Kevin halted at the threshold. He scanned the pleasant, homey décor of the room.

"This is ... unreal. I was here only yesterday. This house was a deteriorating mess but now it's, well, amazing. The renovation must have taken you years."

Laura peered at Kevin from the kitchen. "Renovation? I didn't renovate. Oh God, you don't know, do you? How could you?"

"Oh, I know. You married Paul Calloway. I read the announcement online this morning. You guys live here? In Sullivan's Meadow? That's irony for you." He studied the glossy hardwood floors, avoiding eye contact with Laura. "Where is the old coot, anyway?"

"No, Kevin, you don't know, but you need to know," she said, her voice sad. "You need to hear this. It's a long story, so make yourself comfortable."

She handed him a tall glass of lemonade, and sat in a chair facing him.

Laura took a sip of lemonade and looked into Kevin's eyes. "I'll start where it all started, at the beginning, right here in this meadow."

Chapter 13
1965

Slowly, Laura became aware of her surroundings. She could detect the feathery caress of long grass on her cheek and the pungent aroma of damaged greens. She blinked open her eyes. Her head pounded, her body ached, but she forced herself to sit. At that moment Laura sensed she wasn't alone. She cautiously turned her head to see a young man clutching himself in profound grief, sobbing at the sky.

"Paul?" she attempted weakly. She cleared her throat. "Paul?"

The despondent man pulled his eyes from the heavens and gaped at Laura. "Oh my God. Laura. I thought you were dead."

Once again, Laura's mind attempted to grasp the impossible. Paul was no longer a withered, senile old hermit, but a strong, handsome, virile young man.

With obvious relief, he brushed his black hair out of his radiant blue eyes, scooped her up and embraced her. She surrendered to exhaustion and sagged into his chest, finding comfort in the steady rhythm of his heartbeat. She was back. Back to the very moment in 1965 the first storm took her.

Gingerly, he placed her on the ground and wiped his eyes. "That storm was off the wall," he said with a choked laugh. "Some light show, huh? Let's book, Laura, this place gives me the creeps."

He grabbed her hand and they sprinted to the trail for the Corvair. She wordlessly said goodbye to Kevin as Paul stomped on the accelerator to escape the madness.

"Check it out. The road's completely dry. The storm never left the damn meadow. That's messed up, man. Let's head to Diesel's and tell the guys about the tornado. They'll think I've lost it. You'll back me up, won't you babe?"

"Please take me home, Paul. Really. I should've been home already. You know how my parents are."

He grunted but drove her home, chattering happily about how they braved a catastrophic earthquake and gale force winds. He pulled the car up to the front walk of Laura's house but clutched her shoulder as her fingers grazed the door handle.

"I love you, Laura."

She studied his face, smooth and unlined. She no longer doubted his affection. After all, she had seen firsthand how he had cast aside a life of promise and chosen one of deplorable solitude, all because of his all-consuming sorrow of losing her. What other explanation could there have been for such a choice? It was love, pure and simple.

She hastily kissed his cheek. "See you tomorrow, Romeo."

The following afternoon, Laura was grounded. Twenty years old, and her father actually "put his foot down" and grounded her.

"If you're going to be out, you can do us the courtesy of calling home. There are plenty of payphones in town, use them. Your mother was a nervous wreck, she hadn't heard from you since breakfast. She was this close to calling the police. This close. You need to be more responsible, young lady."

Ultimately, Laura didn't mind being grounded. She was content sprawling on her bed listening to 45s. It was during her fourth play of "Unchained Melody" when she heard knocking on the front door. She ignored the footsteps and voices downstairs and instead raised the volume of her phonograph.

"Laura, honey," her mother called through the closed bedroom door. "Paul's here, sweetheart. Freshen yourself up and come join us."

Laura rolled her eyes, but complied. She was a grown woman, but her life hadn't progressed one iota since her prepubescent years. After passing a brush through her long auburn hair and yanking on a headband, she descended the steps.

At the bottom of the stairwell, Paul was in deep conversation with her dad about the Vietnam War. She thought she heard Paul brag how his father's connections helped him dodge the draft, but she couldn't be sure, nor did she care. Paul grinned when he spotted her, and gave her a polite kiss on the cheek.

"How are your parents, Paul?" asked Mrs. Malone, her voice sweet as honey. She untied her apron, placed it on the back of a club chair, and smoothed the wrinkles from her housedress. She passed her hand over her auburn hair to catch any flyaways. "Is your mother well?"

"They're fine, thank you for asking, Mrs. Malone. My father landed another important client at work, and my mother is busy redecorating the recreation room. She's having new wall-to-wall carpet installed called shag. It's very hip."

"Well, how nice. Please give them both my regards."

"Hi, Paul!" In raced seven-year-old Charlie, wearing a dirt-covered crew neck and dungarees. A trail of muddy footprints followed him.

"Hey, it's the puny fuzz-ball." Paul lightly palmed the top of Charlie's crewcut.

The boy tried ducking out of the way. "I am not a fuzz ball. Come out front and play ball with me, Polliwog."

"Polliwog? Good one, Charlie."

Paul gave the kid's head a knuckle nuggie until Mrs. Malone grabbed Charlie by the arm and propelled him out the front door. "No ball. Go outside and stamp the mud off your feet, mister."

"Ah, gee-whiz, ma."

"Go."

The boy grumbled to himself as he exited the house.

"Anyway, I'm glad you're both home, Mr. and Mrs. Malone. I would like to speak with you."

Laura's heart quickened. What was he up to?

"Your daughter and I have been dating for a while now, and I've come to love and respect her. She's a kind, beautiful woman and the one I'd like to share my life with. It is my hope to ask Laura for her hand in marriage, but first I would like to ask for your blessing."

Marriage? Was he kidding? They weren't even going steady. She stood at the bottom of the stairs, like an outside observer watching her life unfold.

Mrs. Malone covered her mouth with her fingers while her husband answered for the two of them. "Son, nothing would make us prouder. Welcome to the family."

Laura's mother hugged Paul, then extended her arms to Laura and squeezed her tightly. Overwhelmed and bewildered, she weakly hugged her mother in return. She knew her parents approved of this marriage, and her future would be secure and financially stable.

Paul said, "Well, Laura, you're not engaged yet, so don't begin celebrating. Besides, you'll have to wait until you're no longer grounded for the actual proposal."

"I can't ground a practically married woman. Her punishment is formally lifted," her father said.

"That's swell, Mr. Malone. We'd like to paint the town, if that's all right with you. I'll have her back by 10 tonight, safe and sound."

Mr. Malone shook Paul's hand. "Take good care of her, son."

Laura was shocked. Five minutes earlier she was a reprimanded child confined to the homestead, and now she was a woman on the threshold of marriage and bestowed eleven hours of complete freedom. She had no control of her own life.

Chapter 14

As they drove into town, Laura welcomed the distraction of Paul's verbosity. He found an available parking space on the street, walked around the back, and opened Laura's car door. She cringed every time he stopped bystanders on the sidewalk to proclaim his love for her.

"See this beautiful red-haired beauty? She's going to be my wife."

Laura frowned and tugged at Paul's shirtsleeve to move him toward the entrance of the malt shop.

A budding news reporter stood in front of their destination, gathering opinions about last night's planetary light show. One elderly gentleman, clearly disappointed in the outcome, told the reporter, "I was expecting starbursts or comets." As the reporter feverishly jotted down the man's words, Paul barged in between the startled journalist and the man, disrupting the interview.

"On to more important news. This woman is going to be my wife," he said.

"Sir, you're interrupting my interview."

"About what? The alignment? Oh, I can tell you a lot about that fiasco."

The reporter shrugged and dismissed his affronted interviewee without bothering to obtain his name, then focused on Paul.

"Here's the real deal," Paul said. "Did you know there was an earthquake at the time of the alignment? It rattled the earth and created diabolical winds."

The reporter lowered his pad. "Oh, swell. Found myself a publicity hound. Now, if you'll excuse me—"

"Really. I thought we were done for, it was that dangerous. But even with the odds against me, I managed to claw my way out of the storm right in the nick of time to save my girlfriend."

The reporter's brow furrowed. "Who do you think you're kidding, mister?"

"I'm not kidding. It happened. Check it out with your scientist friends at the *Tribune* or something."

Picking up his bag from the sidewalk, the young news writer said, "I intend to," and strolled away grumbling. "Diabolical winds. Man, what a psycho."

Paul shrugged. "Eh, that storm is old news anyway. Come on, Laura, let's grab a table."

She bee-lined to her favorite booth next to the window and he followed closely behind her. A waitress wearing the traditional pink uniform and starched apron rolled up on her skates. Her caramel-colored hair, pulled into a high ponytail, bounced as she skidded to a halt. "Hey, kids. What's happening?"

"Susan." Laura slid off the bench to give her friend a bear hug. "I didn't know you started working weekdays. When did this happen?"

"Sorta recently. I needed a few bucks and Bruno put me in for extra hours. You working this summer?"

"Absolutely." Laura said, as Paul simultaneously said, "Not a chance."

"Oh, you two have your lines crossed. Listen, I'll give you a few minutes to talk it over. Before I forget, Laura, did you hear the news? Bruno is overhauling the malt shop. He says he wants to get rid of the 40s vibe and embrace the modern age. Supposedly he's turning it into a drive-in restaurant. I still think he's behind the times. Isn't that a 50s thing?"

Laura opened her mouth to respond when Paul, drumming his fingers on the Formica, said, "Who cares? Laura and I are getting married."

Susan's expression fell. "What? She turned toward Paul. "You're getting married?"

Laura shot a seething look at him. "Oh, Susan, we're not even engaged."

"Any day now, baby."

"Like I said, I'll be back in a few minutes," Susan said as she rolled away.

"Paul, why are you telling people we're engaged? You haven't proposed yet, and more importantly, I haven't said yes."

"But you will, princess. Hey, I hate to leave you alone but I need to hit the head. Be right back."

Paul dashed to the back of the restaurant, and as he rounded the corner, pinched Susan's backside. Laura frowned, watching her friend giggle in response, batting her false eyelashes.

Turning away, Laura gazed out the diner's window. Paul was being such a clod. Why couldn't he be remotely like Kevin? She inhaled deeply and sighed. God, how she missed him. She hadn't known him for long, but couldn't deny she was attracted to him. Afterall, he was an honest, compassionate man, and it didn't hurt he was remarkably handsome, in a boy-next-door kind of way. Here she was, safely back in 1965, and yet, she felt homesick.

Biting the inside of her cheek, she looked at the scenery outside the window. Across the street, Flip Side had removed its Elvis Presley poster from the storefront window, and a salesboy struggled to hang The Fab Four. She watched the boy, but her thoughts drifted back to Kevin. She wondered what happened to him after she had left. Did he finish his assignment? Did he get back together with the floozy? She felt powerless, as if she had never left the ferocity of the storm.

Later that night, rain battered relentlessly against her bedroom windowpane, making it difficult for Laura to asleep. The howling wind outside her window pounded the side of the house, pummeling the exterior with its powerful fists. She grabbed the wool blanket at the foot of her bed and pulled it up to her nose, creating a cocoon for herself. Tossing and turning, her mind shifted uneasily from one bizarre thought to the next, until she plunged into a fitful sleep.

Somehow, she knew she was asleep and dreaming, but couldn't force herself awake, and it frightened her. She drifted deeper into slumber and realized she wanted her mama, but she wasn't a little girl anymore, was she? She couldn't remember. No, she was an adult. It was 2023, and she was seventy-eight years old. She looked down at herself. Old women shouldn't have smooth forearms, Laura thought, and watched with horror as her skin withered into wrinkly crepe paper. Her mother, who appeared suddenly in an eerie gray mist, chastised her. "You're a grown woman now. Stop your silliness. A storm can't hurl you into the future, but maybe an earthquake can." Paul walked in, the gray mist swirling around his feet. He placed a hand on her mother's shoulder and said to Laura, "you know we're good together, baby." "No! No, we're not." She ran away from him, into a meadow. "I don't belong with you," she shouted.

The next morning, the remnants of the nightmare dissipated into obscurity, like ash in a breeze.

Chapter 15

A week later, Paul convinced Laura to go see *What's New, Pussycat* at the drive-in theater.

"It's supposed to be hilarious. Peter Sellers is in it, and he's a riot. C'mon, what do you say?"

A movie about a womanizer wasn't her bag, but Laura relented. On their way to the drive-in, Paul slowed the car and maneuvered it to the gravel on the shoulder of the road. He turned off the ignition and they sat in silence for a moment, listening to the engine tick as it cooled. Through a gap in the trees, the river sparkled with its unrelenting cheerfulness, a juxtaposition with Laura's pounding heart.

"Look at me, babe."

She peeled her eyes away from the river and looked at Paul. Oh no. He was actually going to propose marriage ... on the side of a road.

"I love you, Laura. I love you so much. I'm over-the-moon about tonight."

"I know, I know. It'll be a great flick. Peter Sellers is masterful." She spoke in a flat monotone.

"Huh?" He shook his head. "Yeah, he is, but that's not what I'm talking about. I've made it clear I want you for my wife, and I will spend my life making sure you have the life you deserve."

He leaned sideways, the vinyl seat protesting with soft creaks, and pulled a ruby red velvet box from his back pocket. Using calloused fingers, he worked to unfasten the tiny brass clasp, and opened the lid.

Laura inhaled sharply. She stared at the most ostentatious ring she'd ever seen. The sheer size of the diamond commanded attention, but apparently that wasn't enough. It sat on a gold band adorned with sparkling diamond accents. The whole effect screamed of wealth and status.

"Ten carats. Nothing but the best for my girl. You'll marry me, right?"

She affixed a smile to her face as her heart pounded against the confines of her chest. She didn't want to do this. He was not the one she wanted to spend her life with. Laura reminded herself of the pathetic old man Paul had become after living decades alone, and felt her face drain of color. He loved her, and someday she'll learn to love him back.

She cleared her throat, and with a strangled voice that sounded a million miles away, Laura replied, "Of course I'll marry you."

He pulled the ring from the velvet slot and slid it onto her finger. "My wife. Man, that sounds good." He pressed a firm, dry kiss against her lips and abruptly withdrew. "We better go or we'll be late for the movie."

After turning into the drive-in, Paul chose a spot in the back of the lot. He unhooked the adjacent speaker from its post, secured it inside the window, and pressed a button. The car reverberated with jarring whistles, deafening crashes, and booming explosions as Wile E. Coyote chased Road Runner.

"Happy, babe?"

She couldn't answer, and stared at the movie screen.

The instant the vibrant, psychedelic words in the title sequence appeared, he draped his arm across her shoulders and guffawed throughout the entire picture. She, on the other hand, was hypnotized by the rock on her finger. Not exactly a romantic proposal, but she was going to marry Paul. She would soon become Mrs. Paul Calloway. She blew out the breath she was holding.

The next few days passed with a flurry of activity. Laura tagged along with him as they drove around to announce their engagement to family and friends. She endured fervent congratulations and hugs, jumped at the explosive pop of champagne bottles being uncorked, and tolerated the laughter and back-slapping. Her fiancé insisted they marry within a couple of months, and she acquiesced.

One evening during a lull in the frenzy, Laura helped her mother set the table for dinner while Paul hung outside with Charlie shooting hoops. Her brother idolized him, though she couldn't figure out why, because Paul constantly antagonized him.

Through the window, she heard her brother whining so she pushed the curtain aside to peek.

"Cheater. That didn't go in, it wasn't even close. Gimme the ball, Paul. Hey. It's my turn."

"Nuh-uh, you little twirp. It was all net, not my fault you didn't see it. My point, and still my turn."

"But it didn't go in. You're cheating."

Paul held the ball loosely on a hip under a dangling arm. "Prove it. You can't, can you? My point, my turn."

She let the curtain drop.

"Mom, can I ask you something?"

Her mother was humming as she worked, and looked up at her daughter. "Of course, honey."

Laura reached for a dinner plate and clung to it. "When you married Daddy, how did you know you were marrying the right person? I mean, you and Daddy were made for each other. But how did you know?"

Her mother studied her. "What's all this about?"

"I don't know. Nerves, I guess."

"Sweetheart, I'm not blind. I can see there are no sparks between you and Paul. He is a little ... much. But he's young. I'm sure in time he'll mature into a responsible man, and you'll fall madly in love with him nonetheless. You can't let this one pass you by, baby girl. You'll be well taken care of, and as your mother, that comes as a relief. Besides, he adores you, and he's really trying to be an attentive fiancé. Give him time."

Laura nodded and rested the plate on the table.

* * *

The following week, the telephone rang and Laura answered it in the kitchen.

"Hello?"

"Hello, dear. This is Elizabeth Calloway, Paul's mother. I presume I'm speaking with Laura? I'm sure you're having a momentary lapse of telephone etiquette due to premarital jitters, and I need not remind you how important it is to identify yourself to a telephone caller."

"Oh, yes, it's me. I mean, this is Laura." Damn, she was stammering.

"Hello, Laura, I hope you're well."

"Yes, I am. How are you?"

Mrs. Calloway disregarded Laura's pleasantries. "I took the liberty of making an appointment for us at Kleinman's Bridal House in Brooklyn. They had a cancellation, which, as you can imagine, is quite miraculous, and they offered the appointment to me. My son is certainly making it difficult for us to prepare a wedding in only six weeks. Men. They don't understand the intricacies of party planning, do they? Of course not. The appointment is this afternoon at 2, and your mother is welcome to join us, of course. I imagine you'll make yourself available, won't you?"

She had originally planned to go dress shopping with her mother next week, but to her surprise, found herself replying, "Certainly. I wouldn't dream of missing it."

"Lovely. Paul is a lucky man to be marrying a girl who is so ... agreeable."

Laura remained silent.

"I'll pick you up at 1:00, dear. Please be sure you and your mother are ready. Kleinman runs on a tight schedule."

Cheeks burning, she carefully placed the phone receiver into its cradle.

* * *

Laura and her mother entered the shop and hesitated a few feet past the entryway. Never before had she seen a clothing shop so extravagant. Without the typical rows of garment racks to clutter the space, the interior of the establishment appeared cavernous. The four walls, painted a delicate cream hue, showcased magnificent gowns in clusters of three. Even the hangers radiated luxury, each thickly padded with cream-colored silk to prevent unsightly lumps in the gowns' delicate fabric. Positioned in the center of the room, cushioned loveseats granted mothers-of-the-bride the ideal vantage point to watch their daughters emerge from the fitting room. As Laura's gaze swept across the room, she noticed multiple mirrors fastened to the walls, but one caught her attention. It was a grandiose, three-way mirror, nestled in a resplendent golden frame. It stood as a centerpiece against the main wall, a circular pedestal before it.

Mrs. Calloway pushed past Laura and greeted a middle-aged saleswoman wearing a white blazer, her name embroidered near the lapel. The woman's brunette hair was tastefully styled in a short beehive. She approached Laura with her hand extended, smiling pleasantly.

"So, you must be the bride." The woman lightly shook Laura's hand. "And, of course the mother-of-the bride. I must say, Mrs. Malone, you are as lovely as your daughter. Welcome to Kleinman Bridal. Allow me to introduce myself. I'm Hilda Kleinman, proprietor, and serving as your Personal Bridal Consultant for the day. My sole purpose is to help you find a bridal gown worthy of your dreams. Your only job is to give me an idea of your preferences, and I will take it from there. Fair enough?"

Laura returned the smile. "Fair enough."

"Wonderful. I will pour the three of you champagne, and we'll begin." The woman went to turn away but Paul's mother stepped forward.

"I appreciate your ability to accommodate us given your busy schedule, Hilda," said Mrs. Calloway. "I'm duly aware it was no easy feat for you to arrange a cancellation for us, but I'm thrilled nonetheless. No bride should marry without the Kleinman experience."

"Right. Now, if you'll excuse me for a moment," she replied. Her words carried a chill.

Returning with three flutes of bubbly champagne, Hilda faced Laura. "Now, tell me the type of gown you've been envisioning for your wedding. Remember, this is the one day in your life you are royalty, essentially a princess. Dream big, and I'll make it happen. Did you bring any magazine clippings?"

"No, I haven't had a chance to look for anything yet, but I was thinking something simple would be nice, like a tea-length dress."

Mrs. Calloway slammed her glass on a side table and the liquid sloshed close to the rim. "A tea-length dress?" She emphasized the word 'dress' with disdain. "Need I remind you, we're not here to find a utilitarian garment. This establishment sells gowns. Bridal gowns. Furthermore, no son of mine will marry a bride in a sundress on his wedding day." She sighed with exacerbation. "Hilda? A little help, please?"

No stranger to familial friction in her shop, Hilda soothed the ruffled feathers. "That's why I'm here, Mrs. Calloway, to listen to all ideas and explore options." She gave her hands a quick clap and stood. "Let me bring an assortment of gowns for you to try on and we'll work from there, shall we? Excuse me a moment."

Mrs. Calloway snatched her glass and took an angry sip.

"Now, now," Mrs. Malone said. "I'm sure Hilda will find Laura a beautiful dress we can all agree on. No doubt we're in good hands."

Paul's mother gritted her teeth. "Bridal gown."

Poised on the edge of the loveseat, Laura sipped her champagne. She deliberately recalled the image of an aged and withered Paul Calloway, and lifted her chin resolutely.

* * *

The wedding ceremony was performed at St. Anthony's Cathedral in Sullivan Township on a sunny, cloudless day in June of 1965. Laura stood anxiously with her parents outside the gothic wooden doors of the church and heard the soft chords of Pachelbel's Canon drifting from within. Seven bridesmaids swathed in pink taffeta strolled down the long aisle and waited at the pulpit. Although not traditional, she had insisted both of her parents give her away. Charlie, of course, was the ring bearer. Earlier, he had whined nonstop as he shoved his arms into the sleeves of the black tuxedo jacket. "I look like a penguin."

A young woman peered through the doorway and whispered, "Whenever you're ready, miss." It was time.

Tightly clutching her bouquet of elegant roses, Laura faced her mother. "Mom, I can't do this. It feels wrong. I can't—"

"Don't be silly, sweetheart. You're feeling those typical pre-wedding jitters. You'll see, your wedding will be the happiest day of your life." She readjusted the veil over her daughter's lush, auburn mane.

Then, without another thought, her parents each grasped an elbow and the three of them strolled through the threshold. Laura's ten-foot regal Watteau train dragged heavily behind her as they moved their way down the seemingly endless aisle. Although flanked by five hundred smiling guests, she ignored them all and fixed her eyes on the carpet before her. Finally, they arrived at the altar. Her parents lifted the heavy veil to kiss her cheeks and smiled at her with heartwarming tenderness. They turned for their seats, leaving her to stand transfixed at the foot of the stairs.

She forced herself to look at her groom. With his hands clasped behind his back, he bore his tuxedo with confidence. He stood tall and proud, his broad shoulders pulled back and his chin held high. His blue eyes sparkled, perhaps with his love for her. She eyed his thick dark hair, meticulously slicked back, and how it accentuated his full lips and chiseled jaw.

She allowed herself to superimpose the sight of this vibrant, young man with the image of the withered, decrepit recluse he would've become if not for this marriage. Her groom's bright eyes withered before her into bleary, bloodshot pinholes, and his magnificent head of hair thinned into limp, yellowed wisps.

Laura breathed in deeply, bid a silent, final farewell to the old man, and extended her hand to her groom.

The entire ceremony progressed in a senseless blur, and then she was married.

The reception was held at the Sullivan Township Country Club, the swankiest catering hall in the county. Tall crystal vases stood as centerpieces on each table, with pale pink roses and orchids cascading from the mouth.

Feeling like a spectator, Laura watched her husband celebrate with his posse. He never stopped dancing except to snag pink champagne cocktails from the passing trays. He entertained his guests by hauling a waitress onto the floor and together they danced a mean Twist. No longer required to remain neatly combed, his curls sprung free from the confining shellac and bounced happily on his forehead. Charlie snuck up behind him and began imitating him, twisting and turning with fervor, until Paul spun around and shoved the boy from the limelight.

At midnight, Laura chatted with Paul's boss from the Esso station. She towered over his small frame, but she liked him immensely. He possessed a contagious grin, and she found herself smiling along with him as they spoke.

"He was a such a little fella when he started working for me, and I tell ya, I didn't think he'd last a week. Privileged kids don't usually like gettin' their hands dirty."

She laughed. "Yet, you kept him on."

"Oh, sure, sure. Paul was different, he didn't mind the grease. I even had him washing windshields and filling up gas tanks, but I tell ya, it wasn't long 'til he was doing oil changes. Still makes me chuckle when I think of the skinny 14-year-old kid traipsing around the station wearing his baggy coveralls." He absentmindedly toyed with his fingers, attempting to remove the permanent stains of grease. "Can't believe he's a married man now."

"Yep, I'm trying to make an honest man out of him."

The man beamed. "Ah, he's a lucky one, that Paulie, found himself a beautiful bride." He patted her cheek. "I'm really gonna miss the boy, but I gotta tell ya, my lady customers are gonna flip a wig when they hear he quit. You might not know this, but he has a way with the ladies."

"I'm sorry, what? He quit?"

If possible, Albert's smile grew to encompass his entire face, contradicting his unfathomable words. "Yep. He quit on the spot. Arrived for his shift last week and handed me his uniform. Said his father was finally going to be training him in the family's financial business, and that— I'll never forget this— Calloways do not make their livings pumping gas. I've been working at the station half my life and managed to support a family of six. Different strokes for different folks, is what I say." He shrugged. "It's kinda funny, when I think about it. Paulie's main reason for working at my gas station was to snub his old man. He and his dad never did see eye to eye. Until now, that is."

She was speechless. Paul never mentioned a thing about resigning from his job at Esso. She knew he would leave eventually, but wasn't that a decision a couple should discuss?

She casually glanced at the dance floor, as the band played a slow version of the Beatles' song, "Yesterday". Several couples swayed together to the ballad, and Laura listened to the melancholy lyrics about days gone by and love lost. Naturally, her thoughts drifted to Kevin, and how cruelly fate toyed with their hearts. She recognized the start of an undeniably powerful connection with him, nothing she had ever experienced with her new groom. But what did it matter now? This line of thinking had to stop, especially on her wedding day. Besides, it wouldn't do any good to wallow in self-pity and dwell on the impossible. Kevin wasn't even born yet, for goodness' sake. Her vision blurred with unshed tears, so she abandoned her thoughts and searched the crowd for her husband.

It didn't take long for her to spot him. She saw him dancing with one of the guests, their bodies pressed together and moving slowly and rhythmically to the music. Laura rose from her chair, ready to cut in and take her rightful place with Paul, when she noticed the woman's hands were placed on his backside. Incredulous, Laura watched the pair while they swayed in a slow, intimate circle. Who the hell was all over her husband on her wedding day? The pair turned in a leisurely circle and the woman's face emerged into view. Laura gasped, horrified, because wrapped in her husband's arms was her good friend and co-worker, Susan, and Paul's hands were reciprocating the favor on her backside. Completely humiliated, she felt the image sear itself into her memory.

Just then, Laura heard Albert mumble to himself, "Yessiree. A way with the ladies, I tell ya."

At the end of the evening, Paul's father sprang up to the microphone, and demanded his guests' attention. With his towering 6'4" frame and iron-colored hair, Mr. Calloway radiated an aura of self-importance.

"Tonight, we are celebrating the marriage of my son to the love-of-his-life, Laura Calloway. May the rest of their lives together be as happy as they are this evening." He paused until the cheers subsided, then continued. "Paul's mother and I have struggled to choose a suitable wedding gift. We are pleased to have settled on, what we feel, the perfect gift for a perfect couple."

He summoned his wife to the microphone. Elegantly dressed in a champagne-colored cocktail gown and her blonde tresses artfully piled atop of her head, Mrs. Calloway played the part of hostess beautifully. She theatrically lifted a large manila envelope overhead before passing it to her husband.

He continued. "It is our utmost pleasure to present to you, Mr. and Mrs. Paul Calloway, the deed to the Rosewood Estate." The partygoers cheered as Paul bounded up to his parents, embracing each one with exuberance.

Laura gathered her long skirts, pasted a smile upon her face, and joined her new family. Had her in-laws handed them a bona fide mansion as a wedding present? Why would they do such a thing? She hugged the Calloways and thanked them politely, when realization set in. The grand gesture gave their guests the illusion of generosity, while keeping a tight grip on the family's wealth.

Scanning the applauding crowd, Laura spotted her own parents standing next to their table with her father's hands resting on top of Charlie's shoulders. Euphoric smiles lit their faces.

* * *

The newlyweds honeymooned in Tahiti and returned to Sullivan Township sporting sun-kissed skin and a calm serenity. Paul had been undeniably loving and attentive, doting on her throughout the two weeks of leisure. Entering the Rosewood mansion completely obliterated any residual contentment. Gaudy, pretentious décor closed in on her, but Laura bit her tongue. It would be ungracious to acknowledge these insensitive thoughts.

Later that evening, as the newlyweds snuggled in bed, Paul yawned and said, "I'm still in shock over my parents' gift. Can you believe this place? It's magnificent. They hired a professional decorator to furnish all the rooms."

"Yes, it's magnificent." She attempted to muster up a smidgen of enthusiasm, but she fell disastrously short.

"What's the matter, babe? You're not happy? Hey, if you don't like the house, that's fine. We can find one that suits your taste."

He couldn't be serious. He was willing to walk away from a grand estate simply because she didn't like it?

"No, it's remarkable, really, but I've always thought I'd choose my own home when I married. I pictured a small cottage with shutters, rows of flowers lining the walkway, and a white picket fence."

He laughed, "You're adorable. A cottage. That pretty much sounds like the kind of thing you'd choose."

She snuggled closer. He really did understand her.

"But you're a Calloway now. We don't live in shacks." He released a boisterous snort while she inwardly cringed.

The following evening, Laura treated herself to a luxurious, fragrant bubble bath. She filled the tub with hot water until is practically overflowed and steam radiated off the water's surface. She eased herself into the tub and leaned back, feeling the heat loosen the knots in her shoulders and dissolve her tension. Breathing in the lavender-scented steam, she closed her eyes. Yes, she could definitely get used to this.

Twenty minutes later, she stepped out of the tub and wrapped herself in a plush Egyptian cotton towel. Steam hovered in the air, and as she realized it would be impossible to dry herself off in there, she heard her husband gently knock on the bathroom door. He opened the door and a billow of steam escaped.

"Got something for you," he said. He pulled an envelope from his back pocket. "A wedding present, from me to you."

"A wedding present? But I didn't get you anything."

"I didn't expect you to. Here, take it."

As she unsealed the envelope he stated, "I know the past month has been absolutely nuts. I mean, my mother monopolized the wedding plans, my father dictated where we should live, so ... I formally bestow upon you ... Sullivan's Meadow."

She furrowed her brow, confused.

He said, "I located the owner and offered him a decent sum of money, and your name is now officially on the deed. If it's your heart's desire to build a little house, we'll hire an architect and a construction crew, everything to be completed to your specifications. It will be your own pet project."

She flung her arms around her husband. "You are incredibly thoughtful. Thank you!" She smothered him with kisses.

Incredibly, the cottage was designed and built within two months. The Calloways certainly knew how to hire people to get things done efficiently. Laura happily spent most of her free time furnishing the home and gardening, and when the last shutter was nailed to the window and the final tulip bulb buried, she pleaded with her husband to drive up to the meadow to see the finished product. He acquiesced, and the two hopped into his brand-new Shelby Cobra. He had sold the Corvair as he haughtily proclaimed the vehicle no longer appropriate, replacing it with one considered prestigious and trendy.

She sat impatiently next to him while he maneuvered his new sports car along the winding trail in the woods. He parked the automobile on the edge of the meadow and she excitedly jumped out of the passenger's side. She dragged her husband by both hands through the field. "Let's go, Paul. Come see. Hurry."

He stumbled through the long grass, complaining. "This place still gives me the creeps."

She giggled. "Stop concentrating on your feet and lift your head." She pointed to an adorable yellow cottage, adorned with flower boxes in the windows and blossoms alongside the brick front walk. "Well? What do you think?"

Her husband smiled pleasantly. "It's beautiful, Laura, as I knew it would be."

She clapped her hands in delight. "So, when do you want to move in? Oh, I have to show you the inside. The master bedroom is huge. Don't let the small exterior mislead you. Come on inside."

"You're a funny one, Laura. Move in? You must be joking."

She ceased all movement. Ever so slowly she turned her head and faced him. "Excuse me? What did you say?"

"We're not moving here. I already told you, Calloways don't live in shacks. Building this house was intended to be a hobby for you, babe, and you've outdone yourself. Truly you have. You can come and enjoy your playhouse whenever you want. Now let's go home, I'm starved."

Did he actually say *playhouse*?

Her feet remained fixed to the ground as an essential part of her shattered. Had she misunderstood his intentions? He told her to build a house and like an idiot she assumed he meant for the two of them. Her stupor transformed into a seething anger. He had called the cottage a playhouse. A playhouse. And, to add insult to her fury, he hadn't even bothered to view the interior.

She stormed over to the car and refused to acknowledge his existence. He was droning on and on, nonsensical dribble, and was absolutely oblivious to her outrage.

The ass.

Chapter 16

Laura enjoyed her privacy in Sullivan's Meadow, and spent many blissful hours over the next four seasons caring for her sweet, little house. The summer of 1966 was exceptionally hot and humid, yet cross-ventilation cooled the cottage to a comfortable temperature. She hummed to herself as she tended her recently added vegetable garden, but was well aware she needed to reclaim a life for herself and struck upon a wonderful idea.

One night at the beginning of August, Laura paced around the Rosewood house wringing her hands, waiting for her husband to come home from work. He eventually staggered in after 10:00, his suit jacket hooked on his finger and flung over his shoulder. She raced to the front door and eagerly pulled him into the foyer.

"What's got into you, Laura?"

"I have a plan I would like to discuss with you. Here, hand me your jacket and have a seat in the living room. Would you like a drink?"

"Uh, sure. Jim Beam. Neat." He no longer drank beer and acquired an aristocratic preference for Bourbon. She returned with a tumbler filled with the dark amber liquid and handed it to him. He took a mouthful, and glaring at her, lowered the glass. "Okay, now or never. What's going on?"

She laughed nervously. "Nothing is going on. I'm excited. Oh, I do hope you approve."

He took another sip and waited.

"Now that I'm no longer working at Bruno's and I can't spend my life gardening in the meadow, I was wondering ... if possible ... if you agree ..."

He raised his eyebrows. "Go on."

"I want to go to college," she said. "I'd like to get a degree in primary education and become a school teacher." She crossed her fingers behind her back and held her breath.

He didn't respond immediately, but set the tumbler on a coaster and approached his wife. Placing his hands on her shoulders, he peered into her eyes. "Honey, I don't know. Going to college? You know it's not as easy as tossing tulips in the ground."

The corners of her mouth twitched, but she ignored his condescending quip. Yet, she stood there restrained by his grasp, aware that Paul, once again, had her future in his hands.

"Well, it would keep you out of the dirt, and a school teacher is a respectable position for a Calloway." He paused on the precipice of his decision. "I think it's a fine idea."

She flung herself in his arms and hugged him with a fervor she hadn't felt in ages. Laura Malone Calloway would be returning to school.

* * *

Laura matriculated in the fall of 1966, and with a pristine notebook in hand, entered her first class at Sullivan U. She gazed anxiously around the classroom looking for an empty chair and spotted one next to an unassuming boy buried in a book, titled *The Time Machine*, by H.G. Wells. The irony wasn't lost on her. She grabbed the seat and immediately introduced herself, hopeful the conversation would lead to time travel.

The boy, startled at the intrusion, snapped his head from the novel. His thin, pale face flushed with the slightest tinge of pink. "Oh, yes, hi. Nice to meet you. I'm sorry, pupils rarely choose a desk next to mine."

He was flustered. How endearing, she thought, and settled into the chair. "And your name is ...?"

"Oh yes, of course. I'm Thomas." He extended his hand.

"Hello, Tom. It's a pleasure to meet you." She loosely shook his hand and attempted to establish eye contact, however he continually averted her gaze.

"No, I'm sorry, not Tom. Not Tommy either. Thomas."

"Okay. Thomas."

The classroom filled with students, brown-nosers sat in the first row and hecklers in the rear. The professor arrived, gathered notecards from his briefcase and placed them under the blackboard on the aluminum ledge. Laura risked a glance behind her. The tough kids in the back rearranged their chairs in a cluster, as if creating a unified offensive operation against the class.

Thomas leaned across the aisle and whispered to her. "They may appear as a respectable, studious group of kids, but they're trouble. Steer clear." One of the boys noticed her staring, and responded by grabbing his crotch. Disgusted, she turned and faced front.

The professor cleared his throat and began his lecture. "Welcome to English Literature 101. I'm Dr. Gordon and I'll be your instructor for the semester."

Laura opened her notebook and eagerly began her academic career.

Fifty minutes later, class was dismissed and Laura suggested to Thomas that they visit the coffee house together. Although stunned by the invitation, he agreed. They began strolling across the commons, and she cautiously broached the subject that was never far from her mind.

"You're reading H.G. Wells? Any good?"

"Oh, yes. The possibility of time travel intrigues me."

"Yeah, me too. I'm sure a visit to the future would be, uh, quite an experience. What's your take on it, though. You think time travel is possible? Or merely science fiction?"

He stopped walking, and rather than face her directly, peered at her sideways. "Science fiction? Um, of course time travel is science fiction. Why would I think otherwise?"

She must have looked crestfallen, because he began backpedaling.

"Well, it's probably science fiction," he said, cringed, then threw his hands up in the air and faced her. "Okay, okay. I mean it's absolutely not science fiction. The evidence is astounding." His speech suddenly transformed into an articulate monologue and she did her best to keep up.

"To begin with, Albert Einstein had developed several theories, several of which relate to time travel. The most well-known is his Theory of Relativity, which claimed that acceleration distorts the shape of time and space. Since space and time curve when they are near an enormous object, the fabric of space-time becomes distorted. If this distortion could be manipulated to overlap, it could be possible to create a connection through time. Einstein also dabbled in quantum physics, which may also play a part in time travel." He stopped a moment, regained momentum, and continued. "I have my own theories. I am convinced gravitational forces from neighboring planets, if aligned correctly, can create a pathway, a wormhole if you will. Of course, I can't properly test this theory, however —"

A rough shove from behind caused him to stumble.

"Am I hearing you correctly? Time travel, dork?" The obnoxious kid from their English class and his thugs encircled them. "What's a fox like you doing with this lamebrain? I saw you eyeing my goods in class. Care for a sample?"

"Get lost, you creep," she said.

"Oh, a feisty one. I'll get to you in a moment. I need to take care of a bit of business over here." He gripped Thomas's arm and twisted it behind his back until he emitted a faint whimper. "Hey,

Diesel," he yelled to another thug. "It's hazing time. We caught you the dork with the freaky eyes, now follow-through."

The dirtbag hesitated for a fraction of a second, then screwed up his face and threw a left hook into Thomas' stomach.

"No!" Laura cried. Her friend hunched over, gasping for breath, and his thick eyeglass frames fell to the dirt. The uproarious laughter of the gang incensed her.

"You scumbags!"

"Oooo, such language from a hot chick. We need to wash your mouth out with soap... or something."

More snickers.

"You're messing with the wrong girl, fellas. My father-in-law is on the board of this school, and he can have you thrown right out."

Relishing the confrontation, the lead moron egged her on. "You're married? And who might your husband be, sweetheart?"

"Paul Calloway, son of Richard Calloway."

She expected him to recoil at the name, to back away and leave them alone. Instead, the jerk burst into hysterical laughter. "Really? Paul Calloway is your husband? You're putting me on."

"I'm serious, and if you don't leave us alone, I'll make sure you're expelled."

The smirk on his face infuriated her.

"Babe, you have more to worry about than a fraternity prank. You better get yourself checked for the clap. I can't get over it. Paul Calloway, married. No friggin' way."

With a wave of a hand, he summoned his boys. "Come on fellas, Diesel has to land one more dork."

Like a mass of locusts that had devoured its prey, they swarmed away to their next victim.

She hauled Thomas him to his feet, handed him his eyeglasses, and peppered him with questions. "Are you okay? Did they hurt you? Can you walk? Your eyes are shaking. We should go to the Health Center."

Thomas coughed and straightened up. "I'm okay. The guy knocked the wind out of me, that's all. I should've known better. Fraternity hazing rituals are brutal for guys like me. We've learned the hard way not to speak in public about science or mathematics, otherwise a bull's-eye is automatically painted on our backs."

"This happened to you before?"

He nodded. "Certainly. But today I had a momentary lapse of judgment when I was walking with you. After all, a pretty girl had asked me my opinion on my all-time favorite topic. I tried not to, but I couldn't let this one pass me by."

She smiled. "I still think we should go to the health center. Your eyes are quivering."

"My eyes are fine, Laura. I have nystagmus. My eyes occasionally dance around involuntarily. I've had it since I was little, it's not a big deal, but it's yet another thing to get ragged on."

A small memory in the back of her mind was struggling to surface, and at last, it materialized. Her breath caught in her throat. "Um, Thomas, if you wouldn't mind telling me, what's your last name?"

"Archer. Thomas Archer."

Laura's jaw dropped. Professor Archer. She envisioned Thomas fifty-eight years older, wearing circular eyeglasses and leaning against a lectern. Without a moment's thought, she threw her arms around him and hugged him.

He laughed. "Wow. I guess getting sucker-punched by a muscle-head isn't so bad after all."

Chapter 17

On a chilly October day, Laura received a phone call from the university. Dr. Gordon was ill and class was cancelled for the day. Without hesitation, she packed herself a picnic lunch and drove the MG Paul had given her to Sullivan's Meadow. She had intended to spread a blanket near the burnt circle of grass and enjoy the bright sunshine and peacefulness of the day. Unfortunately, the air had a chill, so she enjoyed her lunch in the breakfast nook and appreciated the view of her gardens through the picture window. She needed to uproot the weeds because they were choking her flowers.

She hastily washed her plate then headed to the front door for an hour or so of therapeutic gardening. Pulling one of her gardening gloves from the wicker basket next to the door, she remembered the other was missing. With a heavy sigh, Laura figured she'd head to the gardening store downtown for a new pair. She had plenty of time to kill, and besides, she needed mulch too.

She drove to the rear of the gardening store and strolled inside.

"Hi, Henry. You have a minute to load a few bags of mulch in my car?"

The teenage sales boy smiled. "Hello, Mrs. Calloway. How many do you need?"

"I think we'll start off with two."

"Sure thing. I'll meet you out back."

She unhooked a pair of women's gardening gloves from the display and paid for her supplies. As she ventured to the parking lot, Henry finished placing the second bag in her car.

"You're all set. Can I help you with anything else?"

"No, thanks, Henry. I've got all I need. How are things at school? You're, what, a freshman in high school now?"

He smiled shyly. "Yep. Freshman year, bottom of the barrel. Hey, before I forget, I saw Mr. Calloway pull up behind Bruno's malt shop a little while ago, or what used to be the malt shop. You should tell him he better be careful. There's a lot of construction going on there. Bruno has big plans."

"Bruno's plans are notorious for being big. Anyway, I'll deliver your warning to Paul. As always, thanks for everything, Henry."

She jogged across the street towards Bruno's when she heard a familiar voice call her name. Turning, she saw her friend, Thomas, awkwardly waving at her.

"Hi, Laura. What's happening? Feels strange, doesn't it, not going to class today?"

"Yeah, I'm actually feeling a little guilty not opening up my books. Well, not that guilty. It's nice to have a break."

"Do you wanna grab a soda with me? I'm not sure what to do with my free time," he said.

She glanced over at the far side of Bruno's and found Paul's Cobra parked in the back, and shrugged. "Sure, a soda sounds like a great idea."

Thomas suggested they walk to the luncheonette down the block. They chose two stools at the counter and each ordered a large root beer float. Delicious.

"Laura, you know that new television program called *Star Trek,* right? The one about a starship and its voyages through space?"

She nodded.

"There's an unofficial *Star Trek* fan club opening at the university, and, uh, I thought you'd like to join the club with me?" He attempted to peer expectantly into her eyes, but only managed a sideways glance.

She toyed with her striped paper straw as she answered. "You're so sweet, Thomas. Let me think about it, okay?"

"Of course. I thought it was—" He froze, his words hanging in midair. Without blinking, he gazed at the sugar dispenser on the countertop.

One second.

Three seconds.

Five seconds.

Laura called out to him with alarm. "Thomas! Thomas, are you okay?"

Suddenly, the boy blinked, then grabbed a small medicine canister from his pocket.

"Uh, sorry about that."

"What happened to you? Tell me."

"Oh, it's nothing. How's your soda?"

She glowered at him.

"Okay, fine. I don't like talking about this, but seeing that it's you... The thing is, I have a mild form of epilepsy. It's not debilitating, but every so often I get these petit mal seizures. I kinda space out for a few seconds then snap out of it. The medication has been managing the seizures, for the most part. The nystagmus, on the other hand, is more difficult to control."

"Oh, I didn't know. I'm so sorry."

"No, don't feel sorry for me. It's doesn't really affect my life all that much, except when I get beat up by deadbeats who think I'm weird."

She squeezed his arm reassuringly. "Well, I don't think you're weird. You're one-of-a-kind special."

His trembling eyes found hers. "I found a good friend in you, Laura Calloway."

After finishing their sodas, she gave him a quick hug goodbye and backtracked to Bruno's side lot. Henry was correct, the place was a minefield. Carefully stepping around construction equipment, lumber, and the scatter of sharp nails, she eased opened the back door of Bruno's. It struck her how peculiar it was for Paul to even be here.

She advanced inside and halted, ears straining. She heard something, the cries of a wounded animal, maybe a raccoon. The poor thing wheezed and grunted behind the counter, and as it moved in pain, plastic construction sheets rustled and crinkled.

She wasn't sure how she could help it. Maybe it was trapped underneath the plastic. She could lift up a corner of the sheet and let it escape. Hopefully it wasn't rabid. She looked around and her eyes landed on a broom, and grabbed it. Not the best protection, but it was better than nothing. She inched forward, trying not to startle it, and peered around a pillar.

That was no animal.

Surrounded by articles of clothing, her husband lay panting in hedonistic pleasure atop of her good friend, Susan.

Fingers to her mouth, Laura eased her way out of Bruno's, sprinted across the street to her MG, and bolted.

* * *

Later that night, Laura confronted Paul during dinner. She expected him to vehemently deny or rationalize his behavior. Instead, he jeered. "You're a funny one, Laura. You expect me to be faithful? Come on, wake up. You knew going into this marriage that I appreciate gorgeous women. Now, suddenly, it's become an issue? Get off your high horse. How hypocritical can you be?"

She was flabbergasted. "What about our wedding vows? You're aware of what 'fidelity' means, right? I'll grab a dictionary to help you out."

"Don't get caught up with rhetoric."

Her face blanched. It was at that exact moment that Laura knew, in the depths of her soul, she could no longer remain married to this pompous, arrogant, egomaniac.

"I want out, Paul. I can't do this anymore. I gave up my life for you."

"What are you saying? You want a divorce? Is that what you're saying? Not happening, sweetheart. Like it or not, you agreed to become a Calloway. Calloways do not divorce."

"They do now."

She pushed her chair back, rose, and stormed from the room.

He bounded after her. "Don't you ever turn your back on me. Whether you like it or not, I'm your husband, and you do as I say. Since you're the one caught up on wedding vows, let me remind you — to love, honor, and obey. That's right, obey. And as I move up the corporate ladder, you'll be my side each and every step of the way, wearing your pretty little dresses and plastering a friggin' smile on your face. You got that?"

Furious, Laura stuck her palm in his face. "Keep talking to the hand, fella. I'm outta here."

Finding a divorce attorney who was not, in any way, connected to the Calloways was challenging, but Laura managed to hire an experienced, sympathetic man from a neighboring county. She appreciated the man's tenacity, but he was fighting Paul's bullheaded mindset to completely obliterate her. It also didn't help that her husband had all the money in the world. The final divorce agreement was attained twelve months later and she signed despite her lawyer's protests. "We can fight for more, Laura. You are his wife and are entitled to a large portion of his wealth."

"No. I don't want his money. I want out." She signed with a flourish. "There. I'm not his wife any longer. Thank God."

Laura heard through the grapevine that Paul was furious with his attorneys for losing the playhouse and Sullivan's Meadow to Laura in the settlement. His lawyers attempted to explain to him he had presented the meadow as a gift and that Laura's name was on the deed. He had no leverage. Paul also fumed that she'd maintain ownership of her MG and receive biyearly payments from his hard-earned money for tuition until the date of her graduation in 1970.

He was livid, but as of October 31, 1967, she was once again Laura Malone, but the price tag for her freedom was steep.

Chapter 18

Shortly after her divorce was finalized, Laura was forced to return to work at Bruno's, and she soon learned waitressing at a drive-in restaurant was an unusual experience. Her job encompassed roller-skating to customers in their parked cars, taking their orders, and returning with their food on large trays that propped up on their open windows. Music blared from the rooftop of the restaurant, beckoning the locals. Once again, Bruno's was a popular hangout for teenagers, and the burgers were the best in the county. A few weeks into Laura's renewed employment, Bruno invited his employees to his office for an announcement. Hopefully they'd be getting raises.

"As the proprietor of this establishment for the past fifteen years, I couldn't have asked for a better staff. You're all hard-working, responsible young people and I am forever appreciative."

The waitresses, busboys, and cooks waited expectantly. Here it comes, thought Laura, a raise. Come on, say it, Bruno, say it.

"Which makes what I have to say all the more difficult. I won't mince words. I've decided to sell the restaurant and retire. An offer was placed on the table and it was so good I just couldn't reject it." The help began talking at once, distressed. "I hear your concerns, I really do. But what's done is done."

Someone called out a question. "Who's the new owner, Bruno?"

Bruno glanced at Laura, then to the floor. "Richard Calloway."

At that moment, a tall, imposing man stormed through the door. His broad, muscular body and steely gray eyes intensified his commanding presence. Paul's father surveyed the room, located Laura, and affixed a malevolent smirk across his impassioned face.

"Yes, and as proprietor of this establishment, let's get to the first order of business. As of this moment, the employment of the entire staff is officially terminated."

"Now wait a second," shouted Bruno, outraged. "That wasn't part of the deal. You said all staff would remain employed."

"Do you have that in writing?" asked Calloway.

"No, of course not."

"Well then, as I heard you so eloquently phrase it, what's done is done."

The livid ex-employees shuffled out, mumbling obscenities as they tossed their aprons and name tags in a heap.

"And you," Calloway yelled, pointing his finger at Laura. "You, how fucking dare you defile the Calloway name, you money-grubbing wench?" Flecks of spittle punctuated his words. "You infiltrated my family, stole my son's good name. No. This ends here. You may be divorced, but I will personally see to it that my son crushes you, sucks every last penny from you, and ground you into the dirt like dust."

Horror-struck and with eyes wide like saucers, Laura couldn't breathe.

"You started off with nothing and you will end up with nothing. That I promise."

He brushed past Laura knocking into her shoulder and stormed from the restaurant. Laura's breath hitched and she collapsed to the floor, sobbing.

A few months later, after all traces of Laura and her co-workers' existence at Bruno's was mercilessly eliminated, including employee-of-the-month awards, Calloway sold the restaurant. The newest owners began renovating the place into an Italian pizza joint.

The Calloways were true to their word. Paul wielded his family's elevated social stature to demoralize her, yet Laura refused to let her spirit break. At one point, Paul threatened to revoke Laura's matriculation from Sullivan University, however his father decisively rejected the idea.

"No. Absolutely not. You want to tarnish the Calloway name with the school board? You've done enough already by marrying that moneygrubber."

Incensed, Paul focused his energy on harassing Laura's parents and ridiculing Charlie to such an extreme that the family moved from their home in Sullivan Township to a little place in Florida. Her family pleaded with Laura to leave with them, but she refused to follow suit.

"This is my fault, honey," Laura's mother said, between sobs. "I pushed you into this marriage. I thought you'd be safe and secure, but instead of a dream, you got a nightmare."

"Mama, please stop. This isn't your fault. I know you love me and meant well, but we were all blindsided. Paul is a manipulative tyrant, and apparently a masterful one, at that."

Laura had no income and a paltry savings account, yet stood steadfast, refusing to bend. She heard through the rumor mill her former friend Susan was interning in one of Paul's offices. Good riddance.

While attending school, Laura managed to find short-term work but every few months she would be relieved of her duties, courtesy of Paul or Richard Calloway, and forced to resume her job search.

Fortunately, the restaurant formerly known as Bruno's had opened and she applied for a waitressing job.

The new owner, Luigi, was thrilled with her resume, and the interview continued as a friendly conversation. He was a jovial man with a thick Italian accent, and had moved to this country from Italy a decade or so ago, a few months prior to meeting his wife. His salt-and-pepper hair was sparse, but everything else about him was robust.

"My family, I'd like you to meet them. Amelia. Come meet our new girl."

A heavyset women with dark brown hair appeared from behind the counter. "Amelia, come. This is Laura."

The woman grabbed hold of Laura's hand and shook it with vigor.

"Welcome, Laura. Welcome." Laura restrained her giggles, but had instantly fallen in love with the family. "Our son, you have met him? Ronald. Come and meet a beautiful red-haired girl."

An 8-year-old child, maybe closer to 9, obeyed his mother and ran to her side. He was a handsome boy, with a mop of curly dark hair and hazelnut eyes.

"This fine boy is our son, Ronald. He may be filling napkin dispensers now, but you wait. Someday he'll own this restaurant, isn't that right, Ronnie?"

"Uh-huh." He looked at Laura and smiled. "You're pretty. If any customer gives you trouble, you come find me."

His mother chuckled. Laura, on the other hand, gasped, her eyes instantly brimming with tears.

Oh my God, it can't be.

She could barely believe who was standing right before her. Ronnie. Not yet the Ronnie from 2023 but Ronnie nevertheless. It warmed her heart to see him, but yet another painful reminder of the man she had carelessly left behind.

Not long into her employment at Ronnie's, she and a few of the staff were setting up tables for the dinner rush. Laura pushed open the swinging door leading into the kitchen to grab clean silverware when she heard muffled shouts in the back office. She only needed to take a few steps closer to hear Luigi on the telephone, spitting words of disdain.

"How dare you. You don't have the right to tell me who I can hire. You sold your restaurant to me. I am the proprietor."

Pause.

"You threaten me? You who seem like an important man, why you want to waste time harassing me, eh? She's a fine girl and a hard worker."

Pause.

"Say all you want, Mr. Calloway, but hear this. I, too, have connections, and you don't want me to make that kind of a phone call."

Pause.

"Uh huh. That's exactly what I mean. Yes, we understand each other. Good. We clear now?"

Laura crept back to the dining room with the silverware. Her new boss has known her for only a few weeks and was defending her. She sagged into a chair and wept.

* * *

"Why'd you marry him in the first place? He's a cold-blooded brute. Sorry, did I overstep?" Thomas asked.

They were heading to a classroom in Talbott Hall for Laura's first *Star Trek* Fan Club meeting. She didn't want to go, but he insisted. He claimed it wasn't healthy for her to hole up in her house every night.

"It's a long story. I'll tell it to you sometime, but now's not the time. So, what's this meeting going to be like, hmm?"

"You'll see, you'll see. I'm not giving anything away."

The pair walked into one of the large classrooms for the meeting. All the desks were pushed against the wall and about fifteen students were sitting on top of them, chatting in private conversations. A few were dressed in snug, long-sleeved crew necks bearing a "Starfleet" insignia, and one boy had affixed pointy ears atop his own. Laura and Thomas located two empty desks and followed suit by sitting on top.

The boy with the pointy ears slid off his desk and hustled to the center of the room.

"Hello, *Star Trek* aficionados, and welcome to our seventh... it is our seventh, isn't it? Yes, our seventh meeting. For those of you who don't know me, my name is Eddie and I'm the president, or Captain, of Sullivan U's *Star Trek* Fan Club. By the way, members, we still need to agree on a better name. 'Fan Club' sounds too juvenile, so I'd like to hear your ideas next meeting. Tonight, however, we'll be discussing our impressions of the most recent Enterprise mission and what the crew could've handled differently. Then, for the last ten or fifteen minutes of the meeting, let's consider for a moment the gadgets the crewmembers use, and which ones might someday come to fruition. It's going to be a fascinating night folks, so buckle up tight 'cause it's time to engage the warp drive."

Thomas was right. The meeting was fun and a pleasant distraction from the stress of her life.

Fifteen minutes before the meeting concluded, Eddie positioned himself in the center once again. "Great conversation, people. Your contributions to the discussion are inspiring. We've almost come to the conclusion of our meeting, so now I'll toss the reins over to my second in command, Commander Jerry. Go ahead, Jer."

"Hi, all. The *Enterprise,* as we know, is equipped with really cool gadgets. Let's see, they have hand-held communicators, universal translators, teleportation devices, and that's just the beginning. Any of these things seem possible? Let's start with the transporter."

A heated discussion ensued, a few people citing science-based information that teleportation could be on the horizon, and others believing their information was hogwash.

"Get real, people," said one member who wore a yellow *Star Trek* uniform. "There is absolutely no possible way to dematerialize a person, or an object for that matter, and have it appear elsewhere. It's simply not feasible."

"Sure, it's feasible, only not yet. We transport our molecules every day when we walk around. All a scientist has to do is transport molecules over space," a voice said.

"You're crazy. You're comparing the physical act of walking with the dismantling of molecules and living cells? I'll say it again, get real."

Laura was on the edge of her seat, itching to participate.

Yes, it most certainly is possible. I've done it, you guys, I've actually done it. And it hurts.

"Okay, okay. Quiet down, guys and gals. We have time to discuss one more gadget, the communicator. Thoughts?" Another debate commenced. Some people were incensed and practically shouting, but others merely expressed their modest opinion. Timidly, Laura raised her hand, and Thomas, sitting beside her, watched her with surprise.

"Hold on, folks. Our newest member has a contribution." The room fell silent, and all eyes were on her. "What's your name?"

"Hi. My name is Laura, and I know there's a definite place in the future for hand-held communicators. You'll use them like telephones, but they'll do other stuff too. They'll have itty-bitty buttons on them so you can type and instantly send messages to another person. You can also take photographs without the need for film, and the pictures will appear instantly on a miniature screen right on the device. Oh, and you can play music on it too. Press two or three buttons and the next thing you know, there's your song. But it won't be called a communicator, it will be called a cell-o-phone."

They all chuckled, amused. "Well, Laura, I can speak for all of us. Your imagination is staggering, but what you envision is impossible. All those gadgets in one small, hand-held device? No." Jerry looked at his watch. "Oh. Eddie, we have to close the meeting."

Thomas leaned over, whispering in Laura's ear. "Nice ideas, Laura. Good for you."

She shrugged, and the meeting was adjourned.

In June of 1970, Laura graduated from Sullivan U with honors as a certified elementary school teacher. Evidently, Paul's tentacles extended to most, but not all, primary schools. Thomas Archer's father was a principal at Lincoln Memorial Elementary School and gladly hired Laura as a first-grade teacher. From the moment she entered the classroom, she was certain she had found her calling. She adored the children, marveling at their eagerness to learn and creative imaginations. The teachers in the school were lovely, instantly accepting her into their circle.

There was one other first grade teacher in the school, Pearl McKinney, who was a relatively new teacher as well, in her second year. Pearl had a sense of humor that could rival any comedian. Dull, lifeless stories were comedic fodder, for she could twist them into hysterical anecdotes, leaving the faculty in stitches from laughing so hard. One Friday afternoon after dismissal, Pearl stopped in Laura's classroom.

"Laura Malone, my dear, dedicated colleague and wonderful friend, it's 3:30 on a Friday. Get away from your desk and let's make a break for it while we still can. Come on." Her kinky curls bounced.

"I'm coming. Hey, you wanna come over tonight? I know it's kinda the last minute, but we can see if the others can come too."

"Sure, I'll be there with bells and whistles. The other girls, well, they have families to attend to, so it's you and me, kiddo."

"Would you mind if I give my friend Thomas a call?"

"Oh, sure. Please do. I like him. He's not like the other men around here, that's for sure. And he's kinda cute, too."

"You think so? I never looked at him that way."

"Oh, yeah. He's Poindexter cute. You think he'd let me call him Dexter? Poinsy?"

"Doubt it."

Later that evening, the three of them listened to records in Laura's cottage and played a game of Pearl's own invention.

"Okay, here are the rules. We'll take turns imitating a famous dancer, and we each have to guess who the person is, okay? You ready?"

"Yes, with one stipulation. Nobody is allowed to dance The Hitchhiker. It's completely off limits for reasons that will go unmentioned," said Laura.

"Hmm, you can be quite mysterious, Malone, but it's a deal." Pearl snatched a broomstick for a microphone and snarled into it, then began gyrating her hips and shaking her legs like Jell-O.

"That's too easy, Pearl. You're Elvis."

"Well, it's best to start off the game kinda easy. Go ahead, Laura, it's your turn."

They played the game for an hour, doubling over with laughter when Thomas attempted to imitate Goldie Hawn as a go-go dancer on Laugh-in. He was endearingly awkward. His knees were locked so he was barely able to move his legs, and his arms stuck out to his sides like wooden boards. His so-called dance was the complete antithesis of Goldie's free-lovin' spirit. Pearl and Laura applauded his efforts enthusiastically.

"If Goldie danced like that, she'd be thrown out of Laugh-in before she could say, '*Sock it to me.*' You're too much, Poinsy."

Thomas frowned. "Please don't call me that. My name's Thomas."

"Will you settle for Dexter?"

He sniffed.

"Okay, okay. Don't sweat it, Archer," Pearl said with a wink. "I'll come up with something."

Thomas stuck out his tongue and Pearl clapped her hands with delight.

"Another Sloe Gin Fizz anybody?" asked Laura.

* * *

Laura enjoyed her life. She had steady employment and wonderful friends. Pearl had wanted to set her up with eligible men and go on double-dates together, but Laura wasn't interested.

"It's too soon, Pearl. I'm still getting over the divorce."

"Please? With sugar on top? I think you'll really hit it off with this one fella. He's a redhead too. We'll drag Thomas along and he'll be my date. It'll be a riot. Say yes. C'mon."

"Argh. Fine. But don't expect anything to come out of this."

Pearl gleefully clapped her hands. "Of course not. But be sure to name your first born after me."

Laura swatted her friend.

It was one of the most awkward nights Laura had ever experienced. They purchased tickets to see the film, *Plaza Suite*, a three-story comedy about the escapades in a particular suite at the Plaza Hotel. The first vignette featured a married couple's attempts to rekindle their love for one another, and Laura rolled her eyes and huffed throughout it.

At one point, Thomas, who was sitting on her right, leaned over and whispered, "You okay?" but Laura huffed at him too. Her date sat on her left, and he constantly turned to glimpse at Laura after each joke, seemingly desperate to share a laugh together. It only made her skin crawl. After the evening was over and they all parted ways, Pearl called Laura.

"Details, Laura, I want details. Did'ya like him?"

Laura's date, Darren, did indeed sport red hair, but that was the end of the similarities between them.

"The kid was an armrest hog." Laura complained.

"A what?"

"An armrest hog. He kept his arms planted on both armrests of his seat. Doesn't he know the rules? You get only one."

"Okay ...?"

"And how about sharing the popcorn? He kept the bag between his legs the whole time. He didn't think I'd reach between his legs, did he? Gross."

"Uh-huh. Anything else you'd like to get off your chest, Laura dear?"

"Yeah. He kept laughing in all the wrong places. Nothing funny was going on, Pearl, but there he was, heehawing about nothing. Oh, look, Walter Matthau is walking across the room. Oh, there goes Maureen Stapleton, she's about to sit down. What's so funny? Geesh."

"Uh-huh. So you're saying he was annoying because he laughed while watching a comedy."

"I'm saying the guy wouldn't know funny if it hit him on the head."

"Am I wrong to think there won't be a second date?"

"Very funny, Pearl."

For the remainder of the school year, Laura spent most evenings sitting outside on her porch swing with her students' work piled on her lap, leisurely rocking back and forth. She wasn't ready to date yet, and probably never would. She considered herself lucky to have escaped Paul's marital chains, but as her gaze settled onto the charred circle of grass, she was keenly aware of her greatest loss. For some strange reason, nothing ever seemed to grow there.

Chapter 19
2023

"Well, Kevin," Laura said, "you can now see how wrong you were about my life." She stood and walked to the kitchen. Kevin followed and placed his empty lemonade glass in the sink. He leaned against the counter and stared at her.

"Let me get this straight. You sacrificed your own happiness to save Paul from a life of recluse and senility."

She nodded.

"Why didn't you leave him before you married? Surely you saw the signs?"

"I did see the signs, but I was afraid, not to mention young and naïve. I believed if I didn't marry Paul, he would transform into that delirious, jaded hermit. I couldn't live with that on my shoulders."

"Unbelievable." He shook his head. "You are a brave but thoroughly enigmatic woman."

"Don't be ridiculous. I simply had a run-away case of the guilts. If you remember, you and I were convinced Paul's grief for me had poisoned his mind. But I've had decades to mull the events over, and I can clearly see that he never actually grieved for me when I originally disappeared."

He straightened himself. "I don't understand. He was a mess. I can still hear him screeching your name to the gods in heaven."

She absentmindedly weaved a few locks of her white hair back into her braid and smiled slightly. "You see how easily we believed that? It's true Paul was grieving, but not for me. Paul Calloway was mourning the loss of his privileged social standing and subconsciously redirected his profound loss onto me."

He lifted an eyebrow.

"Okay, so I took a couple of psychology classes," she said. "Keep in mind that he was a highly respected, outgoing, attractive young man, and a son of extremely wealthy parents. Instead of a lifetime of privilege, the accusations of his involvement in my supposed murder destroyed his social standing, ripped him away from high society, and left him to rot."

"I see. When you returned to 1965, you prevented Paul's disastrous future from ever occurring."

"Exactly. His climb up the hierarchy of society was no longer in jeopardy, so the cocky, arrogant kid grew into an insensitive, overbearing, entitled cad, and that's the person I guilted myself into marrying."

Nobody spoke. He was trying to reshape his perception of Paul, but could not shake the image of the unkempt recluse he had come to know.

"I need air. Do you mind if we sit outside?" he asked.

"Be my guest. I'll meet you on the porch swing in a moment. Care for more lemonade? How about some butter cookies? My mother's recipe," she said.

"Sounds good, but no thanks."

"You don't know what you're missing, the cookies melt in your mouth. Are you sure I can't change your mind?"

He nodded and pushed open the screen door.

As she ventured into the kitchen, he had a chance to grapple with the old dude's massive transformation. So, Calloway turned out to be a royal dick and she had to pay the price. If she had never fallen into the epicenter to begin with and had remained in 1965, she would have flat-out refused Paul's advances. Didn't she mention the other day she'd known he was a philanderer? So basically, Paul only pursued possession of her because she wasn't succumbing to his charm. Kevin raked his fingers through his hair. This entire ordeal was causing his head to spin.

She returned with a full glass of lemonade. "Last chance for another glass, Kevin."

"It's okay, but thanks anyway. I've been thinking, and you're not going to believe this, but I'm pretty sure I've come up with a plan."

"Whatever you're thinking, drop it. I have no intention of returning to 1965 as an old lady."

"Not you, Laura. Me."

"Am I hearing you correctly? Say that again."

"I intend to go back to 1965."

She snorted. "You must be joking. Why on earth would you do such a thing?"

"Before you dismiss the entire idea, hear me out. If I travel back through tomorrow night's aftershock, I can arrive in time to warn you."

She waited a beat. "Let's say, for argument's sake, you survive that awful trip. I highly doubt the younger me would believe you. The culpability I felt was extraordinarily heavy. I believed with every ounce of my being that I had to atone for what I did to Paul. I had to marry him. End of story."

"Yes, but would it be the same if you'd had a forewarning? You deserve that chance."

"Maybe so. But keep in mind that my life was not horrible after 1971 or so. I had a successful career, wonderful friends, and a beautiful home. I don't want that to disappear into oblivion. I worked so hard to get to where I am, Kevin. Don't you dare take that away from me."

"What about finding love? Having a family?"

"I missed my chance at love. Maybe I'll have better luck in my next life. But I don't want you to mess with this one."

Chapter 20

Kevin drove Lucille back to his apartment barely registering the ride. He despised feeling helpless, but Laura was quite adamant about leaving the outcome of her life alone. He parked the motorcycle in its spot, entered his apartment, and tossed his keys onto the kitchen counter. There had to be a way. Frustrated, he pulled his clothes off and tossed them into the overflowing laundry basket, then crawled into bed.

Surprisingly, he slept soundly and awakened refreshed and rejuvenated. He brewed himself a cup of coffee, adding enough milk to prevent a scalded tongue. Carrying the mug out to the balcony, he settled into a chair, started up his playlist on his phone, and gazed at the river in the distance. A song by Savage Garden started playing, one he hadn't listened to in ages. The lyrics were beautiful, alluding to a man desperately in love.

He smiled as he recalled the younger version of Laura he had come to know. She possessed a combination of sweetness and inner-strength unlike anyone he had ever met. It was that courage, that spirit, that astounded him, even though she doubted it in herself. After all, her safest choice would have been to remain in 2023, but she was determined to push her fears aside to save a man she didn't love from a disastrous future. Being around her was easy, effortless, as if they'd known each other for many years, not mere days. She found delight in simple pleasures, and whenever she laughed, he felt a surge of warmth envelope his heart, that could brighten any day. Not to mention her captivating beauty. There was no doubt about it, he would risk life and limb for her.

He stood up so quickly, knocking his chair over.

"Oh my God," he said aloud, "I'm head over heels in love with her."

He slid the doors open into his living room, rushed to the kitchen and dumped his coffee down the kitchen sink. He decided he was going. After all, she freely admitted that she could never live with the guilt of Paul's deterioration on her shoulders, then neither could he, with her plight. Aware that he and Laura would never share a life together, the least he could do was save her from a meaningless, incomplete life. Besides, it would be interesting to hang out in 1965 for a couple of days then return to the present in the echo.

He showered and shaved, then enlisted Lucille to drive him into town. He felt as if he was preparing for an unusual, supernatural vacation. First, he needed to change his money for bills that predated 1965 and purchase vintage clothing that would blend in with the era. Thankfully, the Past Meets Present thrift shop and the bank were open early, and he was able to stop at both places before lunch. Later, he scarfed down a plate of mozzarella sticks at Ronnie's, and apologized to his friend for not being much of a conversationalist today. He had a lot on his mind.

"Don't sweat it, pal. We'll catch up another time. Here, have a Coke."

Kevin spent the afternoon in his apartment agonizing over how he could convince her to abort her plan to marry the narcissist. Her compassion, typically an admirable trait, would be her downfall, partnered with her obstinacy. He jotted a few ideas on an old notepad, but balled up the pages and trashed them. The issue was not that her life resulted in tragedy. To the contrary, after Paul had finally disappeared from her life, she had managed to create a decent life for herself. He tossed the entire pad in the garbage and made a decision. He would wing it.

In the early evening, Kevin drove to the edge of Sullivan's Meadow wearing his 1965 attire— tan trousers, a light blue sweater, a shirt with navy stripes, and incredibly stiff mock-leather oxfords. He parked his motorcycle next to the oak tree and hopped off.

"See you soon, Lucille. Stay out of trouble."

Soundlessly, he eased his way toward the cottage. One window glowed with a soft, orange incandescence. Laura was home, but he hoped she remained inside. Arriving at the circle without incident, he squatted on the grass using the wrought iron bench as cover. He had enough time to wrench his unyielding shoes off his feet and wiggle his aching toes, but slid them right back on as the sun lowered toward the horizon. He gulped. This was it.

He approached the discolored ring of grass just as the familiar low rumble quivered beneath him. The sky hastily darkened from a pastel pink to a golden umber, so he adjusted his position to ensure he was in the epicenter. The gentle breeze suddenly picked up speed and began blowing steadily and more powerfully. The velocity of the wind accelerated dramatically, whipping debris haphazardly across the fields and roaring with deafening rage. Threatening to break open into fiery chasms, the earth below convulsed angrily. Eyes wide, he could feel his heart battering his chest. What on earth was he doing? Was he nuts? He had to get out of there. Two steps in any direction, and he'd be safe. Just two small steps. As he willed a foot to move, his eyes happened upon the illuminated window. Laura's aged face was pressed on the glass, and she blew him a kiss.

With that empowerment, Kevin vanished.

Chapter 21
1965

Kevin concentrated on breathing. His body instinctively tried to inhale, but the air seemed out of reach. It was as if his lungs had spasmed in a vise-like grip. Wide-eyed, all he could manage was an ineffective gasp. After a few seconds that felt like minutes, his body finally drew a in a long, tremulous breath.

He lay on the grass, chest heaving, when he heard a man's agonizing cry. Kevin turned his head but didn't see a man. Instead, lying beside him wearing her charming, yellow sundress, was Laura. Young, vibrant Laura, with her auburn hair fanned out beneath her. She began to stir.

"Laura?"

She blinked and slowly pushed herself up, sobbing. "Paul?"

"No, not Paul. It's Kevin."

"Kevin? Wh-what happened? It didn't work?"

He sat up and realized he wasn't sure. Images of Laura at opposing ages passed through the fog in his mind. He shook his head to clear his thoughts. Maybe he drank too much wine at the picnic. He wasn't sure of anything anymore.

At that moment, a rugged young man staggered over to them.

"Oh my God, Laura! I thought you were dead. You're all right." He shifted his gaze to Kevin. "Where the hell did you come from?"

"I could ask you the same thing, buddy."

The stranger clapped Kevin roughly on the shoulder. "I have no idea when you got here, fella, but thanks for saving my girl."

"Your girl?" Kevin blinked. "Hold up. You're Paul Calloway?"

"The one and only. Some storm, huh, pal? Pretty much wigged me out." He grabbed his girlfriend's hand. "Let's book, babe, this place gives me the creeps."

"Gimme a second, okay? I'll meet you at the car."

"Fine, but don't take too long." He dropped her hand, and before stepping away, cast a wary eye at Kevin.

Kevin's jaw dropped. He watched the guy strut across the field, exuding a confidence that completed opposed the wither old fossil he knew.

She waited until Paul was out of eyesight, then Laura launched herself into Kevin's arms. "It worked, it worked, it worked! I can't believe it, it actually worked." Grinning, she gave him another hug, then pulled back. "But it doesn't make sense that you're here too. Did you get sucked into the wormhole?"

"Not exactly."

"No? Then what happened?"

He looked into her vivid green eyes. "I'm saving you."

"Saving me? From what?"

Right at that moment, a horn blared from the edge of the meadow.

"Listen," she said. "I don't know what happened or why you're here, but we can't have this conversation now. Come on, we'll give you a ride."

He watched Laura jog to the edge of the meadow, turn around, and face him.

He scratched his head. No sense staying here, and since Lucille was back in 2023, he most definitely needed a lift. He sprinted to the awaiting couple and squeezed his long body into the backseat of a small Corvair.

Paul drove fearlessly through the obstacles of trees while Kevin was subjected to the deafening noise of the engine right behind his head. After a while, they reached the main thoroughfare.

"Check it out. The road's completely dry. The storm never left the damn meadow. That's messed up, man. Let's head to Diesel's and tell the guys about the tornado. They'll think I've lost it. You'll back me up, won't you babe?"

"Please take me home, Paul. Really. I should've been home already. You know how my parents are."

"How about you, stranger? Where you headed?"

"Uh, I guess the nearest Howard Johnson's. I appreciate it, dude."

"Dude? Paul snorted. "Where the hell are you from?"

"At times like this, another planet."

Paul howled with laughter, causing Kevin to shrink back in his seat. The guy was bordering on manic, reminding him of Brittany. Thinking about it now, it was uncanny how both Kevin and Laura got sucked into toxic relationships.

The Corvair pulled up in front of her house. As her fingers grazed the door handle, Paul leaned across the seat and held the door shut.

"I love you, Laura." He glared at her, expecting a reply in kind.

She glanced at Kevin in the backseat and simply replied, "See you tomorrow, Romeo."

* * *

Sitting on a lumpy bed in a Howard Johnson's motel room, Kevin peeled off a shoe. As he rubbed his aching foot, he surveyed his surroundings. The sparse room featured a double bed covered by an unassuming, plaid bedspread of shades of brown, orange, and yellow. Against the far wall sat an oak desk and matching chair, and a black and white television, the size of a microwave, perched on a rickety dresser. An amateur painting hung above the TV, a depiction of orange-hued flowers stuffed in a glass vase. Kevin squinted at the painting, and detected tiny numbers stamped underneath the colors.

He wiggled his other foot out of its shoe and squeezed his toes.

Never one to abandon his modus operandi, he detailed a plan in his mind for tomorrow. First order of business, new shoes. Damn, his feet hurt. It didn't matter if a new pair would cost a couple of hundred bucks, these toe-crushers needed to be tossed. He poked at a blister on his big toe and sighed. Next on his list, he'd track down Laura and work a little persuasive magic. He recalled from her story that she was home the morning after the storm.

Now that he had the semblance of a plan, he collapsed into bed.

The following morning, Kevin limped about a mile from the motel to the center of town and made another executive decision, to rent a car. Walking sucked. First, however, he hobbled down the aisles of Murray's Department Store, a small family-owned place with an eclectic assortment of clothing, housewares, and camping equipment. Industrial steel shelving, four levels high, housed a multitude of unrelated merchandise. A person could find an army canteen or a serrated hunting knife alongside a bottle of Tinkerbell perfume and bobby pins. The shelving units, arranged to create maze-like aisles, allowed customers to view the entire contents of the shop. In the back, Kevin discovered several circular racks displaying sport coats and polo shirts, and to his relief, an entire wall on the right showcasing shoes.

Yanking his oxfords from his tired feet, Kevin tried on a variety of styles, discovering a pair of supple, "black leather inverted seam slip-ons" for less than $20. He pumped his fist in triumph, then meandered to the cash register where he handed his cash to a petite, preteen salesgirl. She could barely peer over the high countertop.

As she counted his change, Kevin asked, "Hey, is there a car rental place nearby, cute-stuff?"

Her entire face flushed rosy pink.

"What's wrong? No car rentals?"

"Umm, what did you call me?" Her high-pitched voice cracked.

"Oh. Cute-stuff. What, is that weird?" He winced. "Oh, man, my bad. Listen, I just need a car. Is there a place I can rent one?"

Silently, the girl pointed her finger to indicate a location down the road, her cheeks glowing crimson. Kevin murmured his gratefulness, accepted his parcel from the mortified girl, and fled.

He entered a white-brick building on the corner, the reception desk unmanned. A squat, balding gentleman appeared from the back, wearing a blue button-down collared shirt open at the neck.

"What could I do you for?" the man asked.

As Kevin stated his purpose, he was astounded how simple it was to rent a car. No background checks were required, only cash. He chose an unobtrusive green Oldsmobile Cutlass.

Driving out of the lot and down the road, it took him a few minutes to adjust to the car, and then he headed for Laura's house. He grumbled and huffed when taking several wrong turns on the side streets, but eventually recalled Paul's route from the previous night.

Finally, he arrived.

He slowed in front of the house, and when he downshifted, the car screeched and lurched, then rolled up and over the curb.

Wincing, he turned off the engine and peered at the Malone's home. He beheld a quaint English Tutor with tastefully manicured landscaping.

Kevin eased open the car door with a loud squeak.

Show time.

Chapter 22

Knocking on the arched, walnut door, Kevin suddenly felt foolish invading the lives of the Malones. He fidgeted as he tarried, shifting his weight from one leg to the other, when the front door cracked open. An attractive middle-aged woman, most likely Laura's mother, greeted him. Kevin arched his eyebrows, taking note of the uncanny resemblance between mother and daughter. The woman wore a simple floral sundress, and her dark auburn hair had a stylish, 1960s' flip. She smiled warmly.

"Yes? May I help you?"

He replied in his best Wally Cleaver impersonation, "Hello, Mrs. Malone. My name is Kevin Donahue and I am a friend of your daughter's. If it isn't inconvenient, may I please have a word with her?"

"Kevin? What are you doing here?" Laura had materialized at the top of the stairwell with "Unchained Melody" blaring in the background.

He stifled a smile.

Mrs. Malone intervened. "I'm sorry, young man, but my daughter is unable to leave the house. Laura, if you'd like, you may take your guest to the sun parlor." The woman faced him. "May I offer you a glass of lemonade?"

He grinned. "Thank you, Mrs. Malone. I would love a glass."

"Oh, brother. Come with me." Laura grabbed his hand and impatiently dragged him to a sunlit sitting room. "My mother can be so annoying."

She directed him to a cushioned loveseat and stood before him. "Okay, spill it. I'm really happy to see you, but what on earth are you doing here in 1965? And what did you mean in the meadow when you said you're saving me?"

He drew in in a long, deep breath. "Laura, the echo worked. You had made it back to 1965 safely. I even know you went ahead and married Paul."

"What are you talking about? I just got here."

"It's complicated. You have to trust me on this."

"Wait. I'm going to marry Paul?

"Yeah, but listen to me. You divorced him after a couple of years, and he resented you for it. He made your life miserable." He wanted to tell her everything, but Kevin pressed his lips together. Giving her any specific details would be a disservice to the older Laura he left behind in 2023.

"Impossible. How would you even know this?"

"You told me. The seventy-eight-year-old you."

She stiffened.

Just then, Mrs. Malone strolled into the parlor with a large serving tray. "Here you are, kids. A pitcher of freshly made lemonade and a few homemade butter cookies."

"Mother. May we please have privacy?"

"Keep in mind your manners, Laura. It's polite to offer your guest refreshments." She looked at Kevin, her green eyes as brilliant as her daughter's. "I apologize for my daughter's rudeness, young man. Help yourself to the lemonade."

Laura rolled her eyes as her mother left the sun parlor. She turned to him and spoke in a harsh whisper.

"Kevin, I hear what you're saying but it doesn't make a difference. I won't let Paul turn into that horrible old man, and if I can prevent that from happening by marrying him, so be it, even if it means a couple of years in an awful marriage. That's a drop in the bucket." She lowered her voice even further as she asked, "Tell me, is my life completely miserable? Do I turn into a senile old lady with a hundred cats?"

Kevin smiled. "No, you weren't unhappy. In fact, you had a comfortable life after Paul left you alone."

"Well, then. You traveled a long way to warn me, and I appreciate it, but I won't change my mind."

At that moment, her father appeared in the doorway. He scowled at Kevin as he addressed his daughter. "Excuse me, kids, but Paul Calloway is here to see you, angel."

"Thanks, Daddy. I'll be right there." She turned to Kevin. "I know you're holding something back. I can tell. You wouldn't have risked your life in that horrible storm only to tell me my life won't be perfect. Whose life is? So, what aren't you telling me?"

He parted his lips, and stopped. The older Laura's last few words echoed in his mind. *I worked very hard to get to where I am, Kevin. Don't you dare take that away from me.*

"Sorry, I... can't," he said.

Laura walked over to him, placed her palms on either side of his face, and gazed into his eyes. "All I can promise you is I'll remember your warnings, and I'll be careful. Get home safely tomorrow." Her lips grazed his. "See you in fifty-eight years."

As the two left the sun parlor, Kevin popped a butter cookie in his mouth and entered the living room. Mmm, they really did melt in your mouth.

"Mrs. Malone, thank you for the refreshments. The cookies were delicious. Laura, it was nice seeing you again." His crestfallen voice cracked. "Take care of yourself."

At the foot of the stairs, he saw Paul yammering away to Mr. Malone. "If my father didn't pull a few strings, I'd be a pathetic army grunt right now. Can you picture me, waist high in a leech-infested swamp? Yeah, I certainly dodged that bullet."

Kevin slipped out the back of the house. "What a dick."

He hopped into the Cutlass and sped away, nearly driving over a kid with a peach-fuzz crewcut who was dragging a baseball bat down the sidewalk.

The aftershock wouldn't occur until tomorrow, so Kevin occupied himself downtown. He had skipped breakfast, so a juicy cheeseburger with extra fries would fit the bill. He chose a restaurant and stood transfixed at the threshold. Although the neon sign indicated he was standing in front of Bruno's Malt Shop, his heart knew he was at Ronnie's pizza place. He half-expected to see his stocky old friend with the greasy apron appear around the corner.

He stepped inside and a pink-clad waitress, whose wide smile looked a lot like his ex-girlfriend's, rolled up to him on skates.

"Sit anywhere, hon."

Kevin chose a small table in the far corner, ordered a burger and chocolate malt, then stared vacantly at the pink and blue swirls on the Formica table. He had failed.

A flurry of activity outside the window yanked him from his reverie. It was Paul, gesticulating wildly at an eager-looking man who was feverishly writing on a pad.

Goddamn it, didn't Paul every go home?

The gentleman suddenly grabbed a worn leather satchel and departed with a disgusted expression on his face. He heard Paul say, "Eh, that storm is old news anyway. Come on, Laura, let's grab a table." Oh no. They were coming in.

Kevin flagged the waitress and requested his meal to go, then lingered anxiously next to the register for his bag. At that moment, the couple entered the malt shop and selected a booth next to the window. Kevin quietly paid the cashier and slipped out the back exit.

Bolting across the street, he barged into a store with a vaguely familiar name of Flip Side, and was greeted by the soulful voice of Mel Carter on hidden speakers. He glanced around the shop and realized he had entered the embodiment of the '60s. Even in the dim lighting, Kevin could see racks of 8-track cartridges serving as partitions between rows of three-foot high showcases. The cases contained stacks of record albums all arranged alphabetically and by genre. Posters mounted on the paneled walls featured The Rolling Stones, The Temptations, Elvis Presley, and the Beatles, while a teenage boy, dressed in a checked button-down cotton shirt and dark blue slacks, sat behind the cash register. Engrossed in a Batman comic book, the kid completely ignored his customer's presence. Another young clerk struggled to tape a Beatles poster to the front window, muttering curses. The top corners loosened and the entire placard flopped on his head.

Kevin stepped over to a display near the disgruntled boy and examined a glass bowl labeled "Plastic Snap-in Inserts for 45s". He wasn't sure what they were used for, but grabbed a handful anyway to purchase. The impassive sales guy completed the entire transaction without removing himself from the comic book.

At that moment, the entrance door opened and Laura ran inside. She catapulted herself into his arms and clung to him, sobbing. "I'm sorry, Kevin. I'm so sorry."

He placed his thumb on her chin, lifting her face from his shoulder. "What's going on, Laura? Did he hurt you?"

She shook her head. "No, no, nothing like that. I was over at Bruno's and saw you come in here, when it hit me. You're leaving tomorrow, and I'll never see you again. I need to tell you that I'm sorry. I'm sorry things couldn't be different between us. I'm sorry that I feel forced to stay with Paul. I'm sorry you traveled back nearly sixty years on a useless trip." She shuddered, but gazed directly into his eyes. "Most of all, I'm sorry I never had the chance to tell you that ... I love you."

Kevin drew her in his arms as she wept on his shoulder. The three words he longed to say in return remained unspoken. It would only bring them pain. All he could do at that moment was embrace her.

She sniffed loudly. "I gotta go. I better buy something, though. He'll wonder why I ran over here."

"Take these," he offered, handing her the bag. "I don't know what they are, but they're cool to look at."

She peered in the paper bag. "You don't know what spiders are? Here, keep one as a souvenir." She pulled one from the bag and handed it to him, planted a quick kiss on his lips, and slipped out the door.

Chapter 23

Kevin existed in a perpetual state of panic and anxiety. He was traveling home tonight, leaving Laura with a dismal future of emotional abuse and disappointment. His darn conscience wouldn't allow him to disclose any additional information. Perhaps his forewarnings would nudge her to make different choices. He'd find out soon enough.

He drove the Cutlass on the rugged trail and parked next to a skinny, oak sapling. He allowed his eyes to drift across the familiar meadow and noted the tall reeds of grass swaying in the gentle breeze. The sky stretched like an ocean of the deepest blue, dotted with islands of billowing clouds.

He approached the discolored circle and squatted on the ground beside it, for there was no wrought iron bench. The yellow grass looked artificial, almost like plastic, so he reached to pull one of the blades to examine it. The blade held fast to the ground, unyielding.

He regarded the splotches of pink in the clouds as the sun traversed toward the horizon, but could only think about Laura.

He knew what the next few years were going to bring her. Damn it, why didn't he try harder? He felt completely powerless, and his heart hung heavily in his chest.

The wind started to howl so Kevin straightened himself and took his place in the center of the circle. The earth beneath him started trembling, and the breeze transformed into mighty gusts. Panting, he willed himself to breathe deeply, but couldn't. Rapid, shallow breaths barely filled his lungs and his vision blurred. The pulsating quakes pounding beneath his feet threatened to split open the earth and devour all it could snare. The wind, gaining more power and velocity, snatched loose branches, leaves, and dirt, whipping them around like hapless playthings.

He had one final thought as reality shimmered his vision.

Oh, God, how can I leave her?

At the last possible moment, he amassed every ounce of strength he had, and stepped out of the epicenter. He fell to the ground, unconscious.

He awoke in the dark. Millions of brilliant stars overhead illuminated the grassy field. Disoriented, he peered around, breathing heavily. He was certain he was in Sullivan's Meadow, but when? No cottage was visible from where he sat, but he could see a car at the edge of the trees. He squinted. The Cutlass. With the realization that he remained in 1965, he experienced a visceral reaction of profound relief coupled with absolute terror. The temporal breach was now sealed. The only means of returning to 2023 was in fifty-eight years through the natural passage of time.

He hobbled to the Cutlass and sat immobile in the driver's seat. He had no plan, knew no one other than Laura, and no place to live. Before he permitted the seeds of panic to take hold again, he started the ignition and carefully drove out of the woods. He returned to Howard Johnson's with only one goal, to sleep.

"Well, Mom," he said aloud as he crawled into bed. "Is this a bold enough choice for you?"

* * *

The start of a new day typically brought the promise of renewed hope, but not for Kevin Donahue. He awoke the following morning in sheer terror, his heart pounding against his ribs like a condemned prisoner beating against the metal bars of his cell. His entire body, drenched in a fear-induced sweat, caused the bedsheets to cling to his clammy skin. What in God's name had he done? He relinquished all that defined him— his independent mother, his friendship with Ronnie, and even his cherished motorcycle, Lucille. Not to mention his academic career. Four solid years of relentless studying with absolutely nothing to show for it.

So, who the hell was he now?

He ripped off the damp sheets and bolted for the bathroom, retching the contents of his stomach into the toilet. Depleted, he staggered to the adjacent sink and clutched the edges of the porcelain in desperation. Whiffs of lemon-scented disinfectant heightened his nausea but he refused to succumb. "Get ahold of yourself," he whispered, but the sound of his own voice drove him further into despair. Here he was, stranded in an era with no computers, no internet, and no cellphones. And, more importantly, no family.

After gulping several lungfuls of air, he splashed cool water on his face, then regarded his reflection. His swollen eyes, normally bright and alert, were bloodshot and dull with grief. Laura hadn't wanted him to stay in 1965. She had pleaded with him to go back through the time echo and let her lead her life. So, why hadn't he? He hung his head into his hands and sobbed. He was trapped almost sixty friggin' years in the past.

But look at Laura. When she was thrown into the future, she managed to keep her sanity. How had she done it? Well, for one thing, she didn't have to navigate the future by herself, she had him. Even so, she had gathered her wits with a quiet strength and forged ahead with enviable determination. Her courage inspired him. He'd find his way home, wherever, or whenever, that home may be. He grabbed a clean towel from the rack.

* * *

After a long, hot shower and a shave, he drove to another county for breakfast. He couldn't chance running into Laura. She needed to believe he went back to 2023 so she can be free to live with that ignoramus, Paul. As he entered a town named Mountaindale, Kevin spotted the familiar logo of IHOP and rolled into the parking lot. He chose a small table near the dessert display, allowing his exhausted body to melt into the orange plastic chair.

A genial waitress approached him with a pot of steaming coffee and a mug. She wore a standard aqua uniform with a frilly white apron tied around her slim waist. She had pulled up her honey brown hair, forming a tight, tidy bun high upon her crown. The girl appeared to be in her twenties, but the severe hairstyle aged her. A tag imprinted with the name 'Maggie' was pinned above her left breast pocket.

"What'll it be, hon?" she asked, while expertly pouring him a cup.

"A cup of coffee for now."

"Not much of an appetite this morning? Let me know if you change your mind." He nodded numbly as he toyed with the ceramic coffee mug before him.

He felt displaced. Alone and unsure how he should move forward. The perpetual hum of anxiety coursed through his veins, desperate to claw its way to the surface. He longed to consult with Dr. Archer, but heck, he was even younger than Kevin at this point. Archer couldn't do anything anyway, as there would be no planetary alignment for another fifty-eight years.

The waitress had turned to leave, but had changed her mind and took a step closer to the table. "Ya know, I may not be a bartender, but I'm a pretty good listener. You okay?"

He lifted his pained eyes to the waitress. "Honestly? I don't know. I lost everything in a blink of an eye."

"Going through a rough patch. I get it. We've all been fired at one point or another, but I'm sure a good-looking fella such as yourself can get a job in a flash." She pulled a *Tenakill Tribune* from the metal rack behind him. "Here. The 'Help Wanted' pages are in the back."

She thought he lost his job. If it were only that simple. Nevertheless, he accepted the newspaper and stared blankly at the year. 1965.

Recognizing he may be in the '60s a while, he nodded to himself and slowly opened the paper. He thumbed his way to the 'Help Wanted' section, and as he skimmed through, he bypassed advertisements for dishwasher, grocery clerk, mechanic, and stock boy. Then he stopped short. This was it.

Wanted: Teaching Assistant

Searching for a qualified Teaching Assistant for Physical Sciences at Sullivan University, a higher-level educational institution. Must have some college experience. Duties include but not limited to writing and grading quizzes and assisting with audiovisual and mimeograph equipment. To apply, contact Dr. August Ryan, Sullivan University Science Department in Sullivan Township at Butterfield5-3126.

Kevin reread the ad, not entirely believing his good-fortune, for this position fit his skill-set perfectly. He jotted down the number and stuffed his hand into his pocket to grab his phone. Right, no phone. He sighed heavily, grabbed a dime from his other pocket, and dashed to the phone booth in the back of the restaurant. After three full rings, a woman answered.

"Good morning, this is Shirley. May I help you?"

"Ah, yes, good morning, Shirley. My name is Kevin Donahue and I'm interested in applying for the Teaching Assistant position."

He chatted amiably with the department's secretary and scheduled an interview for tomorrow morning at nine. Hanging up the phone, Kevin appreciated this promising piece of luck and returned to his table. Seemed like the tides were turning. After taking a sip of his coffee, which happened to be delicious, he beckoned the waitress.

"Any luck, doll?"

"Fingers crossed, Maggie, I have an interview in the morning. But for now, I think I'm ready for breakfast." He ordered the Hungry Man's Special, consisting of a large stack of pancakes, scrambled eggs, bacon, hash browns, and buttered toast.

Maggie chuckled. "Guess you got your appetite back, fella. Lemme warm up your cup of joe, and I'll go put your order in."

He thanked her, and as she scurried to the kitchen with the food order in hand, he spread the newspaper across the table. This time, he flipped to the 'Available Apartments' section. He considered it a good omen that he scored an interview within the first five minutes of searching and decided to try his luck finding a place to live. He had a few possibilities circled by the time Maggie returned to the table, skillfully balancing several platefuls of food and placing them down before him.

"Looking for a pad, I see."

"No, I don't need a pad, but thanks. I'm circling what looks decent."

The waitress broke into a broad grin, the outer corners of her eyes creasing. "No, honey. An apartment."

"Oh, right. An apartment. So far, I'm not having much luck. Most of them are advertised for college students." Using the pitcher next to the napkin dispenser, he saturated his pancakes with the stickiness of real maple syrup.

"Well, aren't you? A college student, I mean. You look like one."

"I was supposed to graduate in a few weeks, but... I've had a change in plans."

"Uh huh. Don't sweat it, I'm not gonna pry. This might actually be your lucky day. Don't know if you'd be interested, but my brother and his wife are looking to rent out a room in their house. You'd have your own bedroom and bathroom but share everything else. Could be a bit of a drag, if you ask me."

Kevin gaped at her. "Are you serious?"

She nodded. "Yeah, I know it doesn't sound like much, but—"

"Maggie, I believe you're my guardian angel. It sounds perfect. Where is the place?"

"Right here in Mountaindale. If you'd like, I can give my brother a call, see if it's still available."

"Sure. Yes. Absolutely," he said.

Maggie disappeared into the back room and returned with his bill and a grin.

"He said c'mon over after breakfast, if you're free."

Chapter 24

A half-mile up the road and down a side-street or two, Kevin turned into the driveway of a large Victorian house with an inviting wraparound porch. He stepped out of the car and a shaggy, smoky-colored mutt bounded up to him, leaping jubilantly on all fours.

"Buster. Get down, you crazy dog." A tall, burly man, probably in his thirties, jogged from the front door to Kevin. He extended his hand. "So sorry about Buster. Hope you don't mind dogs, but he's really friendly. Give him a few minutes and he'll settle down." He held onto the collar of the dancing pup. "My name is Jacob. My sister said you'd be coming over to look at the room, being new to the area and all. I'll be honest with ya, we've been looking for a tenant for a couple of weeks now. Had some leads but as of now the place is still available. Between you and me, I'm kinda glad the other fellas couldn't make up their minds— they weren't too keen on Buster here. Would've made for an uncomfortable situation, now, wouldn't it? Come on in. I hope you like the place." He released his pooch and it bounded up the steps to the porch.

He listened to the man chatter away as they entered the house and into a modestly furnished living room. Buster pranced around in circles in front of them until Kevin stooped and gave the dog's ears a quick scratch. The pup's tongue lolled to one side of his mouth, accepting the stranger's attention.

"So, this is the living room. We have a brand-new color television, but you gotta fiddle with the antenna to get a clear picture. And if you got any records, you're free to use the hi-fi, but please remember to put the arm back. Hate replacing those needles."

Kevin nodded, clueless, and realized Jacob was referring to a phonograph that sat in the corner of the room, nestled between a couple of worn armchairs. Curious, he stepped over to examine it. The phonograph was a large, wooden box, its hinged lid propped open. Inside, there was an empty turntable with a 3-inch metal spindle in its center.

"If you decide to move in, you can use this room whenever you'd like. Let's take a look at your bedroom. Let's go, Buster, lead the way."

The two men followed the gleeful dog down a corridor and Jacob opened the first door on the right. They entered a small but comfortable room with a twin bed and an oak dresser. A single window adorned by a white lace curtain faced the porch at the front of the house, and Kevin's car was visible in the gravel driveway. Jacob unlatched a door in the bedroom, allowing him to inspect a tiny, turquoise and tan bathroom with the expected tub, commode, and sink.

"That there's your closet, and over there leads you out to the side porch. You'd have your own key for that. Come on, I'll show you." Jacob pushed the door and the dog bolted out. The men strode out to the porch.

"I gotta say, Jacob, I'm pretty interested in the place. You live here by yourself?"

He chuckled. "Oh, no, no. You got me and my wife, her name's Anna, and Buster here. Oh, and a little baby in five months."

Kevin smiled, "Awesome. Congratulations. Any idea what you're having, a boy or a girl?"

"Hoping for a boy but don't tell my wife that. She has her heart set on a little girl. I'll tell ya, though, I'm nervous as hell. I'm counting on Buster here to help take care of the baby. Isn't that right, boy?" Panting, the dog looked up at Jacob and wagged his tail.

"Anyway, you'll have free access to the kitchen, but you'd have to buy your own food, of course. Anna will clear a shelf in the refrigerator for you, and you'll have your own pantry. Rent is $82 a month, due on the first. Think about it, but let me show you the kitchen."

They walked back inside the bedroom and down the hallway, past a flight of stairs.

"What's up there?" Kevin asked.

"Bedrooms. Mine's there, a couple of spare rooms, and another bathroom. I'm fixin' one of the spares to be the baby's nursery. You like to paint? I sure could use a hand. Anna's been complaining I'm taking too long. Says if I keep dragging my feet the babe will have to sleep with Buster." He laughed. "Funny woman. But we have five more months to get it done. Plenty of time, right?" He stepped to the side. "And here's the kitchen."

The sizable room featured wood-veneered cabinetry and laminate countertops, with color-coordinated appliances neatly lining the countertop between the sink and the Frigidaire. A round Formica table sat in the center of the room, sported by four avocado-green vinyl chairs that perfectly matched the painted walls.

"No need to think about it, Jacob, I'll take it."

"I was hoping you'd say that." The two men agreed on a move-in date of May first, and after signing paperwork and one last handshake, Kevin departed the house with a smile. Things were looking up. Hey, if this streak of luck continued, he'd consider purchasing a motorcycle.

Chapter 25

The morning of the interview, Kevin donned a new suit he had
purchased at Murray's and drove to his school, Sullivan U. The
buildings he passed on campus will still exist in 2023, although he
noticed many have not yet been built. He strolled into the science
building and introduced himself at the reception desk. A squat,
middle-aged woman, wearing a bright, polka dotted dress and cat-
eye frames, glanced up from her typewriter and smiled kindly.

"Well, hello Mr. Donohue, it's nice to attach a face to the
voice. We spoke on the phone yesterday. I'm Shirley. Please have
a seat and fill out this paperwork. I'll let Dr. Ryan know you're
here." She stood and removed her glasses, placing them beside the
typewriter. "You're punctual. He'll be pleased."

Ten minutes later, Kevin followed Shirley into the exact lecture
hall where he had taken his astronomy class with Dr. Archer. The
professor standing at the podium was quite short in stature, and
boasted a thick head of black wavy hair swept to the side and a
handlebar mustache. The man was fiddling with a rather large,
reel-to-reel movie projector. It shouldn't surprise him there were
no Smartboards, but it did.

"Dr. Ryan? Kevin Donahue's here for his interview."

"Oh, yes. Good, good. Mr. Donahue? August Ryan.
Extraordinarily nice to meet you."

He stretched out his palm and squeezed Kevin's in a firm,
beefy handshake.

"Let's sit in the front row and get acquainted, shall we?" The
professor tossed the circular film tin onto the podium and
extended his hand toward the first few seats, and Kevin obliged.

"This audiovisual equipment is going to be the end of me. Please tell me you know how to thread a film projector."

"Well, honestly, I haven't seen one of those in a while but I'm confident I can figure it out."

The older man turned in his seat and faced him.

"I hope so, I hope so. Now, I have to be honest with you. I haven't taken a look at your application yet, but Shirley assures me you're a suitable candidate. I do value her opinion, but I'd prefer to hear it from you. Tell me about yourself, Kevin, and why you think you'd be an appropriate choice for this position."

He took a breath and imagined telling the man that he had no other options, that he was marooned in 1965 after stepping through a time portal from 2023, all in an attempt to rescue a girl who refused to be rescued. Not the best way to secure this job.

"Well, sir, I'm new to this area, and was hoping to complete my education while working at Sullivan U. I've almost completed my bachelor's degree in geophysics, but I'm a few credits short."

"Indeed? What institution were you enrolled in?"

"A small school. Faber College, in Pennsylvania," he lied, blanching. He had chosen the fictitious school from National Lampoon's raunchy comedy, "Animal House."

"I'm unfamiliar with that particular school, but no matter. It's fortunate that you've taken science classes, as this position is, of course, within the general science department. So let me ask you a few general questions to see what you remember from your schooling."

He swallowed hard. This was a nightmare come true ... taking a final examination without studying.

"Tell me, what is the gravitational force that the earth exerts on any object?"

"That's easy. That would be weight, sir."

"Sure enough. And what would you call the energy of a moving object?"

"Kinetic energy."

"Hmm, excellent, excellent. One more, just for fun. A physical quantity that has both magnitude and direction is what?"

"Magnitude and direction? That would be a vector."

"Well done, Mr. Donahue. You have a grasp of the basics. So let me tell you about the position. First and foremost, it is provisional. You'd have the remainder of the spring semester to demonstrate your value to the science program. At that point, my departmental colleagues and I will decide whether to extend your employment."

"Okay, I understand. What are the duties of the position?"

The professor absentmindedly twirled his moustache. "At first, lots of busy work—mimeographing, typing, that sort of thing. In time you may grade papers, prepare quizzes, and if all goes well, teach a class or two when I'm not available. I do, however, have another question for you, not related to science."

"Oh?"

"Your application indicates you are twenty-two years old, is that correct?"

"Absolutely, as of February 2nd."

"I see. Did you register at the local draft board when you turned 18?"

"Did I ... what?"

"Register for the draft. I'd like to know your status."

"Oh, I ... yes. I have a card."

"Wonderful. May I have a look at it?"

At a snail's pace, Kevin pulled out his computer graphics assignment from his wallet. With an unsteady hand, he extended it to the professor.

Dr. Ryan examined the card, furrowing his brow.

"Ah, I see. 4-F due to a perforated eardrum." He returned the card to Kevin. "I understand your reluctance to show me, Mr. Donahue, but a 4-F is nothing to be ashamed of. You can serve your country stateside. In any case, let me offer you my congratulations, the teaching assistant job is yours, $2.00 an hour. Shirley will iron out the details and paperwork. Do you accept?"

"Absolutely, I accept. And thank you for this opportunity. I won't let you down." He sagged with relief.

Dr. Ryan slapped his shoulder. "You're welcome. You can start on Monday."

As they rose, the men shook hands. Kevin was elated. He arrived in 1965 less than a week ago and managed to land a job and a place to live. Thank goodness the university didn't bother conducting a background check. He was a man with no identity and a phony draft card.

Chapter 26

Time progressed and Kevin adjusted to his new way of life relatively easily. He often thought of Laura but suppressed any temptation to reappear in her life. He was certain he wouldn't be well received. Despite his warnings, she'd been resolute about pursuing a life with Paul, and would be furious if he interfered again. Besides, she was under the impression he returned to 2023 and picked up his life where he left off. Well, that certainly didn't happen.

He also gave considerable thought to his parents. They'd be children now. Should he meet them, somehow figure a way to save his father's life? Realizing any contact with them or even preventing his father's death would jeopardize the entire trajectory of his life and his mother's, he made the heart-wrenching decision not to interfere.

He took his responsibilities seriously at the university, and after proving his competence and exemplary work ethic during the spring semester, his employment was no longer considered provisional. He spent the summer assisting Dr. Ryan's preparations for the upcoming classes in the fall, and was assigned additional classes with other professors. No doubt he made a strong impression with his fund of knowledge and commitment.

The first class of the new school year went off without a hitch. He positioned himself at the doorway of the lecture hall and distributed a list of required reading to the exiting undergraduates. As he listened to their groans and colorful commentary in the hallway, he noticed the professor waving an arm, summoning him to the lectern.

"Professor? You need me?"

"Kevin. Just the man I want to see." He was opening various metal tabs and latches on a film projector to peer inside at the mechanics. "This darn machine, always something wrong with the AV equipment. Aha. A burnt-out bulb. Hand me one, would you? There should be a box under the lectern."

Checking under the podium, Kevin pushed aside a tangle of dusty extension cords, a forgotten Polaroid camera, and a lone motorized roller skate, until he found a box containing a single light bulb. Rather than offering the bulb to the professor, he leaned over and began replacing the nonfunctioning one.

The professor chuckled, warm and hearty. "Thank you, Kevin. Glad I hired you. Speaking of which, I have exciting news to share with you."

What could possibly qualify as good news? He could think of nothing. Did someone finally invent the microwave oven? That would be a relief.

"I had a staff meeting last night with the Executive Dean, six colleagues, and the Board of Directors. We're all in agreement. You consistently exhibit a high level of commitment and fulfill all of your tasks with superb precision, and your background knowledge of the sciences is extraordinary. In as such, the Dean has granted me the privilege of offering you, our well-regarded employee, tuition-free classes to pursue your Bachelor of Science degree." He added that the registrar could not honor his former classes without a transcript, but would permit him to matriculate as an undergraduate. "It's a shame Faber College closed its doors before you earned your degree, and I'm shocked a lawsuit was never pursued. But I digress. If you agree to enroll at Sullivan University, you should expect to complete your academic training in May of 1969. Congratulations, my boy." Dr. Ryan shook his hand, and Kevin beamed. He would be graduating from Sullivan U after all.

Preoccupied with his unexpected good fortune, Kevin departed the science building with a broad grin stretching from ear to ear. Tuition-free. Unbelievable. He didn't think such a benefit ever existed, certainly not in 2023. He strode across campus with a silly smirk on his face, but he didn't care. At the moment, he felt invincible. Why shouldn't he? He was thrown a curveball in life, but managed to knock it out of the park. Nothing could bring him down.

He glanced back at the academic buildings with swelling pride, until he spotted a gorgeous girl with long, auburn hair strolling across the commons, clutching her books across her chest. His breath quickened. Laura. All thoughts fashioned by his bloated ego vanished. Dashing behind a stately elm, he peeked around the trunk.

Her eyes fixed on the pathway before her, she made eye contact with nobody. Why the heck was she here, at Sullivan U? He reviewed her timeline in his head and remembered she would now be attending school to earn her teaching degree. Oh boy. Dodging her was going to be extremely tricky.

"Laura. Wait up," a voice cried.

She turned, casting a half-hearted wave to a slight, skinny kid donning glasses.

Kevin felt a sinking feeling in his chest. He knew she was in for a few rough years with Paul, but looking at her now, he realized the toll on her well-being was far more severe than he thought. As she stood on the pathway waiting for her friend, Kevin couldn't help but notice how her dress hung loosely on her body, emphasizing a rail-thin figure. Even from behind the tree, he could see the weariness etched on her face, her once full cheeks now appearing sunken and hollow. With a heavy heart, he saw a mere shell of the spirited, vibrant woman she was when they first met. That douchebag was decimating her.

He took one step from his hiding spot, but stopped himself from going further, wrestling with his conscience. He knew in his gut he must allow her achieve the goals she was so proud of in 2023, but witnessing the process firsthand? He wasn't particularly confident how well he'd fare as a bystander. The best he could do was keep a distant eye on her and make sure she stayed safe.

Laura and her friend retreated into the Student Union Building while Kevin collapsed on a bench on the edge of the commons. There he was, trapped in the '60s and unable to pursue the girl. The elation he felt earlier with Dr. Ryan disappeared like smoke, replaced by the sharp grip of anxiety that clawed at him, intent on hauling him into the dark, inky well of despair.

Damn it. Why the hell had she insisted he not to interfere? His insides churned. He loved her but couldn't go near her. If he did, the life she was proudly building would never come to fruition.

Body slumped, he turned away, and went home.

Chapter 27

In an effort to avoid downtown Sullivan Township, Kevin spent the majority of his time in the science department at the university or at home in Mountaindale. Kevin and his landlord, Jacob, enjoyed many evenings unwinding on the porch staring up at the stars with Buster snoring contently at their feet. To entertain himself, he once asked Jacob what he thought of that planetary alignment a few years ago. Jacob had puffed on his pipe and replied, "Alignment? I don't know what you're talking about Kev, but I think you're spending too much time in those science books." One time Jacob commented on Kevin's paltry social life and Kevin wisecracked, "Who needs a social life when I get to spend my nights with you and Buster?"

One evening after a long day at work, Kevin pulled his jacket from the hook behind his office door and shrugged it on. He had been grading quizzes for most of the afternoon and was dismayed by the paltry scores. Science Appreciation was an easy course, but he was aware the unit on statistics was more challenging. Apparently, the students struggled with the difference between standard scores and standard deviations. He stuffed a bunch of papers into a folder and headed to the parking lot.

"Hey, Ethel," he said, greeting his bike. No surprise, Kevin had purchased a previously owned, 1963 Triumph Bonneville in jet black. Although not Lucille, he was rather fond of his new set of wheels. The winter was swiftly approaching, and he was certain he'd have to purchase a car, but kept putting it off. "Thanks for waiting, sweetheart," he said to his bike. "Let's go home."

He drove back to Mountaindale at a leisurely pace, then pulled his bike up the gravel driveway. He barely made it up the first step of the house when the front door opened and out bounded Buster.

"Hiya, fella," he said as he squatted next to the squirming pooch. "I know, I know, a back scratch is in order. I'm at your service. How'd you open the door, Buster? You develop thumbs when I wasn't looking? Huh, boy?"

"That'd be a neat trick."

He looked up and saw Jacob leaning against the frame of the door with a lopsided smile of amusement.

Kevin stood, and Buster, satisfied with the attention, padded back into the house.

"What's up, man? Something on your mind?"

"Yeah. Listen, this is not my fault. You know how women are, right?"

"What are you talking about, Jacob?"

"They get somethin' in their heads and there's no stopping them"

"Jacob! Out with it."

The man took a deep breath. "Anna thinks you're lonely.

"So?"

"I can't believe she's making me do this. She says you're lonely, and a good-looking guy like yourself needs a woman in his life."

Kevin sniffed. "An old-fashioned concept, I grant you that. But please, go on."

"She invited her cousin, Barbara, for supper tonight so the two of you can get acquainted. Now, don't kill me. It wasn't my idea. But for the sake of my life, you gotta stop in for supper."

"I appreciate the invite, man, but you know I'm not interested in meeting anybody."

"Yeah, yeah, that's what I told Anna, but she said men don't know the first thing about what they need. Come on, have supper with us tonight, okay?"

Kevin glowered at Jacob and stepped into the house.

"Oh, thank goodness, you're here," said Anna as he entered the dining room. "Come join us. I'd like you to meet my cousin, Barbara. Barbara, may I introduce Kevin Donahue, our long-time tenant and good friend."

Lightly shaking her hand, he peered at the slight young woman, who looked as uncomfortable as he felt. Her silky, cinnamon-colored hair hung to her shoulders in soft curls, and her long bangs extended slightly below her eyebrows, skirting the tips of her eyelashes. She donned a kelly green dress with a rose-scalloped collar, and the hemline rested above the knee. Her natural beauty reminded him of the Ivory Girls in the latest advertisements.

He soon found himself seated at the dining room table with a plate of meatloaf and buttered beans in front of him, and the soft-spoken woman to his right. Piercing a morsel of meatloaf, he cast a quick look at Jacob, who skillfully avoided eye contact with him.

"So, Kevin," Anna said. "Barbara recently received an acceptance letter from the Katharine Gibbs School. Isn't that right, Barb?"

The young woman cleared her throat. "Uh, yes, that's right. I begin my training next quarter."

"Congratulations," he said. "What are you studying?"

Barbara glanced at Anna, confused, then shifted her eyes back to Kevin. "Why, secretarial duties, of course."

"You've heard of Katharine Gibbs, haven't you, Kevin?" Anna chimed in. "It's the best secretarial school in the country."

He sipped his soda. "That so? Fascinating."

Jacob's wife continued. "After the program, she'll be fully trained in typing, shorthand, and dictation. She'll be quite a catch."

"I'm sure she will be." He shifted in his seat. Man, Anna was laying it on thick. What was next? Was she going to whip out the girl's resume from under a placemat? This was going to be a really long night.

"So, Anna," Barbara said. "Did you prepare the dessert tonight? You bake the most delicious pies. You have to tell me your secret."

Kevin turned to her and mouthed, "Thank you."

She mouthed in return, "You're welcome."

As dinner progressed, Kevin realized he was enjoying himself. The young woman's quick wit and contagious laugh left him smiling throughout the meal.

When the two couples finished eating, Anna stood and picked up her plate.

"Why don't the two of you go outside for some fresh air while I get dessert ready."

"Don't be silly, Anna. Let me help clear the table." Barbara lifted her dirty plate.

"No, no. You go enjoy yourself. Besides, my husband can give me a hand in the kitchen."

"My help? Since when have you ever wanted my—?"

"Shh, Jacob. Just come in the kitchen."

"Sorry, Kevin," he said. "The boss needs me." Anna snatched her husband's arm and dragged him into the other room.

"Shall we?" he said, extending his hand to one of the rocking chairs on the porch. She smiled and sat primly on the edge of the seat.

"I have to apologize," she said. "When my cousin gets these ideas in her head, there's no stopping her."

He waved her off. "It's fine. I had a good time tonight."

She blushed.

"But let me be upfront with you. There's a woman I —."

"Ah, I should've known you're taken."

"No, no, that's not it. It's ... well, complicated. I know, I know, such a cliché, but in this case it's true."

He leaned against the porch railing and she gazed up at him, compelling him to explain further.

"In a nutshell, the woman chose another man."

"Oh, I see. And she put you through the wringer."

"I suppose, but I'm not willing to rush into anything, if that makes any sense to you."

"Listen, Kevin. I'm not looking for a husband. I have two long years of secretarial school ahead of me."

"Okay, so if I'm understanding this correctly, neither one of us is available for anything serious."

She smiled. "Exactly."

"Great. What are you doing next Friday night?"

Chapter 28

They courted for several months, enjoying multiple dinners together, a few movies, even a handful of evenings bowling with Jacob and Anna. Kevin grew fond of Barbara. She made no demands and had no expectations. She didn't mind riding on the back of the motorcycle, a definite plus. As the days grew shorter and the air chilled, the time to roll the bike into the garage for the winter was quickly approaching. He bit the bullet after the first sign of snow flurries and visited a Ford dealership. He strolled through the used car lot, unimpressed with his choices of dilapidated cars when he eyed the classic 1964 Ford Mustang in candy apple red. He restrained himself for fear of looking too eager, but the salesman was no fool, he knew he had a sale. With a little negotiation, they struck a deal for a total of $1,900. He thought he bought the car for a song, but the salesman's cocky grin told him otherwise. It didn't matter, he loved his new car.

The night before her departure to secretarial school, Kevin treated Barbara to a quiet, candlelight dinner at a French restaurant, and returned to his house for a nightcap.

"Here. A glass of Chardonnay." He poured a glass of the aromatic wine and passed it to her.

She took a sip, then peered up at Kevin. "Would you mind if I ask you something? I hope I'm not overstepping, but since I'm leaving in the morning ..."

He carefully set the wine bottle on the coffee table and settled in a seat beside her. He watched her swirl the Chardonnay in her glass, creating a mini whirlpool.

"Go ahead," he said.

"Well, we've been having a blast, right? Movies, miniature golf, you name it, they've all been fun."

He nodded in agreement.

"So ... how come I've never seen you laugh?"

Kevin was thrown off. "What? I laugh."

"No. No, you don't. You smile a little, but I've never heard an honest-to-goodness, thigh-slapping laugh. You know the kind, where you throw back your head and laugh with abandon."

"Sure, I have. What was that joke Jacob told us last week? Something about a rabbi, a priest, and a dog walking into a bar? That was funny."

"Nuh-uh, you didn't laugh, that was a polite snicker. Listen, Kev. Whether I see you laugh or not isn't the point. It only tells me you're stuck in the past."

Well, that much was true, he thought.

"I know you never got over that girl who chose another fella. It's as plain as the nose on your face. But for your own good, you might start thinking about leaving her behind so you can get on with your life."

Silence.

She bit her lip. "Will you take me home? I'm tired, and have a big day tomorrow." She placed her wineglass down on the table and stood. "I like you, Kevin. I wouldn't be saying these things if I didn't care."

* * *

A month later, Kevin received a letter in the mail postmarked New York City. He headed out to the porch and parked himself on the top stoop, slit the envelope open and read.

Dear Kevin,

The scribble you see at the top of this page is shorthand. It says 'Hope all is well.'

I've gotten used to the routine here at Katie Gibbs, and have made many friends with the girls. I'm not crazy about my typing class, however. One typo, and the teacher rips up the assignment. Anyway, one of the reasons I'm writing is to tell you I met somebody. His name is Joe, and we kept bumping into each other at the automat. Last week he asked me to dinner and we had a lovely time. I thought it important you know.

As I said at the beginning of this letter, I hope all is well with you. I also hope you have found your laugh.

All the best,

Barbara

Kevin returned the letter into the envelope. Nice girl. It occurred to him he had spent more time with Barbara than Laura, but still, something with Barbara didn't feel right. She was a sock that didn't quite fit.

Lost in his thoughts, he gazed at the trees in the front yard without really seeing them. He thought of Laura and how he had yet to meet anybody like her. She possessed a mix of old-fashioned charm and a zest for life that beguiled him. And what about her courage. Thrown nearly sixty years into an unknown future, she had exuded an incredible strength for self-preservation and survival. Kevin smiled with the memory of her, those emerald green eyes, the gorgeous auburn hair, and the electricity. A light touch of her hand, and electrical currents would spark throughout his entire body.

He missed her. He missed everything about her. Why the hell did she insist he must not interfere? His only consolation was that her life would eventually settle down and she wouldn't have to deal with Paul anymore.

Wait a minute.

His pulse quickened. The older version of Laura mentioned her proudest achievement was her teaching career at Lincoln

Memorial. She completed her first year as a teacher in June of '71 and after that, her life calmed into a steady groove.

He stood up and drew in a sharp breath as realization set in. He didn't have to stay away from her forever. He could wait until her life settled down, and hope that one day, by some miracle, she'd welcome him back into her life.

He felt absolutely buoyant.

Chapter 29

Time marched on.

Occasionally, Kevin snuck into Sullivan Township and could see Laura through the windows at Bruno's Drive-In Restaurant, but as soon as the establishment was moderately successful, the place sold. Kevin's heart soared when he read the sign "*Coming Soon. Ronnie's Pizza and Italian Eatery.*"

Months later, the restaurant officially opened and Kevin made sure he was one of the first customers served. He grinned throughout his entire meal of lasagna, overjoyed to be back in his favorite restaurant eating the best Italian cuisine on the entire planet. With nothing but scant traces of Bolognese on his plate, he summoned the waitress.

"I just wanted to say, the lasagna is out of this world. Reminds me of lasagna I used to love another lifetime ago. Is the owner around? I'm eager to congratulate him."

A few minutes later, a small Italian man exited the kitchen and rushed across the aisle, wiping his hands on his apron. "My girl, she says you like my food, eh?"

"Hands down, the best lasagna I ever ate. I'm Kevin, by the way." He extended his arm for a handshake. "I have a hunch this restaurant is going to be around for a long, long time."

"Your words to God's ears. And I'm Luigi. You, I like. He turned. "Amelia! Come meet our new friend." A stout, lively woman squeezed through the narrow opening of the hospitality counter. Kevin was greeted with a wide smile and chubby cheeks, her eyes crinkling with delight. "This young man, he says he likes your lasagna."

"That I do," Kevin said, "and I can't wait to dive into a bowl of Pasta Fagioli next time I come. Saw it on the menu and it sounds awesome."

"Ah, such a good boy. Grazie." Amelia beamed and leaned across the table to pinch his cheeks. "You cleaned your plate. I go get you more. The gravy, it's my nonna's recipe, from Italy, si? You go to Italy?"

Kevin smiled and pushed his plate back. "Afraid I've never had the pleasure, but I hear Italy's beautiful. A friend of mine used to visit family in Italy and told me all about it."

"Ah, it's a beautiful country. Next time, go with your friend." Amelia nabbed his plate.

"Wait, no seconds for me, I couldn't eat another bite. Thank you, though."

"Nonsense. A little more for you." The matronly woman turned for the kitchen and called over her shoulder, "It'll put hair on your chest, you'll see."

"You need to meet my son," interrupted Luigi. "Ronald, put that down and come. My boy, he's such a hard worker."

A pre-adolescent boy who was stuffing paper napkins into stainless steel dispensers sauntered over. He swiped his dark curls out of his eyes and scrutinized the stranger.

Kevin grinned at young Ronnie.

"Ronald Giordano, say hello to, uh —"

"Kevin. Kevin Donahue."

"Yes. Kevin. This is my son, my pride. A big help at the restaurant." The kid cast a skeptical eye at his father, and Kevin chuckled.

"Nice to meet you, buddy." He shook the boy's hand, knowing exactly what to say to his old friend. "I'd bet all my money you're a baseball fan, am I right?"

"Ah, you know my son already. He likes baseball more than his old man, eh, Ronald?"

Ronnie attempted to play it cool. "Yeah, I like baseball a little."

Kevin grinned, in for the kill. "Uh-huh, only a little. Tell me, how do you think the New York Mets will do this year? They're starting to pull out of their early-season slump, so who knows, they might even make it to the series this year."

Unable to contain himself, Ronnie's face lit up. "The World Series? You really think so? But everybody says they don't stand a chance."

"Yeah, people are saying that, but you know what? I have a strong feeling they're gonna prove everybody wrong."

"No kidding? Well, I think they're the best too. I mean, look at the swing on Ron Swoboda, man, nobody can top that. And now they got this new guy, Tug McGraw. He's 20 and in the major leagues. That's gonna be me someday, you wait and see."

Kevin listened and nodded his head, and heard himself promise to take Ronnie to a ballgame, if it was okay with his folks. What an incredible relief to his soul having Ronnie back in his life, even if he was a much younger version. Another plate of lasagna appeared before him, and Kevin happily ate his second helping with his good buddy chatting away.

* * *

At the end of the school year in 1969, Kevin graduated summa cum laude from Sullivan University and awarded a Bachelor of Science degree. His professors, thoroughly impressed with his continued diligence, intelligence, and commitment, recommended him for a supervised assistant professorship for freshmen science courses. To earn his state teaching certification, he was required to take three additional classes during the school year while fulfilling his duties as an educator. Dr. Ryan confided in him that the school board would be officially voting in July, but the job was essentially his.

After learning Laura had started working at the restaurant, Kevin memorized her work schedule and avoided dining there during her shifts. A few times he treated Jacob, Anna, and their toddler for dinner at the restaurant. Jake Jr., known as J.J., kept himself entertained by dropping ravioli on the floor.

In October of 1969, Kevin took Ronnie and Luigi to Shea Stadium to watch the Amazing Mets play against the Baltimore Orioles in game four of the World Series. He had seen clips of the game on YouTube, but in person? The game was phenomenal. At the end of the ninth inning, Ron Swoboda had sprinted into a fully-extended dive catch, and Ronnie whooped with unrestrained jubilance, shouting his undying allegiance to the future baseball legend. Kevin's heart soared. Lately, he detected traces of the man Ronnie would eventually become, and he sorely missed his old buddy. Ronnie had been Kevin's best friend for years, and it was crushing to be demoted to "the nice customer" at the restaurant. No, this had to change. He needed Ronnie to remain a permanent fixture in his life, so he felt fully justified to target his friend's Achille's heel.

Prior to the World Series, Kevin placed a bet on the outcome knowing perfectly well the Mets would win the series. He used his healthy payout to become the proud owner of 1970 full season tickets at Shea — two prime seats, four rows behind the Mets' dugout, with full intention to invite Ronnie to many of the games. Ronnie was beyond delirious when Kevin gave him a ticket for opening day at Shea.

"I can't believe we're here," Ronnie shouted as they scooted down the row into their seats. "Look how close we are. Man, this is great."

"Geesh, I knew these seats were going to be close but this is unreal. We're practically sitting on the field."

"Pittsburgh doesn't stand a chance," said Ronnie.

"Especially with Tom Seaver pitching better than ever. Wish it wasn't so damn cold, though." Kevin stomped his feet and the soles of his shoes stuck to the tacky cement. Spilled beer from a previous game? Who cares. He breathed in the tantalizing aroma of hot dogs and buttered popcorn, and relished the pandemonium of sounds. The steady roar of the crowd exhilarated him, and when the pipe organ began its six-note chant, *Ba-da-di-duhh-di-dum*, Kevin bounded from his seat pulling Ronnie with him, shouting with thousands of people the final, resounding, "charge!" The crowd went wild.

"Hot Dogs. Get yer hot dogs here."

Kevin dug two quarters from his pocket. "Ronnie, pass this down and tell the guy at the end to grab us a couple of dogs, will ya? Pile on the works."

The money passed hands to the concession man, who slid open the door of his insulated metal box and prepared the hot dogs. Smothered with sour kraut and who-knows-what, the dogs were passed down from person to person.

"Yo, Carolyn," a guy yelled to the pre-teen girl next to Ronnie. "Be alert and pass 'em down." The dogs dripped with toppings, and unfortunately for the girl sitting so close to Ronnie, she got the brunt of the mess. Ronnie half-heartedly apologized and handed Kevin his hot dog.

They munched on their snacks with enthusiasm, and stopped any vendor who wandered down a nearby aisle — popcorn and soda for Ronnie, peanuts and beer for Kevin. The poor girl was getting food and drink slopped on her with every pass, and sat with her arms rigidly across her chest, clearly miffed at Ronnie.

Finally, their beloved team entered the field, and thousands of fans jumped to their feet, except for the sulking girl, of course. Ronnie grasped Kevin's arm, shaking him, as the Mets received their 1969 World Series rings from last year.

"Look! They're getting their rings, Kev. Can you believe it?" And, for their very first time, the Mets raised the World Championship banner. Ronnie's face lit up with awe.

An unpleasant, windblown drizzle chilled Kevin to his core, but he did his darnedest to ignore it. Looking over at Ronnie, waving his arms and cheering, he couldn't help but grin. This had to be one of the most exciting games of the Mets' career, and he shouted along with the best friend he ever had. So what if it was cold. Tough it out.

Ronnie, on the other hand, didn't seem to notice the chill, for he had his sights set on the grumpy girl sitting next to him. Wait, could Ronnie already be interested in girls? Before the seventh inning stretch, the girl expressed an adamant disinterest in the game, yet he somehow managed to befriend her.

"No, of course I'm not having fun," she said flatly. "It's a slow, boring game, and most of the time they're standing around."

"It might seem like they're doing nothing, but watch the pitcher. Look. See how he's eyeballing the first baseman? He's checking to see if the runner's about to steal second."

"Steal it?"

"Steal it. You know, run to another base between pitches?"

"Why would he do that? It's not even his turn."

The poor girl didn't know the first thing about the rules of baseball. Why did someone drag her to game in the first place? Ronnie, at 12 years old, was as patient as they came, and explained each play and what they might expect next. The girl slowly became intrigued.

The Mets lost to the Pittsburgh Pirates in overtime, not the most encouraging home opener. Throngs of people made their way out of the stadium, grumbling about the defeat. Kevin and Ronnie pushed their way through the swarm to the parking lot, searching for the yellow car in the cold, biting rain.

Driving home, the radio softly played The Beatle's "Something," while Ronnie quietly stared out the passenger window. Kevin yawned, content. Life wasn't half bad. He had impressed himself how he managed to carve out a comfortable place for himself here in the past. He had secured employment and had a few solid friends. It was starting to feel like home. Almost, but not yet.

* * *

Jacob and Anna decided to celebrate their good fortune by ringing in the new year with a small party. They invited Kevin, and recognizing his friendship with the Giordano family, placed a call to invite Luigi, Amelia, and Ronnie. The evening was low-key, complete with cocktails and conversation.

"Let's play a game," Anna announced. "Everyone has to share something that happened in 1970 that left an impression. It could be something in the news, something personal, whatever. Who's going first?"

Kevin half-listened to the others. What the heck was he going to say? How he successfully avoided running into Laura? That he finally mastered the art of using a mimeograph machine?

"Hey. Earth to Kevin," said Jacob. "Your turn. What's it gonna be, huh?"

"Okay, okay. Here's something. Watching the Apollo 13 spacecraft land safely was pretty cool."

"Oh yeah, that was crazy, man."

"I know, right?" He ticked off his fingers. "I mean, their oxygen tank exploded, the guys were on the verge of dying, things going wrong left and right, and they were practically stranded in outer space. Even with all of that, they overcame every conceivable obstacle thrown at them and came home safely."

The others agreed, exclaiming it was a miracle the astronauts made it home alive. Kevin, however, marveled at watching history unfold in real time. Sure, Tom Hanks was fantastic in the movie, but personally witnessing history unfold while it was occurring on a telecast? That was truly miraculous.

"Hey guys, you're leaving out the most important thing — Willie Mays and Hank Aaron." Ronnie said.

Luigi threw his hands in the air. "Ah, *figlio*. It's not always about baseball."

"But this is going down in the books, Pops. Willie Mays and Hank Aaron both reached three thousand career hits. You have any idea what an accomplishment that is?"

"Good for them."

"Arrghh!"

"And stop shouting so much. You're getting hoarse and ruining your voice."

They enjoyed a delicious spread of food, courtesy of Anna's hard work. Kevin particularly enjoyed the Whirligigs — meat-filled biscuit pinwheels — but wasn't fond of the grape Jell-O mold with canned peaches. After Anna put J.J. to bed, the guests retired to the living room to watch Guy Lombardo's New Year's Eve telecast.

"10...9...8...7...6...5...4... 3...2...1...Happy New Year! Welcome 1971!"

Kevin blew his horn with his friends, hugged, and kissed, aware of the orchestra playing "Auld Lang Syne" in the background. It didn't take long for J.J. to wail his displeasure from his bedroom.

"Mama. I wanna come down. Mama!" Anna ran upstairs to attend to her sleep-deprived youngster.

It was 1971. Kevin bided his time long enough.

Chapter 30

As the last of the students funneled up the aisle and out of his Fundamentals of General Science class, Kevin snatched his notes and jammed them into his leather satchel. He packed up the filmstrip projector and stored it under the podium until September. Kevin had completed his first year as a fully qualified professor and had relished the experience. He was now able to appreciate the elderly Laura's expressed devotion to education.

Hurrying out of the classroom and down the crowded corridor, Kevin dashed into his closet-sized office. The small room was in disarray, scattered with piles of books and papers, organized in a fashion only Kevin could decipher. The condition of the windowless office reflected the past six years of Kevin's life, an inner turmoil biding its time. He yanked open the bottom drawer of his desk and retrieved a small cardboard box, then rushed out the door.

"Mr. Donahue. Where's the fire?" his students quipped in the hallway. He responded with a wave and jogged to the parking lot. Now that spring had finally sprung, Kevin's apple-red Mustang was safe at home in Jacob's garage. The clean, fresh air carried the scent of blossoming flowers and a touch of warmth. It was clearly motorcycle weather.

"You ready for a mission, Ethel? Let's do this thing."

He donned a shiny black helmet. He hadn't wanted to call attention to himself with an orange one in an era when few riders, apart from Evel Knievel, wore helmets. Kevin fished out his keychain from his pants' pocket. With his prized plastic insert for 45s dangling from the keychain, he slid the key it into the ignition, kicked into gear, and eased out of the lot.

The ride along the thoroughfare was tranquil, and the gaps in the clusters of lush vegetation lining the road allowed Kevin to peek at the river in the distance. Despite the peaceful setting, his heart pounded relentlessly as adrenaline-filled blood surged through his body.

Decelerating, Kevin eased the bike onto a dirt road that meandered through the trees and passed into a denser section of the woods. While negotiating the uneven terrain, he made a conscious effort to swallow the lump in his throat, and arrived at the edge of the thicket. Spanning out before him, the luminous waves of grass in the meadow joyfully greeted him. He removed his helmet and wedged it in the canvas side-bag, then turned to see a cozy, little house in the distance, thankful for its existence.

He approached cautiously, mindful that he had been anticipating this moment for six extraordinarily long and painful years.

There she was.

Laura sat in a wooden rocking chair on the porch, gazing into the far distance, lost in thought. A soft breeze pulled a few strands of auburn hair from her headband, and she tucked the flyaways behind her ear.

His heart stilled. She captivated him, even with this smallest gesture.

As if sensing his movement, she turned her head. Locking eyes with his, her dull green irises transformed into a brilliant emerald.

"Wha ... Kevin?" She stood. The papers on her lap fluttered to the porch floor. "No. I- I- I must be dreaming. This can't be real."

Walking ever-so-slowly, he managed to arrive at the bottom of the porch steps, drinking in the sight of her. "You're not dreaming. I'm really here."

"No. Impossible." She stared at him. "You left years ago." Her chest heaved as her breathing quickened.

"See, the thing is ... I never left. I changed my mind at the very last second." Both of his legs were trembling.

Her green eyes welled with unshed tears, and her voice barely rose above a whisper. "You've been here? All these years? And you let me stay with that monster? How could you?" The breeze captured her loose hair again.

"Oh, Laura, I'm so sorry. I had to. You begged me not to interfere with your life." He felt a tear trail down his cheek. "You were so proud of your teaching career, of the lovely home you built. I had to respect your wishes. Please understand that. It killed me not to intervene." He couldn't stop himself from sobbing.

She studied the long blades of grass playing in the breeze until she lifted her eyes again and peered at him. "Then why are you here?"

This was it. He inhaled deeply. It was now or never.

"It's rather simple, really. You did it, you achieved those major accomplishments you were so proud of, and finally, finally, my presence in your life won't jeopardize them." Cold sweat trickled down his back. "Can't you see? I meant what I'd said to you six years ago. I wanted to save you. I wanted to save you, and myself, from a lifetime of despair and solitude. And, the only way I can see that happening is for us to be together, whether it's in this time or another. I'm in love with you, Laura. Deeply."

She stood motionless.

Twinges of panic stirred in the depths of his gut. Oh no, this wasn't going well.

With a cry, Laura catapulted herself from the porch into his arms, embracing him until he gasped for breath.

"Oh my God, Kevin. Don't you ever, ever, ever, leave me again."

"Believe me, I don't intend to."

With a trembling hand, he tugged a tiny parcel from his pocket, a squashed little box with a pink ribbon tied around it, and handed it to her.

Her breath hitched. It was a single-serve box of Lucky Charms cereal, and there, tied to the ribbon, sparkled a solitaire diamond engagement ring.

He pressed his forehead to hers. "Spend your life with me, Laura, and I promise to make sure all your wishes come true. Marry me?"

"There you go with your promises again." She laughed. "But, yes. Of course, yes!"

After years of longing, their lips finally met.

Chapter 31

On August 6, 1972, Kevin stood next to the Justice of the Peace in the middle of Sullivan's Meadow awaiting Laura's arrival from the cottage. Across the sunlit field, two large audio speakers carried the pure soulful voice of Etta James singing "At Last". Twenty-five of their friends and family rose from their seats, smiling, as the bride emerged from the house with her parents.

Kevin's breath caught in his throat. She was ravishing. Wearing a delicate ivory sundress embroidered with tiny flowers, she had fastened a crown of white daisies upon her head, and waves of her rich auburn hair cascaded down her back. She clutched a tiny bouquet of yellow and white daisies that he was sure her father had picked in the meadow. At the end of the aisle, she kissed her parents and joined Kevin at the altar. Her eyes shone as she gazed at him, radiating a joy that overwhelmed him.

He swallowed hard. Every choice he made in his life, whether in the next century or here in the 60s, led to this very moment.

The wedding ceremony passed in a blur. Before he knew it, the Justice of the Peace declared them husband and wife, Mr. and Mrs. Kevin Donahue.

The celebration continued long into the night. The two clung to each other, and the depth of the joy he felt was overwhelming. He peered at the friends he had made and the family he was now a part of, blissfully aware he was no longer lost in time. He was finally home, for his home was Laura.

He lifted her delicate hand to his lips, barely aware of the music that reverberated from the phonograph. Ronnie and Charlie, who had eagerly volunteered to be the official DJs of the reception, exchanged snickers as they selected songs by Jimi Hendrix and

Janis Joplin. After a few blaring songs, Luigi's voice boomed out. "Ronnie! Charlie! What is this noise. Something romantic. This is a wedding, not Woodstock."

"Okay, okay," Charlie replied, then cued up Jerry Reed's "When You're Hot You're Hot." The boys roared with laughter.

"What is this? This isn't a love song. Boys. Get back here. *Ho un diavolo per capello.*"

Kevin chuckled as he watched the teenagers dash to the side of the house as Luigi chased after them with an album raised over his head.

"Don't worry, guys, I got this," Pearl called out, and she started up Peter Stookey's "There is Love." Curls bouncing, she tracked down a profoundly reluctant Thomas for a dance. The poor guy adamantly shook his head, but considering she already had her arms wrapped around his neck, he lost the battle.

Kevin reached for his lovely wife's hand and drew her close, swaying to the rhythm.

He whispered in her ear, "Look up at the stars, Laura."

She gazed into the heavens and sucked in a breath. "Whoa, there must be hundreds of them, hundreds of tiny sparkles of light. I never saw anything like it."

He reached over and brushed a loose lock of her hair into place. "Well, we both came to Sullivan's Meadow to witness an amazing show of lights. Took long enough, but there it is."

She regarded the glittering stars. "You know, it's crazy to think about, but if it wasn't for Paul taking me here, you and I would never have met."

He pressed his lips to the top of her head. "I wonder what the future holds for him. Do you think he'll transform into that surly old hermit?"

Laura shook her head. "No, I doubt it. Supposedly, he's making a killing on Wall Street with a young investor named Madoff."

"Really? Bernie Madoff?"

"I guess. Why? You know him?"

"Madoff? Uh, no. Can't say that I do."

Laura turned her dazzling green eyes to Kevin. "I'm certain of one thing — this spectacular planetary light show will continue to deliver."

Kevin stopped dancing and raised a quizzical eyebrow.

"Expect fireworks later, my dear husband."

Kevin threw his head back and laughed.

Epilogue
2023

"Honey, would you mind going downtown to pick up a box of Goldfish crackers for the grand-twins? I forgot to buy them earlier." Laura stepped out of the kitchen, drying her hands on a cotton dishtowel.

He pushed himself out of the recliner. At eighty years old, even getting out of a recliner required a bit of effort. "Sure. What time are they getting here?"

"Well, Matt told me around 2:00, but Amy isn't moving very quickly these days. I'm surprised the OB didn't limit her traveling. It's uncomfortable sitting in a car for an hour when you're seven months pregnant."

"I'll take your word for it. Be back in a bit."

Kevin lifted Laura's lustrous, white braid and planted a kiss on her neck. He swiped the car keys from the counter and ducked into the garage. Backing the car out onto the asphalt, he coasted past a magnificent oak and down the half-mile driveway to the main thoroughfare. The dirt trail in the woods had been much too treacherous for daily use, so the Donahues hired a contractor in the mid-70s to widen and pave it.

He ambled into Shop Rite supermarket and stood numbly in the cracker aisle, bewildered by the wide selection of Goldfish. If he selected the wrong variety, the twins would adamantly refuse to eat them. Two years old and his granddaughters had already mastered the art of coercion. He settled for a few variety boxes of rainbow, cheddar, and plain Goldfish, a dozen mini snack bags, and a bag of pretzel Goldfish. After paying for the groceries, he rewarded himself with a visit to Ronnie and a quick slice.

A group of college girls were hanging around outside Ronnie's place taking selfies with their cellphones. Standing in a row, they posed suggestively with their hands on their hips, and lips pouted in a kiss. Kevin excused himself as he tried to push past.

The one with long, black hair called out to him. "Hey, gramps. Take a vid for us? He glanced down at their midriffs and nodded uncomfortably as a cellphone was thrust into his hand. After being subjected to a full minute of belly dancing and twerking, he returned the phone to the Morticia Addams lookalike.

"Thanks, babe. Tootles."

He looked at her, a distant memory trying to take hold, but it remained just out of reach. He shrugged the thought away, walked into the restaurant, and settled onto a stool near the cash register.

"Kevin, my man, what's going on?" Ronnie extended his muscular arms across the counter and hugged Kevin. "I'm surprised to see you. Isn't Matthew and his brood coming home today?"

"Yeah, a little later. You're still coming, right?"

"Wouldn't miss it. Carolyn's bringing her pineapple Bundt cake. Consider yourself forewarned."

"Aw, your wife's cooking isn't so bad, Ron. We've eaten at your house plenty of times."

"Her cooking is fine. Her baking, on the other hand? Well, let's leave it at that."

Kevin laughed. "All right, I appreciate the warning. Maybe she won't notice when I forget to put it on the dessert table."

"That's a good man. She'll be too busy spoiling your granddaughters. She bought each of them a musical, ride-on caterpillar and claims they're educational, but who's she trying to kid."

Kevin snorted. "Whenever those twin munchkins come visit, they own me, and they know it. Hey, Ronnie, do me a favor and throw me in a snack."

"Not a problem. One or two slices?

"Better make it one. Extra pepperoni."

Ronnie grabbed a slice from under the counter, opened the heavy iron oven door, and tossed in the pizza slice. A moment later, a young university student entered the restaurant and sat heavily on an empty stool at the counter. The kid nodded at Kevin as he swiveled around and dumped his heavy books on an empty chair.

"Hey, buddy, good to see you," said Ronnie to the teenager.

"You too. Pop in a couple of slices for me, would ya?"

Kevin glanced at the boy — he looked incredibly familiar but couldn't place him. He was tempted to put on his eyeglasses but had forgotten them on the Camry's dashboard.

"How's that gorgeous girlfriend of yours?" Ronnie asked the boy, who rolled his eyes in response.

Opening the massive oven door to retrieve the heated slice, he placed it in front of Kevin on a paper plate. "Careful, Kev. It's really hot." He grunted his accession, took a large gooey bite and burned the roof of his mouth. Ronnie poured him a large Coke. "Told ya," he whispered, then returned to his customer who was complaining about something or other.

"So, Ronnie," the kid said. "You know I'm taking an astronomy class, right? The preliminary research is due Monday. I don't even have a friggin' proposal."

Kevin felt a chill up his spine with the eerie feeling of déjà vu. He stopped chewing and listened.

"We're supposed to research an interplanetary or celestial phenomenon and its impact on the earth, and I've got absolutely nothing."

He then overheard Ronnie offering a bunch of lame suggestions fit for a fourth-grade science project so he decided to intervene. Besides, he had an interesting perspective when it came to interstellar phenomena. He wiped his mouth with a napkin and walked over to the kid and smiled.

The boy swiveled in his chair and peered up at him. "Sir? Can I help you with something?" The boy was polite, he had to give him that.

"I beg your pardon," he began. "I apologize for overhearing, and I know this is none of my business, but I'd like to offer you a suggestion if I may." The boy grabbed a napkin to clean his face and invited him to sit. He ignored the invitation. Laura was expecting him, and his son was arriving shortly. "Years ago, I used to dabble in astronomy," he explained, and almost began to laugh. He was reducing the extraordinary experience of time travel as "a dabble." He composed himself and asked, "Have you considered researching the planetary alignment?"

The kid appeared confused. "You mean the order of the planets' distance from the sun? That's irrelevant sir."

"No, no, no. The impact of Venus, Mars, and our moon in perfect alignment. This happened fifty-eight years ago, almost to the day. Look it up on your computer." He pointed to the boy's laptop as he moved for the door.

"I apologize sir, I meant no disrespect."

"Apology accepted," he replied. He turned to his friend. "See you at my place in a few hours, Ronnie."

"Stick around a while, Kev. This'll only be a minute."

"Nah, I've got to head back. There's something I need to do back at the house." He reached for his sweater he had left on the stool and departed without another word, heading home to Laura and their family.

He parked the car in his driveway and shuffled over to the side yard. A few weeks ago, he painted the wrought iron bench a cherry red to match their front door then moved it into Laura's flower garden. He nodded to himself, pleased with the timeless charm the bench added to the garden. Appreciating the vibrant colors of the blossoms and their sweet scent, he inhaled deeply, then wandered a few yards to the bench's former home.

The circular scar remained in the meadow despite his countless attempts to remove it. It didn't matter, he realized, the branded circle wasn't to blame, just its location. In any case, the spot was dangerous, so years ago when Matt was a baby, he'd researched plants that sported intimidating and painful thorns. He'd dug a trench around that blasted mark, and despite easing the bushes into the soil with utmost care, he'd suffered over fifty thorny puncture wounds. Laura had dabbed ointment on each cut while he had told her these were his war wounds, and he was darn well proud of them.

His labor paid off. An impenetrable barrier of stinging nettles, rambler roses, and blackberry bushes enveloped that cursed circle. The thick wall was certainly enough to deter curious two-year-old toddlers and any other trespassers from entering. He nodded to himself, pleased. His family was safe.

He started for the house, then slapped a hand to his forehead. He'd forgotten the grocery bag of goldfish crackers at Ronnie's. Rubbing the back of his neck, he called out to Laura, then returned to the car.

Heck, he might as well have that second slice. There was plenty of time.

CPSIA information can be obtained
at www.ICGtesting.com
Printed in the USA
JSHW020155190723
44956JS00006B/13